ARTHUR VANDERBILT

JACK'D

A NOVEL

Jack'd© 2024 Arthur Vanderbilt

.

For more information contact:
Riverdale Avenue Books/Magnus Lit Imprint
5676 Riverdale Avenue
Riverdale, NY 10471
www.riverdaleavebooks.com

Design by www.formatting4U.com
Cover design by Scott Carpenter

Digital ISBN: 9781626016729
Trade ISBN: 9781626016736

First edition, January 2024

Chapter One

As he opens the second set of double glass doors at the Club, the music becomes loud.

Very loud.

Pounding.

Throbbing.

Overwhelming.

As if he had entered a 1970's disco.

At 2:00 a.m.

Past the front counter where the cheery sprite scans his fob— "Good morning, Latham, have a good workout," past the reception area and the door to the rehab center, past the cafe where the young smiler behind the counter is mixing ingredients that will turn into a healthy drink - Green Lightning - the color and consistency of pond slime, (which Latham will buy as he leaves and will drink in his car on the way to his law office), past the large TV screen hung on the wall featuring a continual loop of god-like creatures performing improbable feats, like sprinting across a desert trailing a parachute for added resistance, finally into the cavernous room full of devices that look like they have been de-accessioned from a museum devoted to the Spanish Inquisition. It is a scene that always strikes Latham as being lifted straight from a painting by Hieronymus Bosch, which captured all of the medieval artist's fitful, tormented nightmares.

Latham scans the familiar scene as he walks through the gym on his way to the Locker Room. He is a half hour earlier than usual. This will allow time to get in his daily workout, his customary 10 minutes in the steam room, then shower, shave, and put on his custom-made business suit, gold cufflinks and all the special touches for today and still reach the office before his new clients arrive to be briefed on the tax implications of acquiring the start-up biotech.

A half hour earlier than usual, but as he passes through, the scene is the same as always.

The gym is in motion, filled with bodies illustrating just a few of the infinite variety of ways the human form may miss the mark of the ancient Greek ideal. All in various poses suggesting imminent orgasm or cruel torture, writhing either in ecstasy or pain. Or is it a combination of both? Is this a S&M dungeon? Or an opium den, where, under the power of the music and the smell of the eucalyptus-impregnated towels chilling in the small refrigerators, everyone is under the illusion that, with hard work and dedication, they, too, will look just like the Personal Trainers who wander the floor to dispense, with earnestness and surety, all the life wisdom of genetically endowed 25 year-olds?

Is this Neverland, where one comes to keep from growing old?

Is this the Maginot line of the battle against Eternity?

Such thoughts never cross the minds of Latham, or any of the regulars. They are true believers.

Motion, motion, everyone moving, the music pulsing, blasting what always sounds like the same "song" which repeats the same lyrics over and over, something that always sounds like "monkey chump curry, monkey chump curry." What does that even mean? What do those words mean? They make no sense, yet the noise is so loud the words merge into a primal chanting, "monkey chump curry," again and again. "Monkey chump curry": how many times will it be repeated? It's as if a needle is stuck in a groove on an old vinyl record, and its driving beat is working the patrons into a frenzy.

Latham waves to Joe, a bored Personal Trainer in a clinging black T-shirt which showcases his impressive pecs, and tight workout shorts which showcase his massive quads and bubble butt. Joe is lifting the ends of two lengths of rope, long enough and thick enough to secure the *Queen Mary* to a wharf. He is instructing a middle-aged man who looks like Humpty-Dumpty's brother—who, when he changes in the Locker Room back into business casual, becomes the founder of a multi-billion dollar hedge fund—showing him how to thrust the two ends of the rope up and down, faster, faster. "Choke the chicken," the Trainer encourages him, "choke the chicken," then tries chanting "beat the boss, beat the boss," to a man who is the boss, but who obediently tries, harder, harder. Some huffing, some puffing, sweat beading on his forehead, some reddening of the face, tuffs of frizzled gray hair drenched, eyes bugging out, is something inside him about to rupture? But he keeps choking the chicken, hoping this is the key to ignite his 54 year-old libido.

Latham makes a mental note to stalk him in the Locker Room and talk to him. Humpty's hedge fund may be interested in investing in the biotech, or at least someday need Latham's tax expertise. At $800 an hour. Networking.

Nearby, a kale-fed scarecrow of a woman with tanning-salon skin above her breasts, as dry and crinkled as parchment paper, is tethered to an upright post by a rubber strap around her waist. She is running in place, *faster, faster, legs higher* her Personal Trainer orders her, *higher. Higher.* Arms pumping, eyes frantic as if a mountain lion, or an extra pound of fat, is about to pounce on her.

A lithe Personal Trainer takes off at full speed across the gym, weaving in and out around people and obstacles, show-off-leaping over an incline bench, staying airborne for just a few seconds more than seems natural, landing, racing, leaping again, running back to his client with a flattened medicine ball, showing him how to smash it down onto the wooden floor, pick it up, then toss it back to him. Back and forth they smash and throw, as if on a schoolyard playground.

There's a regular: the woman with the stout legs and a tent-cut skirt ensemble whose weary eyes say, "I gave up a long, long time ago". Latham waves to her as he passes. The regulars feel like family. She has a thick green rubber strap holding her legs together just above the knees. Squatting—how can just the ass get so big, Latham always wonders—she takes baby steps sideways, like a crab, moving as if she has quite a substantial load lodged in her panties, looking up at her Personal Trainer every few seconds for a nod of approval, a word of encouragement, some indication of how much longer she has to keep doing this. Why is she here? What is she hoping for? What is the fantasy that makes her spend $170 a month to be a member of the Club, and $150 more for an hour's time with a Personal Trainer boy who, barring some magical powers, bottom line? can do nothing at all to help her.

Another Personal Trainer nearby watches his client

hopscotch through a rope ladder laid along the floor as the client speaks to his office on his Blue Tooth, barking orders to his grunts who struggle to understand him through his wheezing and huffing and the music's blare. "OK, good stuff," the Trainer says to him, "now try jumping in and out alternate areas." And, like a child hopscotching along a summer sidewalk, he tries, oh, he tries, as if he'll get a popsicle if he does it correctly, all the while chewing out his staffers back at the office who are trying to hear, and interpret, his breathless commands.

Latham glances at the back of the gym where, like caged gerbils on spinning wheels, others are going nowhere on the rows of treadmills, trudging step after step with all the enthusiasm of Volga boatmen pulling canal boats loaded with boulders, plodding along, step after weary step, in no hurry to get where they are going but knowing they must go on. And on.

In the last row, behind the treadmills, others are climbing on the Stairmasters, destined, like King Sisyphus, never to reach the top. Climbing, climbing, up, up, but never higher.

A Personal Trainer suddenly lets out a deep, hollow moose mating call, a WOOOOOOO Woooo, that reverberates around the gym. Another Personal Trainer across the floor answers with the same call. Latham looks and laughs. The Personal Trainers race across the gym, grab each other in a black bear hug, the two of them, still bear-hugging, jump up and down, dancing— as if they hadn't seen each other for an hour— separate, and go back to their clients.

A man built like a Shmoo, wearing a gray T-shirt with black lettering across his chest - "BEAST" - stands in front of the floor to ceiling mirror in the annex off the main floor of the gym, holding a jump rope as if a live wire.

"Here," his adorable female Personal Trainer says, "it's going to be easier to think of this rhyme as you do it. This will set your tempo:

> Five little monkeys
> Jumping on the bed.
> One fell off,
> And bumped his head.
> Mama called the doctor,
> And the doctor said,
> "No more monkeys
> Jumping on the bed."

He looks at her.

She nods encouragement. "Come on. Here we go. This is easy. Ready? Start. 'Five little monkeys…'"

The rope tangles between his feet on his first sweep.

"Fuck the monkeys," he grumbles, then brings the jump rope back over his head, determined to try again until he can master what first graders do on every playground at recess.

Latham does a double take. Over there: in an area where the rubber floor is littered with bodies in various contortions and improbable stretches, looking like the victims of Pompeii, frozen in time when Mt. Vesuvius erupted in 79 AD. There Latham spots the Managing Partner of a politically connected law firm—a power broker courted by every candidate running for office in the northern part of the State, who is consulted by the Governor before he makes any appointment or approves or vetoes any pending legislation. He is flopping—like a manatee out of water—on the floor of the gym. Ahh, so this is when he comes; Latham makes another mental note. He may need him some day to help grease the skids at the State Bureau of Taxation. The Personal Trainer circles him, assessing how he will get him off the floor and into an upright position; in what direction should he roll him? How would a manatee do it?

Walking by with his shaker and white hand towel is the young guy who comes religiously. Every day. Obediently working out with his Personal Trainer. He and Latham nod and smile. When Latham first had noticed him a year ago, in June of last year, he looked like the scrawny kid in the old Charles Atlas ads in the back of trash magazines and comic books—the one lying on the beach with the smirking bully kicking sand in his face. After working out for a year with his Personal Trainer, he looks: exactly the same.

For that matter, so does everyone.

Weeks, months, years, roll by. Day by day. Nothing changes.

Even the members Latham sees every day lifting and pumping and pushing and pulling and crunching and planking and planking with a weight on their backs and squatting and hack squatting and lunging and lunging holding weights and curling and running and climbing and pedaling and jumping and skull crushing and deadlifting—all with an other-worldly intensity and devotion—reveal their pudgy stomachs and rolls of fat under the carpets of scraggly, tangled hair on their backs as they strut smugly naked through the Locker Room. In fact, the only ones who seem to look better and better are the Personal Trainers who, all day, between conducting classes and training clients, are working out (with all the grace and apparent effortlessness of ballet dancers) to perfect what already looks perfect.

Latham—like everyone else—is sure all the other members of the Club are just not trying hard enough. Or just not doing it the right way. That a six-pack, model-worthy look will be his if he could just devote a little more time to his workouts and be a little more conscientious and consistent with his diet. At 44, he can do it. He glances at himself in the floor to ceiling mirror that covers the wall. So close. He is so close. And he considers his time at the Club an investment, an investment in his continued good health to devote to his thriving law practice. And the best way to hold back the frightening hands of Time. He is at the office each day from 8:00 a.m. until at least 7:00 p.m. Most weekends are spent catching up, or handling emergent matters. Now, right now, each morning at the gym, is his one time to zone out and exercise, a time he considers essential to working at peak capacity. And to looking buff like the 24 year-old Latham still sees in the mirror.

As he nears the Locker Room, the Screamer stretches out on his hands and knees in the section of the gym with the rubber floor. In black tights with black gym shorts pulled up over them, and a black tank top, and with his sloth-like frame and vacant eyes, he always looks to Latham like Minnie Mouse. If Minnie had been abusing steroids. For quite some time. And if Minnie was behind several epochs on the evolutionary chart. Prostrate on the floor, he pushes the Ab Wheel ahead of him. Does he think that will help reduce the considerable beer belly that droops over his gym shorts? Is he hoping to exchange one type of six pack for the other? Each and every time he pushes the Ab Wheel to full extension, he lets out a bellow that sounds like he is desperately, though unsuccessfully, trying to pass an unusually hard stool.

At the first bleat, activity in the gym freezes in mid-motion, though by the third or fourth, all is back to normal, and his screams are no more heard than the words of the pounding music.

Latham walks into the Locker Room, puts the hanger with his French cuffed white shirt, blue suit, and yellow silk tie on a hook in his locker, takes his shaker of BCAA from his gym bag, checks himself out in the mirror—not bad, not bad at all— and heads out to the gym.

Chapter Two

"You kiddin me?" Jack said to Ashley and Kaitlyn, the two cute, young Personal Trainers who had been hired with him earlier in June. "Compared to where I was?" They stood around a Stretching Table, folding towels and surveying the gym. "This is epic."

"So you were down at the Shore, weren't you?"

"Yeah. Toms River. Had to get out of there. Big time. That gym, right? It was like in this, a prefab building? In the middle of nowhere. An industrial park. Man, talk about grim. Old equipment. Faded black and white posters of Arnold taped to the walls. Like literally 100 years ago. One prefab shower stall. Literally. One. One toilet. One freakin urinal. No towels, no—"

"What? No towels?"

"You gettin' the picture?"

"So, what did everyone do?"

"They either brought their own towel, or pulled out like a million paper towels from the dispenser next to the sink. If it was even stocked. You know, those brown paper ones? That don't absorb?"

They laughed and watched him as he spoke with his body and hands, illustrating the sad state of the equipment and the patrons, his feet always moving in a little dance routine. They watched him, riveted, taking repeated glances, trying not to stare. Hoping one of his steps would let them get a glimpse of his butt. Could someone really look this good?

"I swear to God, the members were all like, I mean, literally, 80? At least. Every one of them. All of them must have had like quadruple by-pass surgery or something and were there on doctor's orders. To be there. Or else. They all had that look, you know, if they missed coming to the gym? Just one freakin' day? They'd literally drop. On the spot. Dead. Just like that."

Jack pretended he was about to crumple to the floor.

"The personal trainers?" he continued, "they all needed personal trainers."

The girls laughed.

"Big time. Except for my buddy there. Scott. Man, without him? I would have gone postal. I'm serious. We were making, literally, like... nothing. I was renting this shit hole with Scott and this other guy. It was bleak. When we moved in, there were rats. Running all around. All over the place and— "

"Gross." They shivered.

"Tell me about it. They ate everything. Even got into my supplements. And *Cialis*."

"Must've been, like, muscle rats."

"On steroids. With boners."

Ashley and Kaitlyn stole a quick look at Jack's black nylon gym shorts.

"I got those sticky pad trap things? And got 'em. I was so pissed I killed 'em all. With hedge clippers."

They gasped.

"No, no, I didn't like slice and dice them up or anything. Just beat the shit outta them. Till they stopped moving. For good. Fuck'em."

The girls looked faint and kept staring at Jack, devouring him with their eyes and imagining what it would feel like waking up next to him.

"Oh man, I had to get out of there so bad. I kept picturing myself still there when I was what? like, 40 or something. Cooking on a hot plate. Set on the toilet seat."

"Not a pretty picture."

"Let me tell you: It was: The Pits. My old man kept telling me: grow up. You gotta join the workforce, he kept telling me" - Jack made air quotes around the word workforce and rolled his eyes - "and wanted me to work at this lame municipal utilities authority there. A M.U.A. MUA, MUA, MUA." Jack said it so it sounded like a cow in a field.

They laughed and together made the same noise.

The three of them all started mooing and laughing.

"So yeah. My old man? he's been chained to a desk there. At the MUA. For years. I don't know. Decades? A lifetime. In a cubicle? A fuckin' cubicle. Doing what? Shuffling papers around a metal desk. Fuck that, man. Man, you only get one life. Right? Don't waste it. That's my philosophy."

They nodded in agreement. And sighed. And wondered what a lifetime with Jack would be like. He even had his own philosophy.

"My buddy down there at the gym, Scott? He told me all about this place. He knew someone who had been a member here. I floored it up here. And never went back."

"So how come Scott didn't come, too?" (Does he look like you, they wanted to ask.)

"I don't know. I think he was already stuck in that sort of life down there. You know what I mean? It sucks you in. Before you even realize it. You know how it goes: had just gotten married. A kid pops out a month later. Same old story. It repeats. And repeats. The poor guy was already trapped. He was so fucked. Even before he began. He'll probably end up at the MUA."/

They all began mooing again. Jack crossed himself. "May God bless his soul."

"Brian says he has Trainers here making over $100,000 a year," Ashley said. "The ones who can line up a lot of clients. They're the ones."

"And that, ladies and gentlemen, is precisely why I'm here," Jack said.

Ashley went on. "Brian even told me about this one Trainer who used to be here—Aaron? I think that was his name. He landed this one client who turned out to be like a gazillionaire. He and his wife, they flew Aaron all over the world. On their jet. With them. As their Personal Trainer."

"Sweet." Jack again looked out over the gym. "It's out there. A hundred grand. More. I am literally so ready."

Jack pointed to a man in a Penn State T-shirt talking to someone sitting on the leg extension machine on the other side of the gym.

"See that guy? Every day. This whole time I've been here. All he does: walks around the gym. Talking to people. The Mayor, I call him."

Kaitlyn looked. "Yeah. That guy. I've seen him, too. Then after he's made his rounds? He stands in front of the mirror, stretches for a minute—"

"I know, he's the one always prying his gym shorts out of his crack," Ashley said, giving an exaggerated demonstration.

"Nice. Then he goes to change. And leaves."

"Hope he at least showers," Ashley said.

"Quite a workout, isn't it?" Jack said. "Every gym has a mayor. We had the same character in Toms River. It's always the same. There's another," he said pointing. "Look at her. That's another species. A regular at every gym. She comes here each morning, enough make-up and perfume to, I don't know. Go out to a ball? Clearly, she's here to find herself someone attached to some balls. Or better yet, attached to some balls, and a healthy bank account."

They giggled. And dropped their eyes again to look at Jack's tiny shorts.

"She's the one with new sneakers—I swear to God—each day a new pair," Ashley said. "I told her a few days ago I really liked the ones she had on that day. I meant it. I really did like them. Would you tell me where you got them, I asked her. Politely. No, she said. Just like that: no. And kept working out."

Jack and Kaitlyn shook their heads in disgust.

"Bitch on wheels."

"Every gym has at least one of those," Jack said. "Every gym? The same. Different faces? Same types. Look at that fucker seated on the pec deck with his phone growing out of his ear. Like some big, impacted cyst."

"Gross. And speaking of phones," Ashley said, "tell me this, ok? Just tell me: what the hell could be so urgent that everyone here is checking their phones? Like every two seconds?"

"With those oh-so-serious pusses," Kaitlyn added, imitating the expression. "You think they got the nuclear code?"

"You got me," Ashley said, putting her stack of folded white towels on the shelf under the table. She took another batch to fold. "That guy on the pec deck? He'll stay there,

14

right there, a half hour? OK? Doesn't move a muscle. Doesn't give a shit that others are scowling at him. And want to use the equipment he's hogging. Mr. Pig."

Jack looked around the gym. "Look at that poor dude. I see him here every day. Same time. Religiously. Arrives the exact same time. Leaves the exact same time. On autopilot. Does the exact same routine. Every day. No variations. What does he think's gonna happen?"

"Brian told me he's like this—well, he's not some poor dude, that's for sure—Brian told me he's this super successful lawyer," Ashley said. "A tax lawyer, I think he said. Mega bucks."

"He's mine. All mine," Jack said scanning the floor once more. "Hey, how about Mr. Boston College T-shirt. Over there. That guy. There. I mean, look at him. He's good looking. He's got a decent body. Give him that, at least. Probably on some team when he was in college. What do you think?"

"Basketball?"

"Tall enough. But he doesn't look like he's ever seriously trained. He could do wonders with what he's got, right? What we could do with him in a couple months. Literally. Man. But here's what I see him doing. On his own. OK? Does eight reps? Good form. Perfect form, actually. Using decent weight. So far, so good. Good for him. Then after each set of eight reps he takes his little white towel and mops his face and neck as if he's just run a marathon. Then takes a swig of water from his cute little shaker. Then checks his cute little iPhone. Then looks at his watch. 'Wow, look at that, he must say to himself, a full ten seconds have passed since the last time I checked.'"

The girls laughed.

"Then eight more reps," Jack continued. "Then the towel. The shaker. The phone. The watch. For an hour. Sometimes even more. Good for him. Never varies. Always that order."

"I've watched him, too. You're right. It never varies."

"If I could train him, I'd have him so ripped, in six months he could be a model. Literally. Or how about that guy, over there."

"Which one?"

"That guy there. With the white T-shirt that says: 'SHREDDED'".

Jack spelled it out in the air with his finger.

"Is that what you call irony?"

"No. That's what I call: 'a jerk off'. A hundred percenter."

The girls laughed and took another quick glance at the outline of Jack's crotch bulge.

"He spends about 15 minutes in the gym going from friend to friend, socializing. Then, after that vigorous workout, goes into the Locker Room and will spend an hour in there. Between the Steam Room. Shower. Shaving. Trying out all our free products. And I'm sure he tells all his friends at work about his impressive early mornings at the gym."

They looked around the floor.

"You know, you look out there?" Kaitlyn said, looking across the gym, "and somewhere out there, every single minute, I swear to God, some guy's adjusting his junk." She demonstrated how they do it. "I mean, come on, how often does a man have to do that? I mean, give me a break. Are they just trying to make sure it's all still there? What could happen to it in a few minutes?"

They looked to Jack for the answer, but he just smiled and shook his head.

"What if every two minutes I was adjusting?" Ashley said, lifting her breasts. "Men are such oinkers."

"Quick. Look," Kaitlyn said, pointing.

"Have you ever watched that guy? When he finishes on a piece of equipment, look, he sets the weight to a much heavier level than what he was using. Trying to impress—"

"Or intimidate."

"You're right. Impress or intimidate whoever uses it next."

"That is so lame," Jack said, shaking his head and scanning the gym for others. "Ah, yes. There he is. One of my favorites: The Spreader. We can't forget the good old Spreader, over—"

"The who?"

"The Spreader."

"Man, you already got names for every one of these?"

"He's the one over there," Jack said, nodding to the left, "watch this, OK? So, there he is on the leg press. He's put four plates on each side, right? That's a real serious load. And I've got to hand it to him, that guy's a faithful regular. Here every day. Same time. And does a real serious routine. No bullshit there. But watch, OK?"

They watched him complete the second and third sets of twelve reps, then stand up. And walk away.

"See. Look at that. The fucker never puts his weights back. Ever. I guess he thinks that's what the new Personal Trainers are here for, right? To pick up after him".

"Like following around a little kid in kindergarten," Ashley said. "Tommy, put your toys away".

17

"And you should see him in the Locker Room," Jack continued.

"He's got his stuff spread all over the entire bench—clothes, dirty towels, his stinkin' underwear. Products, shoes, socks, everything - so that no one else in that alcove can even sit on the bench. A pig. And when he leaves? he leaves his filthy towels on the bench. Of course. On the floor. All over."

"Ahha. The Spreader. I get it."

"I don't give a shit cause just look out there," Jack said. "Take a look. All those people? All these beautiful, lovely, needy people. Who need, what do they need? They need us. Real bad. They're all ours."

"And we need them," Kaitlyn said. "Those are our lottery tickets."

"Even The Spreader," Jack said. "Every fuckin' one of them. Ready to go out there? And pick our winning numbers?"

"Never been readier."

"Ready to turn on all our sex appeal? To the max? Like Brian told us?"

"I feel so sexy right now, I'd like to do me," Ashley said.

They put their fists together and, on the count of three, exploded them upward.

"Happy hunting," they whispered, making their moo-ing noise and laughing.

Chapter Three

"I guarantee it," Patti said to Anne as she shimmied into her Lululemon tights, then took her sneakers from her locker and laid them on the bench. "You're going to love it."

For each friend she convinced to join the Club that month, she received a $250 coupon for the Club's Spa, which she immediately redeemed for yet another other-worldly massage with Gonzalo.

Anne zipped open her gym bag. "Question one," she said. "What about, should I, do you use a Personal Trainer?"

"I do. I started out working with Jenny. And I have to admit? It made a huge difference. When I started, I mean, I didn't even know how to use any of that stuff," Patti said, waving her hand out toward the gym. "All those weird-looking contraptions? Give me a break. They intimidated me. Seriously."

"I can see how."

"OK, so it was my first day here and I didn't know what the hell I was doing out there. So, I sat down on the pec deck and—"

"Girlfriend, I'm impressed. The pec deck. Look at you."

"Yeah, well, it might just as well have been the poop deck for all I knew. Back then. I just wanted a quiet place to sit. With the emphasis on 'sit'. Out of the way. So, I could see what other people were doing. And try to imitate them."

"That would be me, for sure."

"So, I'm just sitting there, minding my own business, and after a while thought I better at least sort of look like I was at least doing something? So, I grabbed hold of these metal things and just sort of was pushing slash pulling at them, when I look up and this Personal Trainer is standing right in front of me."

"Uh oh."

"Uh oh is right. She was smiling but she wasn't laughing or anything like that, but just said to me, very quietly in this kindly soft voice? Like she's talkin' to a little kid? So, she says to me, 'has anyone shown you how to use the equipment?'"

"Ouch."

"I didn't know her name back then. It was Jenny. I didn't want her to see what a helpless little girlie I was, as I was watching all these Amazons in spandex swinging kettlebell weights in between their legs and everything. But I think I just shook my head no. And she says, here, let me show you, and she's pointing out that this piece does this, and that does that, and you put this here, and sit this way, with your feet pointed like that, and your wrists like this. Way too much information. Too fast to absorb. I'm sitting there nodding like an idiot and looking enlightened like I'm getting it all. And thanking her profusely."

"So, initiation by fire."

"Well, hardly. The minute she walked away, and I knew she wasn't going to look back to see how I was doing? I dismounted as if I had just completed 100 reps. And slunk away into the crowd. It was months before I went anywhere near the pec deck again."

"That would be me."

"Jenny was very kind and looked after me for a while. I didn't want to, you know, get stuck in one of the machines. Or anything like that. Can you imagine having to call for help? Making a scene? Looking like a total a-hole? Jenny really helped me get started."

"Would you recommend her? For me?"

Patti thought a minute as she tied a sneaker. "Jenny's a sweetheart, but no, I don't think so."

"No? Why not?"

"I may be a slow learner, OK? But I'm not stupid."

Anne laughed. "Far from it, Miss Vasssar."

"So, you're paying a lot each month. To be a member here, right? Why not take advantage of all the Club has to offer?"

"Makes sense. So?"

"So go right for one of those young stud Personal Trainers."

Anne looked at her and raised her eyebrows.

"I'm serious. They're here for us. For you. May as well take advantage. Take one."

Anne sat down on the bench next to Patti and stared at her.

"Girlfriend, do you even realize how politically incorrect this conversation is? You're objectifying the lads. You're talking about them as if, as if they're like that poor Ken doll you used to make do all sorts of, I don't know what. Unspeakable things. Remember?"

Patti laughed.

"These guys," Anne continued, "are someone's sons, someone's brothers, someone's—"

"No, see, I really don't think they are. You're gonna find out."

A woman outside their alcove turned off a hair dryer and hooked it back on the wall next to the mirror. Patti lowered her voice and continued.

"They're a whole new species. A species you've, we've, never encountered before. Ever. Visitors to planet earth. They were created just to please us, they—"

"Hmmm. Think you may have been sitting in that Steam Room just a bit too long, love? OK, I cannot believe I'm even asking this: so, which of these young studs, as you call them, would you recommend? For me?"

"Oh boy. That depends, what you're into." Patti grinned at her. "No. Seriously. It's like in a supermarket out there. Just go up and down the aisles. Select whatever looks good. To you."

"Can we squeeze them?"

"What?"

"You know, like in a supermarket. To check freshness and everything. Give them the smell test, all that? Like with an avocado, a cantaloupe?"

"Kiddo, you are as sick as I am. You're gonna fit in so well here. You do whatever you have to do. But it's sort of like *Whole Foods*: everyone out there—on display—has already been sorted and selected to meet the Club's high standards. Before they are even put on display and offered for sale." Patti thought for a moment. "You're going to see this out there. They're just standing around. Striking poses. As if they're on display."

Anne smiled. "I think I am going to like this place."

"See? Have I ever led you wrong?"

"Never, girlfriend."

Anne glanced out at the aisle and whispered, "Who the hell is *that*?"

Patti looked. "Oh, her. That's just Little Miss Ponytail Swisher."

"Is she a Personal Trainer?"

"No. Could be. Looks like one. But she's just one of us."

"Oh really?"

"Well, perhaps just a better, younger—"

"Much younger."

"OK, much younger version of us. Probably no husband."

"For starters. And no kids to age her."

"Or pets. Ahh, freedom, oh freedom," Patti said.

"Unfair competition. People who look like that shouldn't even be allowed in here. And the same time as us. Or they should have their own gym."

"I know. Or at least special hours. I forget her name. I've talked with her a couple times. She's actually very nice. A real estate agent in town."

"So, if we workout with a Personal Trainer, will we look like that?"

Patti tied her sneaker. "Well, I guess if your Trainer can also dip you into the Fountain of Youth. If we were to be really, really serious," Patti continued,

"Yes?"

"Brutally honest, right?"

"You go, girl."

"If we really had our druthers, every—"

"Druthers. Love that word: druthers. See? You've been hanging around me too long. Picking up all my British expressions. Who, but you, today, would ever say: druthers? That's why I love you. Pretty soon you'll even pick up my accent."

"You don't really have an accent."

"A little?"

"Maybe just a little. I guess I'm so used to it. So, if

23

women had their druthers," Patti winked at her, "let's be frank: we all, long, long ago, would have gone for one of those guys, wouldn't we? Someone like them. Years ago. Though I'm not sure they even existed back in our day. They are like ideal husband material."

"Or maybe ideal fantasy husband material?"

"Perhaps. Perhaps. But, alas—"

"See. There you go again. Alas. There's another one of what you used to call my quaint words. That, over the years, you've appropriated. Are you quite certain you, too, weren't born around Lancashire? Maybe we were neighbors there? Back then?"

"Alas, no. New Jersey born and bred. Yes, there's a load of compromising everyone has to make along the way and—"

"Well, yes, but if these guys had their own— druthers—wouldn't they be marrying their female equivalents, don't you think? Like that one. The one you called the Ponytail Swisher? Not one of us, for sure."

Patti shoved her gym bag into the bottom of her locker.

"No. I'm not so sure. I think they have to be the prettiest, don't they? They don't want wives who, you know, upstage them. Take the spotlight off them, right? But, yeah. I guess the world ends up with a load of compromising on both sides. Which is OK. It can work. A husband with more hair coming out of his nostrils and ears—enough to braid—"

"Thank you for that visual."

"—more spouting there than on his head, he may be a really good provider. May be a really good father. May even be a lot of fun? I guess. I don't know. I mean, that could happen. Couldn't it?

"Sure," Anne said. "On occasion. I guess?"

"See, that's the sorry lot of most of us. But don't you think that, that somewhere, deep in the recesses of our horny, bitchy, little raggy brains, we never forget that certain guy? Who was our lab partner in our 11th grade chemistry class? Or that we saw that summer at the shore?"

"How did you know about Chuck?"

"Who?"

"My lab partner. Chuck. Remember him?"

"Ahh, Chuck. Yes. Who could forget?"

"Oh my God, he was so perfect, I—"

"Cause we've all had a Chuck in our lives. They are out there, always, somewhere deep in our dreams, aren't they? Probably even someday, ages hence, when we're sitting together? You know, lined up side by side, in our wheelchairs? Out in the sunny corridor of our nursing home? Can you see us? Heads bobbing, eyes flickering?"

"Too vivid an image, Sister. Reel it in."

Patti ignored her.

"Our own Chuck's beautiful image will flash through our demented, drooling minds. And we'll think "what if…""

"So true. So true." Anne looked off into the distance. "He was so beautiful. He smelled so good. I would just sit there, just inhaling him, as Doc Woodside droned on about—"

"Shhh," Patti whispered.

Into the Locker Room, into the alcove right across from them, came a gaggle of women who has just finished a Hot Yoga Class, obviously—from their chatter and laughter and questions and answers about weekend plans—good friends.

25

Patti tilted her head toward the group and motioned for Anne to listen.

"Oh-my-God," one said, "your underwear is Fab-u-lous."

The gaggle began gaggling, talking over each other, whooping and shrieking in delight.

"Your husband must love it when you wear those," said another.

"Look at the front," someone said. "It says 'Gobble. Gobble.'"

More gaggling, shrieking, laughter.

"Ah that would be: a big NO. These are *not* for Alex," the wearer said. "He'll never even see this pair."

Knowing oohs and ahhs, some more gaggling, then the chatter continued.

"Hmmm. I rest my case,"

Patti said to Anne, "welcome, my friend, to the real world."

Anne leaned against her locker, pretending to steady herself.

"I had no idea, I mean, do you hear stuff like this here? All the time?"

"Sweet, innocent little lamb, you have no idea."

"Just that is worth the price of admission."

"A lot more to come, kiddo. Fasten your seatbelt."

Anne pantomimed pulling her seatbelt tighter.

"So," Patti continued, "if we can't have our own Chuck in real life, why not at least sample the goods here? Right now? For each hour you're here: live your fantasy. Get to know, get to be with—a real man. Get one of those guys out there. Just waiting to help you."

"OK. Sold. I guess. But Jenny maybe to start me off? Just until—"

"Oh, for goodness sakes. Don't be such a wuss. Grow a pair. Live a little, honey."

Anne pulled a light lavender Lululemon tank top from her gym bag and held it up against her, walking the few steps to the corridor to check it out in the mirror, peeking around the corner to see if she could see the gobble gobble underwear, then coming back to their alcove.

"Patti, what do you think? Is this OK?"

"It's gorgeous, honey. Whatever you wear? It always looks like you're walking out of the pages of the latest fashion magazine. It makes me barf chunks."

Anne put it on, then did a few steps of a runway walk past Patti.

"OK?"

"You pass," Patti said. "With flying colors."

"Do my boobs look OK in it?"

Patti rolled her eyes and gave a dramatic sigh.

"Sweetheart, are you even listening to the words of wisdom I'm tossing your way?"

"Of course I am. I just want to make sure I don't stand out. Out there."

Patti laughed. "You still don't you get it, do you girl? No one, and I mean no one, is even gonna be looking at you. The Personal Trainers are the bowl of eye candy out there. They are the objects of desire. Get it? You could strip naked out there. Stand on your head. Do a pole dance. Whatever you want. No one will notice."

"No, I understand. Just want to make sure I fit in."

"Girl, you could roll out of bed and come straight here in your PJs. With a volcanic mud face mask an inch deep on your face. And no one would even look. Everyone is too busy checking out the hotties. Who, by the way,-are checking out each other. And themselves. Mainly themselves."

"Love it," Anne said.

"I'm serious. Have you ever seen any other place of business with mirrors covering, *covering* every friggin' square inch? Except maybe a whore house?"

"Never actually been in one of those."

"Neither have I. But just watch. And you'll see these cute guys taking furtive glances at themselves. All day long. It never stops. When they think no one is watching? They'll be flexing, posing. And, every once in a while—and this gets a little spooky—they'll start staring at themselves in the mirror and become so transfixed it's like, I swear to God, they can't stop. It's like they're entering into the mirror and want to melt into the lovely vision before them. I've even seen one of the guys get a boner doing that and—"

"Shut up."

"Well, it sure looks like they're about to. Mirror, mirror on the wall? Who's the most perfect? who's the prettiest? the fairest? the sexiest of them all... If they didn't think anyone else was watching? I could see them having a hands-free ejaculation. Right at their mirror image. Splat."

"You're nuts."

"Am I?"

Anne laughed. "Richard's hasn't shot far enough for a good solid splat in, good Lord, I don't know how long. Can't even remember that far back. Don't tell anyone I said that."

Patti looked at her. "Hey, if a teeny, tiny dribble drips down Fletcher's shriveled weenie? That's like an occasion for fireworks."

The friends smiled.

"Patti, I'm so glad you convinced me to try the Club. Just to be here, with you: this is fun. To get away from everything. To escape my regular life? I needed this. So bad."

"Right back at you, friend. We need a place like this to blow it out and re-charge."

Anne closed her locker and fluffed her hair.

"Heaven is right out there." Patti pointed. "Let's go out there. And once you select which one you want, it's going to get even better."

"No way. How could it possibly get better?"

Patti shut her locker door.

"Oh, it can. And it does."

Chapter Four

Jack, Ashley and Kaitlyn looked around the gym. Each headed out in a different direction: Ashley over to pick up a stack of neatly folded small white towels under a Stretching Table; Kaitlyn off toward the darkened Spinning Room where the Staff all day placed fresh piles of towels on the shelves above the sink; and Jack to the sink area outside the Pilates Room, where he picked up a stack of towels and cradled them in his left arm, holding a folded one in his right hand.

He began at the treadmill closest to him.

"Good morning, sir," he beamed at the overweight man, tired, bored, straining on the treadmill. Brian had told his new recruits that on the strength and sincerity of their smiles depended their success, for the name of the game was hustling clients for Personal Training sessions, from $40 an hour to learn how to use the machines, to over $200 an hour to learn how to use the machines with a Personal Trainer who happened to look like a god or goddess—your choice.

"Would you like a towel?"

The man grunted and returned his gaze to the overhead row of flickering television screens.

Jack moved on to the woman on the next treadmill: "Good morning, ma'am. Would you like a towel?"

She took out one ear bud back as she kept almost - jogging.

"May I give you a towel, ma'am?" Jack repeated.

She put the ear bud back in and shook her head "no", pointing to her towel already draped over the treadmill bar.

"Ma'am?"

She took out her ear bud again and looked at him with a hint of annoyance.

"Would you like a *fresh* towel?" He held it out.

She placed her ear bud in and continued fast walking.

Jack walked past the next treadmill being cleaned by the Staff guy who was proceeding down the row of treadmills with his bucket and mop and cleaning cloths, part of the squad moving around the gym all day, dusting, cleaning, picking up dirty towels, bringing out piles of clean, warm towels from the laundry room, polishing the acres of mirrors, mopping the locker room floor, closing locker doors.

Jack did a double take. On the next treadmill was a rarity at the gym: a young woman, perhaps late 20's, who looked perfect.

Running full speed.

Perfect form.

While checking and sending texts with one hand.

Her iridescent spandex tights and tank top highlighted a perfect body.

Her blonde ponytail swishing up and down in perfect rhythm.

She saw Jack approaching and before he could say a word, smiled a perfect smile at him, shook her head "no" and looked away, never losing her rhythm.

He walked by, turned to look again, just for a moment, moving on before it was obvious he was staring. Brian had warned them not to stare.

Jack had noticed the next man every morning at the same time, always on the same treadmill, a section of *The New York Times* always folded lengthwise, held by one hand across the top of the treadmill, the other hand always holding a buttered bagel which now and then made its way into his mouth, all the while walking, duck-footed, as if on a leisurely Sunday stroll. As Jack approached, the man put the bagel in his mouth and held it between his teeth, reached for Jack's towel, wiped around his mouth with it, wiped one hand, then the other, and tossed the towel back to Jack. All without saying a word.

It wasn't until his sixth or seventh attempt that Jack could interest someone. Those who had been around a while knew what the offer of a towel meant: a brand-new Personal Trainer wanted to talk with them, to chat them up, to befriend them, and ultimately to try to hustle them. It was a lot easier just to say "no thank you" to the kind offer of a towel than it was to listen to their spiel and end up crushing their dreams of finding a paying client.

Anyone who didn't realize this was new enough to the Club to be an easy mark. Or turned on enough by the looks of a new personal trainer to want to see where a chat might lead. If a member accepted the towel, and did anything more than grunt, the door was wide open for the new recruit.

"What are you training?" Jack asked, as if the panting man was a professional bodybuilder, and, now, his new best friend. "Cardio? Great. I wish I could do more of that. I've got to start building that into my routine. I'm really weak there." (Show empathy with the mark.) "Very smart of you. Are you going to do just treadmill today? Or something else? Just the treadmill? Excellent. How long have you been coming here?"

"Oh, about a month I guess."

Bingo. He was talking. A great prospect. A newbie. Just starting off. Doesn't know what he's doing. Needs some guidance. Needs a program. Needs Jack. "That's awesome," Jack said. "Good for you. Have you had your personal assessment done yet?"

"Nah. I don't wanna do that," the man responded, as if Jack had proposed an immediate rectal exam. On a Stretching Table. In the middle of the Gym.

Jack laughed. "It's free. Doesn't cost a thing. I know, no one seems to want one. But it's painless, I promise. And free. No charge."

"I know, I know. I just don't want to find out how bad I am."

Jack smiled his I'm-your-best-friend smile. "I'd say you're not only not bad; you are *good*. Number one, you're smart enough to come to a gym. That's a big first step the majority of people are too lazy to take. Number two, you're wise enough to know the importance of cardio. Everyone should fit that into their routine."

The man at least was listening.

"My name is Jack, by the way."

Jack held out his hand. The man looked at it, then shook it.

"I'm Phil," he said.

"Any day you'd like, Phil, I can set up a time with you. To do the assessment. It's easy. I'll walk you through it. Then maybe we could just sit down and discuss your goals, all that good stuff? And work out the best way for you to achieve them? Whatever they are. Whatever you want. Phil, what do you think? Does that sound like a plan?"

"I don't know."

"You don't know?" Jack grinned as if Phil was joking with him. "Would you do something for me, Phil?" Phil looked at him. Good. Eye contact. Reel him in. "Just think about it; I'm not going to bother you any more today, OK? Fair enough? But just think about it. Will you do that for me? Phil? I'd love to work with you to get you started on the real road to fitness. OK?"

"Sure. Let me think about it."

"You got it." Jack smiled and gave him a fist bump as if this stranger was now his best bud, ceremoniously draping a towel over his treadmill—a special gift to cement their new friendship—then moved to the next prospect.

The man had observed what had just happened and was prepared.

"Sir, good morning," Jack said, giving the man his best 24 year-old smile. (After a few days, the regulars could predict, by the sex appeal of these smiles, which new Personal Trainers would succeed in developing a client base, and who, inevitably, soon would be gone.) "Would you like a towel? No? OK. What are you working on today?"

"Biceps/triceps," the man said. "As soon as I've burned off 200 calories here."

"Good for you." Jack said. "With your biceps workout, what are you trying to achieve?"

The man checked him out. "I want mine… to look like yours."

Jack looked pleased and unconsciously ran his right hand over the bicep of his left arm cradling the towel pile. He flexed it a little without thinking.

"Except," the man paused and looked again at Jack's arm, studying it, "to tell you the truth? I'd like mine to have more of a peak than yours." He paused again. "And I'd like more definition. Than yours."

Jack looked as if he had been sucker punched.

He turned around and walked into the Pilates Room, which was vacant, stood in front of the mirrored wall, dropped the towels to the varnished wooden floor, then flexed his right bicep. Hard. Harder. He looked at it from every angle. He turned so that his back was to the mirror, flexed, quickly spun around to check the bicep reflection. As if it might disappear in the mirror. He did a double bicep flex. Staring at the mirror. Staring. He rubbed the palm of his right hand over his left bicep, then changed hands and ran his left-hand palm over his right arm bicep.

What was the matter with the peaks? Was he losing his pump? Was he losing definition?

Jack left the pile of towels on the floor and trotted toward the Locker Room, making a plaintive mooing noise as he passed Ashley and Kaitlyn.

Chapter Five

They walked from the Locker Room into the deafening chaos of the gym.

Patti sensed Anne holding back.

"I know, I know," Patti said. "It's overwhelming. The first couple times. But you'll get used to it. I think it would behoove us to just take a walk around. So, you get the lay of the land?"

"Sounds good to me, Sister Behoover. See all the great words you've learned from me? That they never taught you at Vassar? Lead on."

Patti started off around the perimeter of the gym, weaving in and around the scurrying motion.

"Hey Patti," a Personal Trainer called out from atop a Stretching Table where he was kneeling, holding up a woman's leg cradled between his shoulder and neck, his arms wrapped around her thigh, easing it toward him, as she lay serenely on the table.

Patti waved. "Austin, hi. This is my good friend, Anne." She put her arm around Anne's shoulder. "First timer."

Austin grinned, and the overhead lights gleamed on his perfect white teeth.

"Hi Anne. Welcome to the Club."

"Thank you."

They walked on.

Anne squealed.

"Who was That?"

"Down, girl. That, my dear, is one of *Them*. A Personal Trainer. That's Austin."

"What a cutie. I think he's the one I want."

"Lordie, girl, don't go settling for the first you happen to see. There are lots more where he came from."

"Do they all look so, so squeezable?"

Patti smiled. "I know. And so, so squeaky clean. Such tasty morsels laid before us."

"Oh man, you know we are so sick, don't you? Can you imagine if our kids heard us talking this way?"

"Mine? They'd be making those really gross gagging noises. And saying they're going to pitch. Or barf chunks. Aren't they sweet? But don't think the managers of this Gym don't know exactly what they're doing. They hire these kids, profile the ones with quote, *The Look*, close quote, and set them out there posing like works of art around the gym to entrap us."

"I'd be very happy to walk right into his trap. Like a little helpless fly. Right into the spider web."

"Beware, fair maiden. The spider spins its web around and around its prey and squeezes it to death."

"Ahh, what a way to go. To be squeezed in the arms of one of those cute hunks."

A man with a kettlebell in each hand passed them again as he made yet another circuit of the perimeter of the gym.

"Much more to come, girlfriend. We're just starting our tour. But Austin is a real sweetheart. In the afternoons, he's like an assistant coach at the high school he used to go to."

Anne stopped. And looked at Patti.

"You talk with them?" Anne sounded incredulous.

Patti laughed. "I know this may amaze you, my dear young lady, but some of them even know how to talk."

"You're cruel."

"I don't mean to be. But come on. Guys who look like that? Don't have to talk. Or anything else. All they have to do? Stand there and strike different poses. By the equipment. As inspiration. And motivation. They're paid for that."

They started walking again.

"So, tell me more about my next husband: Austin."

"OK. You like his buzzcut?"

"Mmmm."

"So, he told me his mom works in a beauty parlor, and she cuts his hair, cleans that up for him. Once a week. Always looks real sharp like that."

"His mom?" Anne sighed. "That's just so adorable. I'd run my fingers through it. All day. Do you think he'd let me?"

"I'm sure. If you ask politely. And hire him as your Personal Trainer. But slow down, girl. I mean, always keep somewhere in mind what we're here for. Yes?"

"Remind me?"

"To keep in shape, remember now?"

"Oh yeah, that's right. But I've got to ask you this. Exactly what was it that Austin is doing with that woman? That strumpet. She should leave my husband alone. I ought to yank her off the table."

"Strumpet. That's one of your words, I love. Strumpet."

"Whatever he's doing to her? Me next."

Patti laughed. "I think this may be the perfect time

to just take a quick little detour of our grand tour. For this one, you need to sit down." They were passing the Café. "Here, let's sit in here for a second. This you'll like."

They sat across from each other at a table in the small room as the blender whirled, mixing up a Blue Lightning for the man waiting at the counter.

"Ah, yes. So, the Stretching Tables intrigue you? I thought they just might. Your personal young stud *if* you've been a good little girl during your workout with him. Have you been?"

"For him? I do anything."

"Good. So, he's going to say these magic words to you: 'OK, Anne, now let's get you on the Stretch Table for 10 minutes.'"

"OK, so I don't know what that even means—*yet*— but I think I may like 30 minutes?"

"I think you may. OK, so after your training session, they have you lie on one of those tables—"

"I'm getting the shivers already." Anne feigned a full body tremor.

"Sounds like you already have your Personal Trainer in mind?"

"May we try out a different one every time?"

"No, you pig whore. You cannot. And what happened to your husband, Austin? Man, that affair didn't last long."

Anne sighed. "It was fun while it lasted."

"OK, so your own Adonis makes you lie on the table and gets you all real comfortable and maybe he'll put a rolled-up towel or two under your head as a pillow."

Patti made the motion of rolling up a towel and laying it at the end of their table.

"Oh yes." Anne looked off toward the gym.

"Slow down girl. He's just starting. Then he'll gently place a cool fragrant moist towel over your eyes."

"Oh baby, momma's moist already."

"And ready for this?"

"Oh, am I ever."

"So, he's gotten you nice and comfortable on the table. Then, guess what? He mounts the table."

"Slow down, girl. Slower. Go slower!"

Patti laughed. "You horny bitch. Get that filthy mind out of the gutters. This is serious. So, he's on that table with you. Straddling you."

"Just like we saw Austin?"

"Bingo. And starts gently massaging and stretching an arm here, a leg there, asking you how it feels, pressing more, putting more pressure on it, pressing deep, pushing hard." Patti showed how with her hands. "Just doing his job."

"Love that job." Anne folded her hands on the table and rested her head on them.

"A little harder," Patti continued. "Harder. Always deeper. Nice and firm. And he's so close to you now, he's leaning right on top of you, so close the tip of your tongue could easily touch the tip of his tongue if—"

"May we try that?" Anne looked up at Patti.

"So, close you can smell how good he smells. And now you're inhaling deeply. Greedily. Trying to draw in the wonderful scent of, of—I don't know. Youth? That scent of a beautiful young man? And it's giving you a buzz. And you feel the warmth of his breath. Like this very gentle summer breeze. After a shower. And you try to draw it in. And hold it."

"Mmmm. I'm holding it. It's giving me a buzz."

"And the smoothness of his muscled arms as he

presses one onto yours, harder, deeper, you're really feeling it—"

"Girl. I am so ready to go out there and select my dream boat, I mean—you know, Personal Trainer."

"Slow down, girlfriend. Don't get your panties all bunched up till I finish. So, you'll know exactly what's in store for you out there. You don't want to miss out on anything."

"There's more?"

"Oh yes indeed, there's more. What do you think: I'd take my best friend to something like the iHop of gyms? This is a Five Star Restaurant, girl. Seven courses."

"Yum." Anne raised her head and sat up.

"I'm going to let you in on a little secret," Patti said. "Just between us girls."

"I'm all ears."

Patti leaned across the table, closer to Anne, and whispered.

"If you can get that Joe one? If you can get him to service you. On the Stretching Table, OK? And if you take off your sneakers? He will kneel at your feet, for 20 minutes massaging—just your feet. The soles. The arches. Every little toe. Big toe. Little toe. In between toes. The, *this little piggy went to market* toe. Anointing each with oil. Twenty minutes of undivided man-attention."

"Sounds like our young man, this Joe, may be working through a pretty serious foot fetish?"

"That may well be. That may well be. And all the better for us. The woman on the table always starts making little noises of contentment as he's doing it. And so does Joe."

"Talk about a win/win."

"I digress. Excuse me."

"No need to apologize. Loved that digression. I think I like the Joe one already. Be sure to point him out to me."

"I will. So, if you obey your Personal Trainer, which ever lucky lad it might be, and if you've done just what he told you to do or—and this is the really, really good part. Listen up, girl: you really don't have to succeed; as long as you try. OK? Or... even better yet, *look* like you're trying."

"I can do that."

"Of course, you can. That's how you and I made it through eighth grade phys ed with Miss Landry. Remember?"

"Oh yes. Do I ever. In a million years, I never could ever have somersaulted over her stupid vault box. Was she insane? No matter how much she scowled at me. And blew her friggin' tin whistle."

Patti laughed.

"Me neither. Remember all that shit? So, if you just make an effort here, like you and I pretended we were doing for Cruella, there's no scowling. Just the opposite. Lavish praise. So, get this—"

The blender shut off. Patti lowered her voice.

"I'm all ears."

"I'm sure their PT training manual, or the pointers they get from Brian when they first start off, emphasize the importance of physical contact with the client."

"Beyond that stretching thing?"

"Oh, girl, poor little girl, that was mere gym foreplay. They'll help you get up from the lying position and sit right next to you on the edge of the Stretching Table. Side by side."

"Sweet chicken."

"As they talk with you about anything and everything *you* want to talk about. And, unlike our dear husbands, they really listen. And care. They are so there for us."

"Or, at least, maybe are really, really good actors?"

"That may be. But who cares? Compared to our husbands? They are all Academy Award nominees."

"My husband couldn't even make the cut for a middle school play."

"Mine? I'm pretty sure he was cut. As a tree stump. For his fifth-grade play. So, these guys are not only Academy Award worthy; they've got these incredible film-worthy looks. The first couple sessions, they'll fist bump you when you leave. Then, you graduate to a really nice warm bear hug, so you feel them all around you. Holding you. Squeezing you. Hard."

"Heaven. I'm all for the squeezing."

"I'm gathering that. Which is just the right way to end a good workout session, isn't it?"

"It certainly is."

"And get you incentivized to come back for the next, right? Good business practice, right?"

Anne luxuriously stretched and sighed, as if greeting the most beautiful June morning. "How many times a day can we come here?"

"Whenever you feel the need, cutie pie. No limits. Spend the day here, if you like. Set up your beach chair by the pool. Stop in here for all your meals. Breakfast. Lunch. Dinner. It's now your Club. But hang on. Hang on—"

"More?"

"Of course, more. You'll reach the point pretty

quickly when you graduate from the bear hug. And then… they'll kiss you goodbye."

"Ahh, a smooch on the cheek."

"No, I don't mean a little peck on the cheek. Like from your great aunt Lenore. With her smudged lipstick on her teeth. No. I mean right on the mouth. And you'll feel, and taste, the softness of what? Voluptuous. Tender. Young. Lips."

"They're allowed to do that?"

"I think they're even encouraged."

"Tongue?" Anne giggled.

"Well, were you a good little girl who worked hard during your session? And tried real, real hard? Then… their tongue is yours. And tell me: is there anything more wonderful, more delicious than a hot 24-year-old stud's tongue?"

"I don't know. But I'm so ready to find out."

"Good. So now that you're fully prepped, let's get our sorry little asses back out there. And complete our little tour. And maybe even spot just the perfect Personal Trainer. To help you with our fitness regime."

"Let's not tarry," Anne said.

Patti laughed. "I'm going to make that word my own. Love it. Tarry. Remind me when we're back in the Locker Room to show you the little dark private spa and massage rooms. Way back in there near the pool area. You'll like those."

"Don't forget. I don't' want to miss a thing."

"Did I tell you about my last massage back there? With Gonzola?"

"Details. Details."

"He had me way out there. Far, far beyond the solar system. Soaring way out along the Milky Way…"

Chapter Six

Jack came out of the Locker Room wearing his black hoodie and white Adidas work-out pants with a black stripe down the sides, walked over to the pull-up bar between the two lat stations and the two rowing machines, looked up at it, and, in a movement barely perceptible, was holding the bar and executing perfect-form pull-ups.

One. Two. Three. Seven. Thirteen. Fourteen.

Those nearby now were watching. And silently counting.

Seventeen. Eighteen.

There wasn't a Personal Trainer in the Club who could do ten. Ten was a lot, even for someone in really good shape, and if they could squeeze out 10, it invariably involved a lot of leg flailing, as if the air below them would somehow provide support to help get them up there, and their heads never got over the bar on the last several counts, and their form deteriorated so that they looked like pieces of meat on a hook, straining and shaking, their bodies trembling.

Twenty. Twenty-one.

With everyone else, Latham was watching.

That amazing young god, he thought, was still going strong, still maintaining his clock-like rhythm, maintaining his form, exhibiting no signs of strain, no sign of not being able to go on and on for as long as he wanted. He was flawless. He was the most perfect human being Latham had ever seen. Anywhere. He couldn't be real. He was a living fantasy.

Twenty-two. Twenty-three. Twenty-four. Twenty-five. Twenty-seven. Thirty.

He alighted on the ground as gracefully as a cougar. His feet kept moving, always, in that little dance step of his, as if every cell of his body was surging with energy. He peeled off the hoodie and cast it to one side, straightening his gray tank top across his shoulders, clasping his hands behind his back and flexing his triceps, hard. He looked up at the bar, then put his hands on the opposite sides of the bottom of the tank top, and in one motion, like a stripper, pulled it over his head, crumpled it into a ball and tossed it on top of the hoodie.

In less than a minute since executing the 30 pull-ups, he was up on the bar again, pulling himself up and straightening his legs until they were parallel to the floor, then circling the lower half of his torso, first all the way to the right, holding it, then all the way to the left, holding it, his abdominal muscles popping, showing their definition as if Michelangelo had lavished months of attention on chiseling each individual ab out of marble.

All activity in the gym slowed. It grew quiet. All eyes fixated on the show. Back and forth. Back and forth as he worked his obliques, his body from the waist down moving with his complete control over every individual muscle.

Once more on his feet, he walked over to the floor-to-ceiling mirror that extended the length of the long wall behind him, clasped his hands behind his head and twisted his torso, one way, then the other, examining it as if a fine art expert critically evaluating the look of each ab. He pushed his workout pants a little lower around his hips to reveal more of the deep V cut of his obliques, then did the same flexing movement, checking each side, seeing what work, if any, still needed to be done to come even closer to the perfection he craved. He ran his hand down his flat slab of stomach over the hint of a trail of pubic hair that led straight into his workout pants.

If Jack could see in the mirror how many eyes were riveted on him, he gave no hint that there was anyone else in the gym. It was his. He was God, creating Man. He pushed his pants a touch lower for a closer inspection, looked again in the mirror, then, satisfied that his creation was perfect, pulled them back up to almost cover the top of his black Under Armor compression shorts, doing a double bicep flex into the mirror, and bringing the flex down lower in the competitive body builder's classic pose. He held it, making a war face at himself in the mirror, shaking his arms loose at his sides, grabbed up his tank top and hoodie, then walked across the gym with a roll of the hips just this side of a swagger.

The crowds parted to let him pass.

He stopped at the section of the gym where two long ropes—shoulder width apart—dangled from the high ceiling. He looked up to the top of the ropes where black clamps attached them to the highest metal grid that ran across the ceiling. He rubbed his hands together, then rubbed them vigorously down the sides of his workout pants. Looking up once more to the distant ceiling, he flipped off the *Cloud Surfer* sneaker on his right foot with his left foot, then pushed off the sneaker on his left foot with his right foot, kicked the sneakers out of the way, then lifted each foot and stripped off the low-cut black athletic socks and tossed them on top of the sneakers. He looked up at the ceiling again, rubbed his palms, and pulled his workout pants to around his ankles, kicking them off toward his growing pile of workout gear. He adjusted his compression shorts which admirably were performing the job they were designed to do: accentuating his bulge and butt.

He walked between the ropes, turned around to face the gym, shrugged his shoulders as if to say "what the hell", and grabbed a rope in each hand, instantly starting the climb, one hand pulling him up on one side as the other hand let go and reached higher on the opposite rope, up, up, higher and higher, scrambling up like a monkey, his rigid body swaying side to side with each higher grab, up, up, past the line of fluorescent lights, higher, past the gray plastic heating/cooling tube, up toward the grids which crisscrossed the ceiling of the gym, up to the very top where the metal collars secured the ropes to the ceiling near the skylight.

He hung there, motionless, and looked down.

"How ya doin?" he asked the crowd gathering below, gawking at him.

He started to reverse the process, letting the ropes slip a few inches through his palms, stopping, lowering himself a foot more, stop, another foot, stop, descending until he was halfway down, then reversing course and scooting back up to the top again.

The gym broke out in applause.

He favored the earthlings with a God-like grin, lowered himself a quarter of the way down, steadied himself and pushed his arms straight out into the Iron Cross position.

And held it.

Arms quivering. Mouth set. Teeth clenched, eyes concentrating. Holding the position. The ropes shaking.

A minute? Two minutes? He pulled in his arms and began lowering himself to the half-way mark, then stopped, raised his two legs parallel to the floor, and began circling his lower torso in the ab-tightening oblique-stressing motions, back and forth.

He steadied the ropes; then continued to lower himself, legs outstretched parallel to the floor, all the way down until at last, he was standing, holding the ropes as they stopped moving.

He gave a war whoop, and seeing everyone staring at him, seemed, for a moment, embarrassed. He looked around, saw Pony-Tail-Swisher on her treadmill smile at him and give him a thumbs up. He looked back at the ropes, kissed his right bicep and smiled back at her. When the onlookers cheered and applauded, he raised one arm in the air, giving a Mr. Olympia fitness show flex, then performed the same flex with the other arm, relaxed, laughing at his pantomime.

Anne broke out of the crowd and walked right up to him.

"That was quite impressive," she said.

He looked at her, grabbed the ends of the two ropes and brought them to her.

"Wanna try?"

"How very thoughtful of you. But no, I think not. Not today, thank you. In my eighth-grade gym class, I was much too scared even to just grab on. To even try going up one bloody foot. No way. Still the same. Heights freak me."

"No big deal," he said, looking up at the ceiling. "Here, let me show you. I promise I won't let anything happen to you."

"Well... if I was going to try with anyone, I suppose it would be with you. But actually, truth be told? I'm sweating, just looking up there. I was sweating watching you."

He laughed. "Here, look," he said, clasping his hands over his head so his shaved armpits were right in her face. "No sweat at all. See? Touch 'em.'"

"No thank you," she said, looked, then lightly ran her palm over one armpit, her hand slipping up over the solid mound of tricep. Then touched his other armpit.

"That's unnatural. Don't you sweat?"

"Not that much. More with cardio. When I try going flat out?"

"I don't want to learn how to scramble up those ropes. Like a monkey But, can you teach me anything else?"

"Sure. Ma'am, you looking for a Personal Trainer?"

"Maybe. Yes. I'm pretty sure I'm old enough to be your mother, but I don't want people to look at me and call me: ma'am. I want them to look at me and call me: Anne. Can you help me get in that type of shape? And maintain it?"

"Ma'am... I mean Anne. Piece of cake. I'm Jack, by the way."

He held out his hand and they shook.

"Jack, a pleasure to meet you."

He looked her over with approval. She was trim, her skin young, supple, unlike so many of the weathered, parchment paper hags he saw there, her sleek, short dark hair glistened with life in the light. He was fascinated by her slight British accent that made everything she said sound classy. And smart.

"A walk in the park," Jack said. "You look in really

good shape. Already. I've got some openings. Would you want to give it a try? And see if the chemistry's there?"

"You certainly look like you know what you're doing and—"

He flexed and grinned at her. He gathered up his gym gear and jogged toward the Locker Room. "Think about it," he called back to her.

She stared at the way his body, from his shoulders to his waist, formed the classic V shape, how his ass cheeks moved up and down in precise, perfect rhythm. Like pistons.

"I am," she called after him.

Chapter Seven

On his spinning bike, Latham had watched the rope climbing exhibition, savoring the view looking up between Jack's legs, had observed Anne go over and speak with him, and now, the moment he saw Jack scooping up his gear from the floor and heading toward the Locker Room, had gotten off the bike, picked up his towel and shaker of BCAA, and followed him in.

From observations since that first day, he had seen Jack in the gym, Latham knew which alcove in the Locker Room Jack preferred, and made it a point always to find a locker right there.

Damn. Mark was there, too, but it looked like he was getting his stuff together to leave. He was rubbing some product through his hair, and Latham knew it wouldn't be much longer before he packed up and left for work. Mark was telling Jack that he, and his girlfriend, were going to run in a marathon in Rhode Island that weekend.

In bits and pieces of guarded conversations over the last several months, Latham had pried out of Mark that he was 23, had gone to Roger Williams College in Rhode Island on a wrestling scholarship, and was working at Merrill Lynch in the same office park where Latham's law office was located. But most of all Latham had learned: Mark had a "girlfriend."

Young, handsome, with a wrestler's build, had Mark found he needed this word as a shield? Latham wondered. It popped up in every other sentence. Whoever he was talking with. Did he worry that his looks sent out the wrong vibe? Had he discovered how powerful his looks were? He covered them up—baggy white sweatshirt, loose work-out pants—offering forbidden glimpses only when he changed, taking care always that the large white towel was secured around his waist before he slipped his underwear off, and that it was securely around him before he put them back on after showering.

As Mark picked up his gym bag and threw his towel in the hamper on the way out, Latham again checked out how well his business slacks cradled his wrestler's butt. Not bad at all.

Jack also was watching Mark's exit, then looked over at Latham.

Latham felt his eyes on him and froze.

He had never spoken with Jack, had never even made eye contact. He hadn't wanted to spook Jack by coming on too fast, too strong, by revealing in any way how fixated he was on him. Better just to get him used to his presence for a while. That had been his strategy: to gradually get to know him. More natural.

Look up, look up, he now thought to himself, and in an act of will raised his eyes from Jack's crotch to Jack's face. *Keep eyes on face. Eye contact. Hold it there. Hold it.*

Jack's lips were smiling.

Jack winked at him.

"So," Jack said, "did you hear he has a... girlfriend?"

Latham stared. His brain sprung back into gear. He laughed.

"Oh yeah, I think I may have heard that. Once or twice."

"I mean what the fuck, is every other word out of his mouth 'girlfriend'? What does he think? We're gonna toss him over that bench and gang bang him?"

Latham rolled his eyes and slipped off his Nike workout shorts.

"I mean, he is sort of good looking and everything," Jack continued, "but fuck-worthy? Come on. Give me a break. His girlfriend can have him."

"You know, when someone talks that much about their… girlfriend," Latham said, making air quotes, "that's probably exactly what he wants."

Jack shook his head, and in one quick motion peeled his compression shorts down his quads, over his calves, and off, tossing them on top of his pile of workout gear he had thrown under the bench, as if trash.

Latham's eyes were drawn to this pile of treasure under the bench which was attracting him as inexorably as a magnet attracts iron filings, all the while memorizing from one quick glance everything about Jack's penis, the look of the neatly trimmed patch of light pubic hair over it, the heft of his shaved testicles, the symmetry of his smooth ass, before Jack had tied the large white towel around his waist and shut his locker door.

"You here tomorrow?" Jack asked as he walked out of the alcove.

"You bet," Latham said. "Always come before work. I actually got a membership while this place was still under construction. I may very well be the first paying customer here. I think I may be."

"Good stuff. A founder. Where do you work?"

Latham was buttoning his white dress shirt, then adjusting the French cuffs.

54

"I'm a lawyer, a partner in the firm in that office park down the parkway. So, this is a real convenient way to start the day. Get the old engines revved up. Without this? I couldn't work all day. That's for sure."

Jack stopped. And looked at him. And smiled.

"Excellent," he said. "So, Mr. Attorney. Tell me: what kind of lawyer are you? I mean, like, you on your feet in court? All day?"

"No," Lathan said. "Nothing so glamorous. I'm a tax lawyer. So, I sit on my ass in an office all day. That's why I need this."

Jack again looked at him and did a double take. And smiled again.

"Good stuff. My name is Jack, by the way." He walked back into the alcove and shook hands. "I'm a new Personal Trainer here. Just started."

"I'm Latham. Jack, I've seen you around. Your rope climb was truly amazing."

"You saw that?" He grinned. "Thank you. Still working on refining it a little."

"Looked perfect to me."

"Hey, if I can ever help you, Latham, just let me know, OK? Any time."

"Thank you. I may take you up on that. I think I may have hit a plateau and—"

"Everyone does. At some point. I can help power you through, if you want. Switch up your routine. Kick it up a notch, if you'd like." Jack looked him over as if evaluating his build. "You've got a really good base. I can tell."

Latham looked up at Jack. And vacuum sucked in his stomach.

"I could help you transform yourself," Jack

continued. "If you'd like. You've got a real good build to work with. Just give me the word. I could have you looking like me in no time. If you want this sort of look."

Latham stared at him. "You messing with me? Man, I'd be here 24/7 every day if I could do that."

Jack laughed. "You're funny. But if you'd like to try and see what we can do, you know, together, let me know, OK? I've seen you out there and you're basically doing the exact same routine. Each day. I mean, it's good, you've got really good form, but I can walk you through a bunch of different stuff. New routines that will trick your muscles. Like never before. You'll be surprised how fast just that will grow them."

"Guns like yours?" Latham said, looking at Jack's biceps.

"You want this look?" Jack said, flexing one as he held the towel around him with his other hand.

"If you can do that?" Latham said, pointing, "for me? Guaranteed? I'll hire you on the spot. As my Personal Trainer."

Jack beamed. "You are on. Want to start tomorrow? This time slot?"

"I'll be here."

"Great. See you tomorrow," Jack said, and bounded out to the hall.

He stopped. Walked back into the alcove. And fist bumped Latham. Then walked back out to the corridor, heading through the Locker Room toward the Showers and Steam Room.

Latham didn't open up his fist. He looked at it, then felt it with his other hand. From his time at the gym, he knew a fist bump was the gym equivalent of a warm hug. Jack had fist bumped him. Jack had noticed him out in the gym. Jack was offering to remake him. In his own image. *This*, he thought, *is a great start to the day*.

From his reconnaissance work the past week, since the day he had first spotted Jack and felt like he had been hit in the stomach with an elephant gun—what his eyes beheld, and devoured, knocked the air out of him—since that day, Latham had memorized Jack's routine to the minute: exactly how long he would stay in the Steam Room, then in the showers, then, white towel around his dripping torso, stand at the sinks, take one of the disposable razors in jars along the counter, pump out a handful of Barbasol and spread it on his face, then shave, in between strokes feeling his chest and hitting a few stray hairs around his nipples with the next stroke, (passing behind him as close as he dared while pretending not to look, Latham had noted that his skin was flawless, not a mole, not a freckle, not a hair, from a foot away it looked like polished marble if marble could have a light tan), splashing water over his face, pumping out some mouthwash into a little cup, running a comb back through his wet hair, again and again while watching himself in the long mirror, mesmerized. Sometimes, in front of the mirror, he would strike the contrapposto pose of an ancient Greek statue and take a selfie, before heading back to his locker.

That period of time gave Latham enough of a window right now to get into the custom-tailored blue suit he had ordered hand-made for special meetings like today's, knot his yellow silk tie, adjust his bull and bear gold cufflinks, then do what he had wanted to do, had thought of doing, had dreamed of doing since the first time he had seen Jack. He was in a rush today to get to his office to be ready for his new clients, he was distracted, but there was no telling when the fates again would converge to give him an opportunity like this. A clear shot. Now or never.

He stepped out of the alcove, looked down the hall toward the sinks—two men shaving—looked along the corridor—for a rare moment it was quiet, no one coming, no one going, just one man standing in front of a mirror, lifting the front of the white towel around his waist, completely absorbed in circling a hair dryer around his crotch—back to his alcove where, in one rehearsed motion, he reached under the bench, grabbed all of Jack's gear—no time to pick and choose, such a chance only comes once—shoved it all into his gym bag, zipped it up and walked toward the door out, his heart pounding as if he had set the treadmill to the steepest incline, knowing that if seen, if confronted… At that moment, it didn't matter.

Dan was coming in, soaked from his jog outside, a towel around his neck, eyes glazed, about to say something funny like he always did.

"Gotta run," Latham said, rushing by. "See you tomorrow?"

"God willing," Dan said, but Latham by then was far down the corridor toward the door out.

He fast walked across the parking lot to his Beamer, tossed in the gym bag, and, rather than sitting there to drink his protein shake, as he always did, took off.

It wasn't until he was at the first stop light that he zipped open the bag next to him, felt still the warmth of Jack's gear. Delicious. How was it that really good-looking guys always smelled good?

The light turned green.

Chapter Eight

The door of the Steam Room closed behind Jack, deadening the blare of the music in the gym with the soothing dreamy exhalations of bursts of steam, swirling wraiths of which filled the room like a warm, wonderful, all-embracing cloud.

Jack felt his way along the wall to the tile bench, climbed to the upper level, pulled off the towel from around his waist, positioned it in the corner and sat down, leaning against the warm dripping wet walls. He closed his eyes, breathing slowly, deeply, the soothing moist heat relaxing him and sending him into another world, wondering if Latham was indeed the lawyer worth gazillions that Brian had mentioned to Ashley, thinking of what to say to him tomorrow, what to do to seal the deal and become his Personal Trainer. And fantasizing where that might lead.

Every once in a while, whatever generated the steam paused to stabilize the temperature, the soothing sound stopped, the clouds of steam drifted, the room became less impenetrable. Jack was about to climb down and put his hand out the door to turn the dial to keep the steam coming up when he noticed against the opposite wall two men.

Sitting.

Masturbating.

Their eyes locked on him.

Jack closed his eyes. Opened them. Looked again. They were still there. Still working away, still aimed directly at him. No one said a word.

"Is this by any chance the 'Develop your Forearms Fast' class?" Jack joked.

No reply. They continued on.

He tried again.

"Or is this the 'Clean and Jerk Class'"?

Nothing.

No one else in there.

Jack hoped the door would open and someone would walk in. Come on. Anyone. Where the hell was Austin? Any Personal Trainer. Please. They had to see this. No one would believe him. Where was everyone? Didn't anyone want to take a steam? He looked at his watch. He had planned to stay 15 minutes. It had only been what, six? But this was getting way too creepy. He got up, held the towel around his waist, climbed down and exited into the cooler fresh air of the Shower Room.

He passed Harrison in an alcove, changing from his official Personal Trainer outfit into his own workout gear, and reported what was going on in the Steam Room. As the head of the Personal Trainers, he would know what to do.

Harrison looked at him.

"They're what?"

"You know, fapping?" Jack made the motion with his right hand.

Harrison looked at him as if he was an alien.

"You kidding me with this?"

Jack looked at him, uncertain what to say.

"What are you," Harrison said, "like a Cub Scout? Working on your Anti-Fapping Merit Badge? Where have you been, boy? What the hell do you think goes on in there? I mean, not all the time. OK? But at least a few times a day? Easy. Every day. Man, you *are* a newbie. Didn't Brian mention that as one of your duties? As a new recruit? Get in there and clean it all up, boy."

Jack stared at him.

"Give them a few minutes. Wait till they come out. Then go take care of it. You've gotta be checking all day, man. If anyone goes in there? and slips? or complains? it's on your watch, man."

Jack kept staring at him.

Harrison pointed. "You'll find all the stuff you need to clean it up in that maintenance closet. "Over there," he said, "next to the scale."

Chapter Nine

Anne was hanging around near the entrance to the Men's Locker Room when Jack came out, now wearing a newbie Personal Trainer periwinkle blue T-shirt and black gym shorts he had found in Austin's locker. He spotted her.

"Hey."

"Hey you, Monkey Boy."

"You must really put in a lot of time here. Anne."

"Thank you for not calling me ma'am."

"You're welcome, Anne. So how often do you come to the Club, Anne?"

"Actually, this is my very first day. My friend Patti brought me."

"Cool. So, welcome. To the Club."

"Thank you. I think I'm going to like it. So, I've been thinking over what we were talking about, over there", she said, pointing, "and I think… I'm maybe sort of ready? At least to start? You know, give it a try?"

"Great."

"Any chance you have an opening for a brand-new beginner client? Who has nary a clue what she's doing?"

Jack smiled. "Nary. That's a funny word."

"Oops. Sorry about that. Born and raised in England, so I still have to translate a little."

"No, no problem. It's cute. Nary. So sure. Nary a problem. I can work you in. What are like, your goals? You know, what would you like to accomplish here?"

Anne looked at him and thought for a moment.

"Hmmm. OK. I'd say: holding the line. That may be the best way to describe it. I'd like always to look like a few years younger than I am. So, when my husband comes home from a hard day's work? Or my kids come home from school? They don't see an old crone flying around the kitchen. On a broomstick."

"Somehow, I don't think that's gonna be a problem. Nary a problem. So, you're married? With kids?"

"Yes, and yes. Two kids. One just finishing her second year in college. Georgetown. That's Meghan. The other, Walker, he's a senior at Delbarton; counting down the last few days left until graduation. June 20th. Next Thursday. He's been one of the lacrosse stars there. I don't even understand anything about that game. I should. I pretend. I am such a bad mother."

"Sounds like your son's very athletic. Must have gotten your gym genes."

"I doubt that. His dad was a good athlete at college. Track. You wouldn't know it now, though. What was once a six pack is now... a great big one gut."

"That does happen."

Jack absentmindedly lifted the lower corner of his T-shirt and ran his fingers slowly up and down his abs. Anne watched.

"Still six," he said when he realized she was staring. "Gotta keep counting. If you're not careful, one'll disappear on you. I gotta say, I'm shocked your kids are that age, those ages. I'd say you're already winning the battle. Of looking younger."

"Oh boy, you are good. I love you. Does that count as a training session? That's all I need. Because I would pay for that one. I'd pay a lot for that one."

Jack smiled.

She liked the way his lips looked always ready to grin, as if he saw the humorous side of everything. She liked the way they looked so nourishing.

"No, no such luck. That was not an official work-out. If you're really interested, we can find a time slot that's good for you, for both of us."

"Perfect."

"Give it a try. I always tell all my new clients—that would be like," he raised his eyes towards the ceiling as if trying to recall the precise number, "that would be like, about, literally: three. So far. If no one quits".

He crossed himself and folded his hands in prayer.

Anne laughed. She liked the way he joked around and didn't take himself seriously.

"I always tell them we can start off and you see if the chemistry's there," Jack continued, "if we're meeting expectations. All that good stuff. So, no commitment. Some Trainers want you to commit to, like x number of sessions? Or a certain number of weeks? I think that's bullshit. If it's not working for you, all you gotta do is say so. Fair enough?"

"That's more than fair."

She looked at him and liked the way his hair—the color of thick dark honey—dropped in wet ringlets over his forehead, around his head, down the back of his neck. Like a halo. Like a marble bust of Apollo.

"And I feel the chemistry is going to be there," she added.

"Well, we can find out. If you want to give it a try, I'm game."

Jack pulled his iPhone out of his pocket and started scrolling through.

"Hey, here's an open time slot. Here's, like—a lot of open times. Literally, a whole lot. You like early mornings, I'm guessin'? This sort of time?"

"Perfect for me. If it is for you. A good start to the day."

"When do you want to begin?"

"I'd say right now, but I have to run. Tomorrow?"

"You got it."

She turned to head to the Women's Locker Room.

Jack called after her. "Hey, Anne. Don't you want to know my hourly rate and everything?"

Anne looked back. "If it works, then not a problem. Right? Whatever."

Jack looked at her. "This is your lucky day. I'm just starting out. So, mine are the lowest Personal Trainer rates you can get here."

"I think you're right," Anne waved as she got to the Locker Room entrance. "This is my lucky day."

Patti was at the mirror by their alcove, blow drying her hair as she brushed it out.

Anne jumped up and down behind her.

"I got one," she shouted.

"What?"

"I got one."

She took Patti by the shoulders and shook her, jumping around her.

"You got one what?"

"I got me a real live Personal Trainer. That Jack one."

"Bitch. You rock, girlfriend. You just got yourself a real stud muffin Trainer." Patti looked at her in the mirror and paused. "Now you're not gonna Mrs. Robinson the poor boy, are you?"

"No way, girlfriend. He's training me. He's going to train me. Starting tomorrow. Patti: thank you. My first day, and I've already got myself a real honest to goodness Personal Trainer. This is going to be fun."

"Just remember, you cradle robber: you can look all you want, but no touching."

"What?"

Chapter Ten

Just beneath the surface chaos of the Club lay predictable patterns, regular rhythms, so on the same day, at the same hour, the same people would be doing pretty much the same things.

The next day Latham at once sensed that regular rhythm had shifted.

When they thought no one was watching, one Personal Trainer after the other would try to scale the ropes. Try. They sheepishly asked Jack for pointers, he'd show them, they'd try again, and look as awkward, as frustrated, as a new member of the Club. They would try his ab flexing routine on the high bar but couldn't come close to the effortless control he exhibited. They pow-wowed with him, asking for tips, listening to him, absorbing what he was telling them, then try again.

Jack kept upping his game. He'd be talking to someone as he casually leaned against the pole that supported the high bar, and while he was talking, grasp the pole in a certain way and perform a flagpole, so that his entire body extended parallel to the floor, holding that rigid position for longer than seemed possible. As he kept talking. Other Trainers would attempt it, yet couldn't get into position, heaving out their legs and tumbling to the floor, in a heap.

Every once in a while, if a song he liked blasted through the sound system, he would launch into a break dance that had him spinning on his head, then moonwalking from one side of the gym to the other, pushing off from the wall with a running start and cartwheeling back across. He'd get on a treadmill and continue his break dance routine, sideways, backwards, spinning through the bars, standing on his hands, all with the fluid grace of a modern dancer.

When a group gathered around him to chat, he would do something so that his feet appeared to rise several inches off the floor, float there for a few seconds, then gently descend, which creeped everyone out. Who was this guy?

In the Personal Trainer lounge, he took the deck of cards on the table, tossed them up in repeated elaborate air shuffles, then asked someone to pick one at random, without showing him. He somehow would extract an identical card from his underwear.

When he felt things in the gym were becoming too routine, dull, stale, he'd dream up a challenge: which Personal Trainer could get on a Treadmill, set it to the steepest incline, and run flat out, full speed, for the most minutes? Which Personal Trainer could then do the most pushups in one minute? The two with the highest numbers would then compete against each other for the most pushups, but this time with a female Personal Trainer stretched out on their backs, encouraging them, slapping them as if on a horse, as the onlookers placed bets on the outcome and cheered their favorites. Which Personal Trainer could bench press or curl one of the female Personal Trainers the most times? Jack could make everything fresh.

A Personal Trainer across the gym seeing Jack arrive

in the morning would whoop the moose mating call—
WOOO WOOOO— and wait for Jack to echo the greeting.
As Jack walked toward the Locker Room, others made a
point of dropping what they were doing, coming over to fist
bump him and hug him, whispering something to him,
waiting for a smile or joke or piece of gossip, like puppies
waiting for their master's pat on the head.

More of them were slinging their photo IDs on the
lanyards over their backs as Jack did, and when they had
time-off to work-out themselves, would emerge from the
Locker Room wearing the same style black stringer and
tiny *Gym Shark* shorts that Jack favored. They saw what
brand cologne he used and soon wraiths of it drifted
around the Locker Room.

It was clear to any observer that—without fuss or
bother—Jack had toppled Harrison from his position as
High Priest of the Personal Trainers. Jack was their new
Messiah.

And any member of the Club, who fantasized, in
their middle-aged imaginations, that they, too, could pull
it off, started wearing stringers and *Gym Shark* shorts, the
same colors as Jack's, and soon everyone was wearing
Cloud Surfer sneakers, gray with the orange soles and
laces. When they thought no one was looking, they stared
up at the ropes and would give it a try, sliding back down
after gaining a foot.

* * *

As he was spinning, Latham eavesdropped on the
conversation of two women on the bikes next to his.

"Look. He's coming," one squealed under her breath
like a teeny bopper.

"Oh. My. God. How do I look?"

"Quick girl. Head erect. Boobs up. Faster. Pedal faster. He's coming."

They looked straight ahead as if nothing was happening.

"Excuse me," Jack said, "are you Merle?"

The first woman blushed and giggled.

"I'm not either," her friend jumped in, "but I could be. Anything interesting?"

"If I can't find Merle, maybe you wanna sub in for her?"

"Any time."

"I'm supposed to meet a Merle here for her first session, but I can't find her. Anywhere. I'll do the circuit once more. Sorry to bother."

"Please. Bother. Any time. No bother. At all."

Jack smiled.

"If I can ever help you gals, any questions, anything at all, just give a holler, OK? I'm here for you."

"Thank you," they each said, pedaling faster and watching him walk away, and when he was a good distance across the gym, giggling again like teenage girls.

They slowed back down to their regular pace.

"Oh, come to momma, baby boy.

"Did you hear that? He said he's here for us."

"I'm here to nurse you, you beautiful baby boy, 24/7."

"When he asked if we knew Merle, we should have said, 'oh you mean that smelly skank?'"

"Lucky Merle, the big bitch. Merle the Bitch. I hope she cuts a wicked fart every time he has her lean over."

"I hope she feels a lump and has a big fat smelly wet turd drop out."

70

"Girl, you be vicious. But I second that emotion."

"That hunk of humanity should be ours. All ours."

"May a snot ball fling out of Merle's nose when he stretches her."

* * *

Anyone watching—and that was just about everyone in the gym—saw how much fun Jack was having with each of his clients. How he was introducing brand new techniques and routines, tailored specifically to whoever he was with. How he really seemed to be enjoying himself. And really cared about what he was doing. It wasn't long before anyone with a serious interest in fitness, and anyone who wanted to join in the fun, and anyone who just wanted to be with him, was signing on as one of his clients.

Jack's days of passing out towels and swabbing down the sticky Steam Room floor were over before they began.

He now had the best book of business and wore the black T-shirt of a senior Personal Trainer.

Chapter Eleven

Jack gunned his Jeep up the cobble-stone driveway. Where to park? Where to park? He saw two wide flights of stone steps, each leading to impressive double doors. Which was her front door?

It was a stately brick Georgian manor, three stories presiding over a ridge, surrounded, and shaded by venerable old oaks.

Anne called from an open door: "You found me. Come in. Get out of that bloody wicked heat."

Jack bounded up the stone steps.

"Please excuse my appearance," she said. She was barefoot, in short shorts, a large loose tank-top hanging almost to the bottom of her shorts. "Just finishing up tiling a bathroom. Almost."

She brushed the hair off her face.

"I'm impressed," he said, and gave her a quick kiss.

She led him into the reception hall.

He pivoted, staring.

"Are you kidding me? Think you got enough room here?"

Anne looked around.

"It was a broken-down old pile when I first saw it. No working heat, no working plumbing, no working electricity. In a good half of the house."

"Really?"

"Walls falling down. Everything. But I fell in love at once. It has such beautiful bones. I had to save it."

ack was looking, whistling in awe at the high ceilings, the massive carved limestone fireplace, the grand staircase.

"Your husband has got to be like super smart to afford all this. Where'd he go to college?"

"Harvard."

"Figures. He's gotta be, like, genius level. Literally. To have a house like this."

"I don't know about that. He's bright. But he's had a good run of luck, too. That's important. For sure. Right places, right times. That's when luck comes in."

"This sure looks like a whole lot more than luck to me. So, how'd he do it? Harvard, then what?"

Anne led him into the oval music room.

"Well, then he went on to the B School—Harvard Business School—then through some contact of his dad's got a job at Goldman Sachs. And did pretty well there. As a trader. I guess he has some sort of innate feel for it. So, he and a couple pals broke off and started their own hedge fund. And the thing did well right from the start."

Jack sat down at the grand piano and played the first few notes of "Chopsticks".

"Can you play?" Anne asked.

"You just heard my entire repertoire." He bowed. "That be it."

"That's about my speed. Meghan's actually pretty good. She took lessons since the second grade. Walker? He wouldn't even sit down there. We should play a—"

"So, then what did your husband do? I interrupted. I'm sorry. I shouldn't do that. But this piano is awesome."

73

He pretended he was playing an elaborate concerto that took his long fingers up and down the keyboard, over all the keys.

"No. That's OK. So honestly? I still don't understand exactly what it is Richard does—I joke with him that he's some sort of money changer. Sometimes I tell him he must be a money launderer. He doesn't like that, but whatever it is, it's working. And keeps the wolf away from the door."

"I'd say the poor wolf is nailed to your door. Paws stretched out. So, Harvard."

"Where did you go to college?"

Jack looked away. He got up from the piano bench.

"I didn't," he said quietly, from a place far away. "My parents never even talked to me about going."

"Are you serious?"

"Not once."

"Jack, I—"

Suddenly Anne saw him not as a young god, strayed from Olympus, but as someone's lost boy. She circled him in the hug of a mother and held him. "I'm so sorry," she whispered into his shoulder. "I—"

"No, no, it's OK. I got out of there the minute I got out of high school. My old man told me I had to grow up, join the work force he kept telling me, spend the rest of my life sitting at a metal desk. Like him. No way. I ran so fast. Never looked back." He came back from wherever he was. "It's worked out OK. So far."

"You should be very proud of what you've done on your own. I'd say you've got super street smarts. My bet? You'll always land on your feet. You could do anything you want."

Jack looked embarrassed and looked away again.

"I don't know. I don't know about that. I'm really happy just doing what I'm doing. Maybe it'll develop into something. I'd like maybe to open up my own gym. Someday. Maybe."

"That would be wonderful," Anne said, grasping his arm and shaking it. "I can see you having a whole chain. Give the Club a real run for its money. You can do it. Let me know, whenever you're ready, whenever you want to give it a go. I can get Richard to—"

He looked at her.

"No, no. I don't know. That's a long ways off. I'm just starting out. Gotta see how things work out for now, just one day at a time."

"That's a good philosophy."

Anne suddenly wished her house wasn't so large and decided not to give him her usual grand tour.

"I really appreciate you coming over, its—"

"Are you kiddin? Not a problem. Not a problem at all. Literally. I've got some down time right now anyhow."

"I'm going to pay for your time, just like—"

"No, comeon. No charge for consulting work outside the office. For me? This is fun stuff."

"It's just I want to surprise Richard when he gets home. He may as well get something out of this whole project," Anne swept her hand to encompass the entirety of the house, "and I thought a home gym would be perfect. But I don't have a clue what sort of equipment would be best. What to get. Where to get it. What to do. How it should look. So, I go to the expert."

"Great project. I love it. So, how long is he gone for?"

"Well, he's got work over in Singapore right now, so he's going to hit a bunch of Asian cities as long as he's there. Then over to Dubai. Bottom line? As Richard would say. He always says that: bottom line. Drives me crazy. We've got a couple weeks to get it done. Possible?"

"No worries. Easy peasy."

They walked into the two-story library paneled in French polished mahogany.

"I had just finished renovating our house when I saw this one," Anne said as they walked. "Halfway up the driveway I knew—something in me just fell instantly in love—I knew right then I had to possess it. I called Richard and told him about it. The poor man. I think his exact words were 'Just tell me where to fax my signature.' I'm pretty sure he was happy to give me something new to work on. To keep me out of his hair."

Jack smiled. "So, you did all this?"

They walked through the library and out into the conservatory with its Palladium windows.

"Well, of course I didn't do it, but no, I take that back; I actually did do some of it, at least. You'd be very proud. One of the workmen taught me how to tile and I really tiled—am tiling—a couple of the bathrooms—"

"A couple? How many are there?"

"Seven. And a half. I think. I'm getting pretty good, fairly good, at wallpapering. And painting. Tiling and wallpapering. If Richard ever has a really bad year, I guess I could always find work doing that."

"Don't' see a bad year coming. But if it ever did? Don't forget, you could always get a job at the gym."

Anne smiled. "Not exactly sure that I have much to offer there. I guess I could be at the front counter, check everyone in? Tell them to have a good workout?"

"Believe me, they got a lot of positions there. I can help you."

Anne looked at him. "Jack, thank you. You are so sweet. But maybe I should keep refining my construction skills? Just in case?"

"Never hurts, I guess."

"I guess what I really did, on this project," Anne continued, "was to find the best people for each of the jobs. And then—and this of course is always the really hard part—I had to make sure they actually did what they promised to do."

"I know."

"And even harder? To make sure they did what they were supposed to do, *when* they were supposed to do it. I had to ride their bloody tails. Hard. I've heard every excuse in the book. Where the hell are you, I'd ask when they were no shows. 'Ma'am, can't come today; my balls ache.'"

"No way."

"Oh yes. A pimple in the nose? My hair hurts. I've heard every one of them. I should have made a collection."

Jack looked out the large windows at the back of the living room to the lawn that rolled past a fountain toward flower beds, as perfect as if from a garden magazine, and, behind the beds, majestic oaks.

"Do you play badminton?"

"Does that surprise you? I'm British. I was born with a badminton racket in one hand. And a croquet mallet in the other."

Anne made the motions of swinging her racket and then hitting a croquet ball.

"No, I mean, you just really don't see many, literally any, badminton nets anymore. Are you any good?"

"Excuse me? I, young man, was the captain of the Bryn Mawr badminton team."

"Well, excussse me. I had no idea. So, you're pretty good then?"

"I think I can hold my own, yes."

"Oh, you do, do you? Against me?"

Anne snorted. "Oh, come now. Please don't tell me a big strong strapping young man like you plays a little girly game, like badminton?"

"Am I sensing a challenge?"

"Oh, any day, Monkey Boy. Any day. Bring it on, bring it on. Badminton, my dear young man, is a sport that does not depend on the show-off popping muscles of a pumped-up brute. It depends on, on balance, on hand-eye coordination, on finesse, on outthinking your opponent, on—"

"You're on."

"Oh, this is going to be such a magnificent slaughter. When are you ready to walk right into this bloodbath, sonny boy?"

"Now. Right now."

"Now? My, my. Aren't you the brave young lad. Don't you have to stretch first? And get all pumped? And chug your witch's brew of powders. And potions. And take a fistful of supplements to give you the stamina you shall need to play against a helpless little girl? I would not want to take advantage. I'm surprised all you big, strong men don't need naps before you work out. And after. I know it must be really tiring to be such a strapping young man. It just wouldn't be fair to—"

"Where are the rackets?"

Anne led him down the stairs to the recreation rooms, decorated like a country club, picked up two rackets and a tube of shuttle cocks, and led him through the climate-controlled wine cellar tasting room out to the terrace, into the steamy heat of the late June afternoon.

"You really wanna do this now?" he asked. "The heat may muss up your hair and everything."

"Up yours. What's the matter, Mr. Personal Trainer? Afraid to get your rock-hard ass whipped by a sweet, helpless little girl?"

"I don't have the right clothes. Nary a thing."

She looked at him and gave him the finger.

"Oh, bloody Jesus. What do you need?" Anne said. "Your official little badminton skirt? The one with the lacy border? Stitched with pale pink primroses?"

"It's just that it's too hard to move fast in jeans. They don't give you the flexibility—"

Anne looked at them and playfully patted his butt.

"I mean, my God," she said, "yours could not be any tighter if they were sprayed on you."

"No, no, it's just there's no give. And sandals. Especially on a stinkin' hot day like this and—"

"Here, I'll get you a pair of Richard's tennis shorts; he hasn't worn them in years, but—"

"No, that's OK. OK if I just take this off?" he asked, pulling the black stringer over his head.

"Be my guest. Of course, it's OK. Get comfortable. I'm playing barefoot anyway."

"Good idea." Jack kicked his leather sandals around the post holding up the net, and pulled off his jeans, tossing them on top of the sandals.

"Hope this is acceptable official badminton attire?" He pointed to his striped boxer briefs.

"Quite acceptable on a day like this. But they better be your magic undies. Cause if they're not? There is simply no friggin way you can ever win."

"Whatever you say—Ma'am."

"Did you just call me ma'am? Game on. Let's see if

you can even get your fuckin little shuttle cock over the net."

"Excuse me. My what?"

"I said: Your fuckin' little shuttle cock. Fire away."

"Oh. You mean birdie."

"Oh, sweet Jesus. Are you too shy to even say cock? You probably still call yours your 'tinkle thing'?"

Jack fired the shuttle cock straight at her: warp speed.

Anne moved a fraction and slammed it right at his head.

Jack was ready and sent it soaring high over the net, as high as the oak branches.

Anne waited for its descent and spiked it directly at his crotch.

They placed it in the back left, the back right. They raced up to the net and tapped it just a touch over to the other side. They kept each other tearing back and forth, trying sneak attacks, slow shots, fast shots, high, low.

The match quickly degenerated into what to any observer would have seemed a battle between two bratty, foul-mouthed 13 year-olds.

"Suck my shuttle cock," Anne called over.

"Hey, FYI douche: you don't even have a cock."

"Did you just call me douche?"

"Sorry, Ma'am. I meant bitch."

"Balls up your fuckin ass."

Jack doubled over laughing, clean missed a shot and fell to the grass, banging his racket, laughing, crying, "No. No."

Anne rushed over and waived her racket triumphantly over him.

"Sudden death, Monkey Boy."

She tumbled down on the lawn, gasping for breath.

They lay there on the cool grass, in the dappled shade of the old oaks. It was one of those "what is so rare as a day in June" days that promised that every day, day after day, would bring the same magic, all summer long.

"Oh my God, I have never laughed so much. Or so hard." Anne said. "I'm crying. I'm drenched. I hope that counts for some cardio."

"Oh yeah. That was our cardio for, literally, like a whole week. Two weeks."

Jack spotted a hose coiled on the terrace, jogged over, turned on the spigot and gulped and gulped at the stream of water gushing out the end, hauling it to Anne to let her drink.

He put his head under the hose and let the water pour over him, shook his hair out of his face, then put his finger over the end and sprayed himself, front and back, cringing.

"Fuck that is fuck-in free-zin."

He looked over at Anne.

"Don't even think about it, Monkey Boy."

She had stood up, coming at him.

Jack sprayed her, trotting backwards as he did. She lunged at him to grab the working end of the hose out of his hand. Back and forth they wrestled it, shouting, shrieking, laughing, both drenched. As Jack threw the hose to the side, turned, pulled off his underwear, balled them up, wrung them out and draped them over the net, Anne grabbed the hose, jumped on his back, her arms around his neck, her legs wrapped around his waist in a strangle hold as she sprayed his head. He fell to his knees and rolled over to toss her off. In an instant, she was on top of him, her knees digging into his chest, her hands pinning his wrists to the ground as he struggled to reach the hose. In one motion he flipped her on her side, then onto her back, lying on top of her to hold her down.

"Uncle?"

She pushed with all her might. Not a budge.

"Uncle? Are you willing to concede Monkey Boy won, at least this wrestling match? Fair and square?"

She stopped struggling and lay there, every muscle relaxing.

She kissed his face above hers.

She felt him relax, his arms cradle her head, his tongue flicking over her lips, finding its way into her mouth (it was more delicious than Patti had imagined) until she was somewhere else, drifting above the lawn, swimming as she always swam in her dreams: a languid fluid slow-motion breaststroke across a room, several feet above the floor.

Chapter Twelve

"Do you use steroids?"

They had dried off after showering and had pulled on their identical black Under Armour compression shorts, and had let their towels drop to the floor.

Jack looked around their alcove in the Locker Room and put his index finger against Latham's lips. "Shhhhh."

Latham closed his eyes. Then opened them to look around.

Jack did one more quick check.

"OK, I think by now we know each other pretty well. Right?"

"Sure. Very well. You've been my Personal Trainer for, what, like a couple weeks?"

"Bro, you were literally? My fifth client. You saved my sorry ass."

"Hey man, you're really changing my life, too. I feel so much better. I think I'm even doing better work at the office. Better focus. More stamina."

"That's what I live to hear. Cause it means I must be doing my job right, right? And I'd like to think we've become bros, too?"

"Forever."

Jack fist bumped Latham.

"OK, and I think you're old enough to know the facts of life, so I'm—"

"Oh, yeah; I'm old enough."

"So, I'm going to tell you."

He stepped closer to Latham and put his arm around his shoulders and pulled him in close so that he was talking very softly right into Latham's face.

Latham inhaled.

"OK, so there are two types of Personal Trainers out there," Jack continued, pointing out to the gym with his free hand; "those who use steroids, OK?" He paused and then continued. "And those who say they don't."

"So you're saying…?"

"No. Don't get me wrong. I'm not saying there are guys out there who are literally on steroids. You know what I mean? On them." He emphasized "on." "At least right now. But they've all experimented."

"Have you?"

Jack looked at Latham.

"Sure. Everyone in this business is curious. To see just how far they can go. With my genetics? I could literally become one of those pumped up, freakoid monsters. If I abused them. But hey, that's not my thing. I don't wanna look like that. I want this look." He waved his hand from his face to his feet. "The natty look. Natural."

"So, you did try—"

"Yes, I got to admit: I did try them once. Just for what? Maybe a week? Like every few days. For a week or so."

"So, tell me: what did it do? How—"

"Oh, it was good. Let me tell you. Real good. I've never felt better. In my life."

"Is it like, a high?"

"No, not at all. It's just this tremendous dope feeling,

84

of, of, you know, sort of like general well-being? Energy. Like you're, I don't know, Superman? Maybe that's the best way to describe it. Like, you know, like I literally could go out there and rip the equipment right out of the floor? And toss it around?"

"Sweet."

"Man, let me tell you. On the juice? I was going to the gym early in the morning, burning up those weights. Two hours. Easy. No sweat. And in the afternoon would want to do it all over again. Two hours more. My muscles were so pumped they felt like they were ready to burst through my skin."

Latham absorbed each word.

"And then I'd jog for an hour. OK? And come back and swim laps for an hour. And then wake up at 5 a.m. literally bustin' to do the whole thing. All over again. But this time heavier weights. More reps. More focus."

"Sold. I'm ready. Give me some juice."

"Slow down, cowboy. Aren't you even curious why I only did it a week?"

"Well—"

"I'll tell you why. I'd be driving around town and be stuck at a light in a line of cars. Right?"

Jack rubbed his deodorant stick under each arm.

Latham noted the brand. He'd buy some at CVS on the way home tonight.

"At a red light?" Jack continued. "And the instant the light changed? The instant. I'd be banging on the steering wheel. Yelling, literally yelling at the top of my lungs: 'Move it, you fuckin' motherfucker. Move it!' All of a sudden, I realized I had roid rage. And thought 'hey, this is not smooth. I don't need this.' And that was it. For me."

"So never again?"

"I'm never gonna say never. Ever. If I feel like I'm hitting a plateau? I'll go on the juice for a cycle. But then stop. Cold turkey. It seems to work. For me at least."

Jack picked up his towel and rubbed his hair.

"Would you want to try it," Jack said. "Once? Just to see?"

"Hey, you're my Trainer. I do exactly what you tell me. You tell me jump? I say 'how high? How many times?'"

"That's what I like to hear. Well, trust me, this is not in our manual. This is like, waaay outside the manual. This is like a huge no-no. I'm pretty sure I'd be thrown out of here if Brian ever heard about this. But I think anyone serious about fitness today? OK. Should try. Just for, say, like a week? Just to see. And it would definitely jump start getting you to the next level. That I guarantee."

"Sounds good to me. Count me in."

"Really?"

"Really."

"Wanna think about it overnight? You can read up on the internet. All the pros and cons. That's what lawyers do, right Mr. Attorney? Weigh all the evidence?"

"Hey, Mr. Personal Trainer, I'm ready right now. How soon can we do it?"

"Well, actually, right now. If you're really like, ready, ready? I don't wanna push you. Austin always keeps some in his locker."

"Oh, I am so ready, Coach. Let's go for it."

Jack led Latham in their compression shorts and bare feet to an alcove closer to the showers. Looked around. The coast was clear. He opened a locker. Wrong one. He opened the one next to it.

"Pay dirt. Sweet. We're about to transform you into:

drum roll, please" - Jack did a quick roll with his fingers on the locker door - "a Super Man."

From the top shelf of the locker, he took a bottle of rubbing alcohol, and from a plastic bag extracted a cotton ball.

"OK, man, you ready? Don't do this for me, OK? This is for you, right? You're sure you really want this?"

"Ready."

"OK. Step One: Drop trou."

Latham laughed. "It always starts that way."

He pulled his compression shorts to below his knees.

"Now lean over the bench, bitch."

"If someone walks by now, we got a lot of 'splaining to do."

"Let's get this done, like fast. One minute."

"Don't rush. I want to savor my initiation."

Jack tipped the bottle of alcohol over the cotton ball, then swabbed the wet ball back and forth over a small area of Latham's butt.

"So far so good?"

"So far, real good." Latham stood up. "All done?"

"Dickhead. What are you, some kind of jerk off? I gotta jab the fuckin' needle into your fucking ass meat. You'll know when I'm done, dildo. Scared?"

"Jam it in," Latham said. "I'm ready."

"That's what she said."

"Jam it in real deep."

"Fuckin pig."

From the clutter on the top shelf of Austin's locker, Jack found a hypodermic needle sealed in a plastic sleeve. He ripped the cover open with his teeth and pulled out the needle and showed it to Latham, pushing the plunger up and down a few times.

"Still OK?"

Latham stared at the working end.

"Are you sure you know what you're doing? Could anything go wrong here?"

"Ahh. There's Mr. Lawyer's Voice. At last. Sure, something always could go wrong. Mr. Attorney, you should know that. Like if I shove the needle in the wrong spot? If I'm off just by a teeny tiny fraction? You'll be paralyzed. From the waist down. Would you sue me? Isn't my defense, like, consent? Can I hire you to represent me? Or is that a conflict? We could say the batch of juice was tainted, right?"

"Paralyzed?"

"For the rest of your life. A quad."

"Are you shittin me?"

"No. But my aim usually is pretty good."

"Usually? Pretty good?"

"Well, let's just say: so far. Ready or not?"

Latham could see himself in a wheelchair, his life changed, forever. Just because he wanted to please Jack. Just because he wanted to look like Jack. Just because he wanted to be Jack. He looked up at Jack and his faith in his gym god for a moment tipped the scales. He would do anything for him.

"Ready."

"Atta boy. Here it is. Here's the miracle juice."

He showed Latham the tiny dark brown bottle from Austin's locker, unscrewed the top and showed him the rubber seal over the top.

"A new batch. This is good stuff."

Jack inserted the needle through the seal, into the bottle, and slowly lowered the plunger. He extracted the needle and held it up to the light, then poked the needle into the bottle again and drew in a little more. He held it up again to check the level, flicking it with his finger.

"Oh yeah. This should do it. Real nice. Ready to become a real man?"

"Ready."

Latham didn't sound as ready as he had been.

"Jesus Christ, would you fuckin unclench your fuckin butt?"

"Sorry."

"I swear to God I'm not about to fist ya. You're clenched tighter than a horny virgin. If I ever tried to ram this into solid ass muscle? It's gonna literally hurt. Like hell. What have you been doin' out there? When I'm not training you? Like 3,000 squats? They ought to put you in charge of the 'Best Butts Now' class."

"Sorry. I didn't realize I was doing that."

Jack massaged the area where he had swabbed the alcohol.

Latham began relaxing, thinking less about spending the rest of his life in a wheelchair and more about how good it felt to have Jack touching him.

"OK. Ready? Here we go. No more bullshit. Count of three. OK? One? Two… Three."

Latham felt the needle enter and could sense Jack gradually pushing it in deeper as he pressed down on the plunger.

"You doin' OK?" Jack asked.

"Yeah."

"It takes a little time to get all the juice in. Just relax. Keep breathing. Breathe real slowly. Deeply. Slowly. Stop holding your breath, dickhead."

"Sorry."

"Deep breathin'. Come on. Let me hear you breathing. Let your body receive it. And distribute it."

"All good."

Jack slowly extracted the needle and playfully slapped Latham's ass.

"You were very brave out there. On the front line. Gold star. Stay put just a minute."

He rubbed the wet cotton ball around the area.

"Not a bleeder. No blood at all. Hey, I'd say I'm gettin' pretty good at this. Knew I shoulda gone to medical school. Maybe one of those Caribbean ones. Get some sun and fun."

He closed Austin's locker.

"OK," he continued, "moment of truth: can you even stand up? Or did I miss my mark by a fraction of a millimeter? Let's see if you can even move your lower extremities. If you have any feeling there. At all. Or if it's all numbing up on you. As paralysis gradually sets in."

Latham slowly stood up, wavering, pulled up his compression shorts, then pretended to topple onto the bench.

"Fuckin' douche," Jack said. "Don't fuck with me like that."

Latham laughed.

"Just for that?" Jack said, "I'm gonna work your sorry ass so hard at our next session, you're not gonna be able to walk. For, literally, like a week. Better get yourself some crutches this afternoon."

Jack looked at Latham's compression shorts and smirked.

"Well, will you look at that, will you? At least we know your fucking dick muscle is still working. Maybe for you, does like the juice goes directly to the dick?"

"Oops. Sorry, man," Latham said, pressing down on his erection. "You did a great job. Didn't feel a thing. How soon does it work?"

"It takes a while. Not all at once. But when you come in here tomorrow morning—we're still on for tomorrow, right? Wednesday—"

"I'll be here, God willing. Same time. Same place."

"Good. When you come in here and see what you can do, you're gonna be amazed. Literally. I want you down on your hands and knees saying—"

"Hands and knees? I'm liking this already."

"Perv. Hands and knees, worshiping, saying 'Jack, All Powerful, you are the greatest Personal Trainer in history.' No. Just kidding. Don't do that. Not a word about our little session. Mums the word. Don't tell any of your lawyer buddies."

"Those desk pussies?"

"Just let me know how you feel tomorrow. I'm gonna be able to assess pretty quickly how you're responding. And man, believe me. If it hit? You're gonna get the best leg day workout you've ever experienced. Maybe in history. You're gonna be so sore, but you'll be begging for more. OK?"

"Sounds good to me."

"Don't thank me yet," Jack said as they walked back to their alcove. "Here, may as well share all the trade secrets at once. Now that you've been initiated. OK?"

"Yes, please."

"OK. So, a half hour before you come in here tomorrow, I want you to take all this stuff too."

Jack took an empty shaker from his locker, looked in, blew into it and shook it out, then from a collection of containers on the shelf of his locker, filled it with a scoop and a half of Blasto Nuclear Preworkout Powder and, like a medieval alchemist, dropped in a scoop of Beta-Alanine, two scoops of Citrulline Malate, and one of Taurine.

Jack looked Latham over as if evaluating him to figure out how much of each ingredient to add.

"So OK. For you? You're gonna need almost a full scoop of AAKG and—"

Latham pulled up his business slacks, tucked in his shirt. "And, what the hell might AAKG be?"

"You know, Arginine Alpha-Ketoglutarate?"

"OK, well of course I knew that. I guess. What are you, like a pharmacist on the side?"

Jack tipped the scoop into the shaker.

"Anyone interested in a fitness lifestyle picks up on these tricks of the trade. AAKG you can literally take a few times a day."

"If you say so. But no way can I remember all this shit. You're going to have to write it all down for me sometime."

This is it, Latham thought. At last, at long last, the secret formula to how the fitness models look like that. So, it wasn't just endless jackknives and pull-ups and platforming after all. It was this combination of secret ingredients. Of these exact supplements. In these exact proportions. The magic formula. He felt like he had just been handed a map, leading to the long searched-for buried treasure. A month? Two? Max. Following this regimen? He would be transformed. Shredded. Ripped. Sexy as hell. Hot. Just like Jack. He would be able to pass for 24 again. Twenty-eight for sure. Twenty-eight would be good. To hold that age.

"You'll learn it. Homework with pop quizzes. Here's one I know you like: ALCAR."

"Oh, yeah, Alcar, that's a real good one."

"Do you even know what Alcar stands for?"

"Of course. Everyone does."

"Tell you what. If you can even tell me what it stands for, I will be—" Jack thought for a moment. "How about, I'll be your personal slave boy? For a day? How does that sound?"

Latham thought and looked at him. "Do you mean just the working hours, nine to five? Or do you mean like, a full day?"

Jack smiled. "You're really thinking about this, aren't you, Mr. Esq.?"

"You better believe it."

"I guess maybe I should be thinking of my safe word?"

"Just a little pointer here? OK? On real master-slave protocol? Slaves do not have safe words."

"Shit. And by the way, you seem to know a little too much about all this stuff. Scary."

"Damn right shit. So, you're talking about an eight-hour day? Or a real honest to goodness day?"

"OK, OK, a full day. Your slave. You can make me do whatever you want done."

"Dear Lord," Latham said, looking up toward the ceiling, "I don't ask you for much, you know that, but: please, help me with this one." He finished buttoning his dress shirt. "OK, this is easy, that Alcar thing stands for... Alpha L'carton."

"Well, nice try. The real answer is Acetyl-L-Carnitine."

"Oh man, I knew that. That was going to be my second try. I did get the L right. Does that mean you'll be my slave, like, for an hour?"

"In your sick wet dreams, buddy. Tell you what: if you can even tell me what Alcar does for you, the bet is back on."

"Oh, that is so easy. Promotes muscle growth. What day are you available, slave boy?"

"Not so fast there. You certainly get an A for effort, but the correct answer is: it burns fat, improves performance and maximizes focus."

"I knew that."

Jack screwed the top on the shaker, shook it and handed it to Latham.

"So tomorrow morning, a half hour before you leave home to come here, here to worship at the Temple of the Gods, fill this little fucker to the top with *Evian*. Got that? It's gotta be *Evian*, only *Evian*. That's the only one that works. Got it?" He smiled. "So, shake it real well. That's your pre-workout drink. Pre-workout. To get you pumped up to work out. To max capacity. And chug it."

"Got it."

"And whatever you do, do not—I repeat—do not: mouth fuck it. No matter what. I repeat," Jack said each word slowly: "do-not-mouth-fuck-it."

"What does that even mean? I don't even know what you're saying. Sounds good, though."

"You'll see some of the jerk-off Personal Trainers around here doing just that—drop all that shit into their mouths, dry, then chase it with some water? They think it will all mix up in their stomachs. And they'll get a more powerful hit. There's always one who ends up flopping on the floor. Puking their guts up. In agony. Do not try that. Just chug it. Mixed with *Evian*."

"Got it. No mouth fucking."

"Chug it. With these."

Jack opened up a plastic divider of pills on the top shelf of his locker, looked them over, selected a handful from different compartments—three hard red ones

94

("these are Nitric Oxide; they open up your veins for the best pump"), one with blue stripes, "two of these black beauties—boost the almighty T juice—testosterone," a clear gel one, a hard white one, over a dozen in all, and handed them to Latham, who fingered them like lucky charms, then dropped them into his pocket.

"OK", Jack said, "all set?"

"Got it. Where do you even get all this stuff?"

Jack looked at him, pulled him closer and whispered, "I'm gonna introduce you to my pusher."

Latham looked around.

Jack shook his head. "Just shittin; you, man. GNC, man. That's gonna be your new pharmacy. From now on. Your new health clinic. Your new medical group. Your new doctor's office. Your new home."

"That GNC in the strip mall?"

"Sure. Or once you know what you're doing, you can get it all online. So, tell me: what are you having for dinner tonight? This is a test."

"The usual, Sir, per your orders. Exactly what I've had since you became my Personal Trainer. Grilled chicken, steamed broccoli florets, sweet potatoes, a glass of ice water. With lemon squeezed in. Love it. Can't get enough of it. Delicious."

"Very good. Pop quiz: Abs are made—where?"

"Abs are made in the kitchen, Sir."

"Very, very good. Quick learner. And dessert?"

"One red grapefruit, Sir."

"Oh, and one more thing, dickhead, OK? This is important. When you finish a workout like today's, your muscles are screaming for nourishment. Like, literally, they're starving. So, what you want to do is flood them with protein, literally flood them, within a half hour of the end of the workout. The sooner the better."

Jack looked in his locker and pulled out a shaker. "Do you mind sharing mine? It's the only other one I have here."

Latham looked at him. "Not a problem. At all."

From the bottom of his locker Jack pulled up a large canister of Gold Standard Whey Protein.

"This is the one I recommend. Double chocolate."

He twisted off the cap with both hands and pulled out the scoop.

"Two scoops." He dropped them into his shaker. "That's 50 grams of pure protein you're gonna deliver directly to your stressed muscles. Then add to that a scoop of Creatine Monohydrate." He pulled out the container and tapped a scoop into the shaker, "and one scoop of Glutamine, just like this. And you're good to go. Lemme fill this up for you."

Jack returned, vigorously shaking the shaker, up and down, sideways, back and forth, and handed it to Latham, who was putting on his Gucci loafers.

"Cheers. Pound it. We're gonna make a Personal Trainer out of you before you can say—Citrulline Malate—"

Latham chugged it and wiped his mouth. "Shit. This is complicated. This is a lot of shit you have to take. To look like you." Latham looked once again at his fantasy. "Is it all safe?"

"Safe?" Jack rolled his eyes and shook his head. "That's the wrong question, lawyer boy. You think it's easy to look like this? You think all this just… happens?"

Jack flexed both biceps, twitched them in rhythm and grinned at Latham. "Here, feel those guns. Come'on, feel'em. You know you want to. Everyone does."

Latham felt the solid mound of each bicep, then ran his hand back and forth over them.

"I'm in," he said. "See you tomorrow?"

Chapter Thirteen

That next Monday, Latham noticed at once that Jack was wearing a new watch.

His black sports watch with the black rubber watch band: gone.

Replaced by a Rolex Submariner with the deep blue face and gold band.

As Jack stood in the corridor outside their alcove in the Locker Room and went through the swing of driving a golf ball, the Rolex caught the overhead lights.

The gold glistened.

Latham stared at it. And realized at once that Anne had given it to him.

That. Filthy. Bitch. Whore.

He knew he had to up his game. A lot.

"Are you a golfer?" Latham asked.

Jack leaned on his imaginary driver and looked over at him.

"No, not really. I've played literally only a couple times. Just learning. But I want to."

He swung again, staring off into the far distance where his ball was heading. "I think I'm getting addicted."

"That can happen. Real fast. Where do you play?"

"Austin and I go to that par three place down the road? It's pretty lame. I know. But the price is right. You're a big lawyer boy. So, you must be a golfer, right? Golf outings. That's all I hear the lawyers in here talking about. Every day. A golf outing here. A golf outing there. I'm going to this one. Are you going to that one? Not a bad life. Is that all they do? How do I get in on that racket?"

Latham laughed as he adjusted the knot on his tie.

"I know. Their poor clients. You wonder when any work gets done."

"So that's not you? You're not one of them?"

"I wish. No, not one of that racket. I only play once in a while," Latham said, exaggerating the truth even with that statement. "I'm not very good. But I enjoy it. I go out there just for fun. I would never play with any of that golf outing crowd. They take it much too seriously. And I'd never, ever, take my clients out there. Or, God forbid, potential clients. In fact, I would lose every client I ever had if they ever saw me in action. They'd say, 'who is this dufus?' I try to find partners my own speed."

"Sounds like we'd be a perfect match. But I bet you're much better than you say you are. Where do you play?"

"I'm a member over at Haverhill?" He buttoned his collar, "So I play there. Whenever I can."

"Holy shit. Sweet chicken. You're a member? There? Didn't they just have the PGA there?"

"Yeah. That was last summer. They've had the US Open there sometimes, all that, all the big names have—"

"You kidding me? I know. That place is famous. It's literally like probably the number one golf club on , like, the entire East Coast? Literally. Maybe the whole country.

"It's up there."

"Do you think—" Jack looked at Latham and tentatively started again. "Do you think, maybe, we could play there? Sometime? How cool to say: 'Indeed, I play

Haverhill.' Like Tiger. Well, not like Tiger. But at least I could say I played it. That would be way cool. 'Oh yes. I play Haverhill,'" he said again, in his imitation of an obnoxious WASP country club voice.

Jack swung again, a mighty drive, and looked like he heard the roar of the spectators.

"Sure. As long as you realize really I'm no good. At all. So don't expect—"

"You think you're bad? You're gonna feel like you're playing with a kid. Aiming for the clown's mouth. That was my speed in Toms River. When Scott and I played miniature golf. Pretty lame, I know. Now? With Austin? I never can tell if it's gonna be a great shot, or like, a total dud. I can't quite get it. Yet. I think if I can spend some more time—"

"Hey, you're a natural. You're a born athlete. We'll have some fun, no matter what. Right? Just to be out there. On a beautiful summer day like today. Let's do it."

"Really? You serious?"

Jack looked as excited as if he was watching his putt roll toward the final cup that would win him the Open.

"Absolutely. This'll be fun."

Jack bounded over to double fist bump Latham, doing a little touchdown jig in their alcove.

Latham suggested a date which gave him enough time to get to the Pro Shop, buy two sets of the best clubs, two golf bags, a few boxes of the balls guaranteed to work miracles, play hooky from his law practice a few afternoons to take lessons from one of the Club pros, and get in a couple practice sessions on the driving range and on the practice putting green. Rusty. Not good. At all. But not hopeless.

The afternoon came when it was now or never.

Chapter Fourteen

Latham slowly circled the gym's parking lot until Jack came trotting out, taking exuberant running leaps toward Latham's car.

Shit. Jack was still wearing his Personal Trainer gear.

He had neglected to tell him the Golf Club's dress code. OK, no problem. The Pro Shop. They'd buy some stuff for him at the Pro Shop. But Jack wouldn't even be able to walk down the path from the Golf Club's parking lot to the Pro Shop in his stringer and tiny gym shorts. He'd be stopped and turned back before he made it 10 feet.

When Jack got into the car, Latham explained the need for a slight detour to his house to get one of his golf shirts and a pair of his chinos for Jack to wear even to get into the Pro Shop. There he could pick out some appropriate clothes for the afternoon and evening.

Jack looked around Latham's living room filled with nineteenth century nautical antiques and China Trade pieces.

"You've got a lot of awesome stuff here."

"Oh. Thanks."

Latham looked to see what had caught Jack's eye and considered asking if he'd like to have it.

"It's pieces I've collected over a whole lot of years. You know, things whose beauty attracts me, calls to me. I had to have them. I had to possess them. I had to bring them home. To be mine. Sort of a sickness I guess, right?"

"Looks like you know just what you want."

"When I see it, I know. Instantly. Just like that. No debating. But I do think everything sort of fits in together, like pieces of a jigsaw puzzle. Like they belong here. To me at least, that's the way it seems. At least that's what I see. But I'm pretty sure most people see a house jammed with much too much… stuff. One step away from a hoarder."

"No, it's really amazing stuff," Jack said, examining a sailor-made model of the whaling bark, *Wanderer,* on top of the glass-fronted barrister's bookcase, and picking up the large piece of scrimshaw next to it. He held it up to his mouth, letting it hang down like a tooth.

"My, what big teeth you have, Grandmama," Latham said. "Hey, you know what that is? Right next to it?"

"What? This?" Jack picked up the long-bleached bone lying by the ship model.

"What do you think that is?"

"Not a clue."

Jack ran his palm down the smooth length of it.

Latham laughed. "Well, I'll tell you this: the whale would be mighty happy—like I mean *real* happy—to have you doing just that. That, my lad… is a whale's penile bone."

"No fuckin way." Jack put it down on the bookcase and stared at it, then picked it up again and held it out in front of his crotch. "So, Moby Dick's dick. Not that big…"

"To be exact: 23 inches. Plus."

"Fuck. Talk about a boner. Two fuckin feet of whale dick meat. Look at the girth of that mother."

Latham followed him as he walked from the living room into the study, then out to the sunroom, taking it all in, excited by each exotic treasure he spotted, picking some up, pointing to others, asking the value of some of them.

"So, where'd you go to school?" Jack asked Latham.

"What?"

"Where'd you go to college?

"Oh. Amherst?"

Jack looked uncertain.

"You know, in Massachusetts. Amherst, Massachusetts?"

"That's a real good one, isn't it?"

"It's got a good reputation."

And then what, so you decided to become a tax lawyer?"

"Well, not quite as fast as all that. First, I had to go to law school. And pass the bar. Exam."

"Was Amherst your law school?"

Latham looked at him. "No, that was just college. Then further north, to Cornell, for law school. Cornell Law School. Three years."

"No way. Three fuckin years?"

"You said it. Three *fucking* years. Of cruel torture. Water boarding."

"Man, so let me get this straight. So, you're saying, like four years of college? Plus, plus then three more years of school? For law school? So, seven years in a classroom? Before you even make your first dollar?"

"You got that right. Seven years in a gulag, doing hard labor. Seven years on a chain gang. And then a bar exam to pass before you even get your license to practice."

Jack stared at him. "So, what happens if you don't even pass that exam? You're out?"

"Bingo. The big nada."

Jack looked around and whistled. "Looks like it was worth it."

"I don't know. No one today even wants to go to law school. Everyone today wants to be an investment banker. And make a shit load of money. Real fast. Our gym is full of those wannabees. You can spot them a mile away. Or, if they have balls, like you, do what you're doing. And have fun. But not sit on their asses in a law office. Billing away hours of their lives."

"The work force, right?

Latham looked at him. "Yeah, I guess you could say that. A little cog in a wheel at a desk."

Jack's eyes scanned the room.

"Somehow, I don't see Mr. Lawyer Boy here sitting at a metal desk. In a cubicle."

"Well, maybe a fancy cubicle with nice furniture. And a wooden desk, you—"

"A desk like that?" Jack said, pointing to the carved mahogany landing field desk in the middle of the den.

Latham grinned. "Well, maybe not *quite* like that. I inherited that from my grandfather. That was a whole different world. Back then. But bottom line? I'm siting all day, at a desk, in a cubicle. You're free, man. Freedom. Savor what you have. Savor what you have. I hope you realize how blessed you are."

Latham selected from his closet a golf shirt and pair of chinos and tossed them to Jack to put on.

Latham watched.

Jack was undressing. In his house.

Jack was putting on his clothes.

His clothes fit Jack so well he looked like a model for them, a spokesman for the brands.

This outfit got Jack into the Golf Club's Pro Shop, cool and quiet on that July afternoon, the wood paneled rooms filled with a quality selection of country club attire.

"Pick out whatever you'd like, for today," Latham said. "Try it on. Check the fit."

With the eyes of a professional buyer, Jack looked over the stacked tables and crowded racks, feeling the fabric, comparing colors, patterns, checking sizes, pulling aside a few that struck him. He took off Latham's golf shirt, and started trying them on, right there in the aisle.

A young sales associate came over to help.

"Don't you just hate people who look like that?" she stage-whispered to Latham, "guys who look perfect in every single thing they try on? Everything. It's just not fair."

They shook their heads.

"Tell me about it," Latham said, "I've certainly never had that problem."

Jack was debating among three of the golf shirts, holding them up, looking in the mirror, trying the next, asking Latham and the saleslady their preferences.

"Let's get them all," Latham said, "you can always use a few."

Jack looked at him. "Really?"

"Sure."

"Man, thank you so much. Thank you." He put his arm around Latham's shoulders. "Are you sure that's OK? Thank you, man."

They picked out a pair of golf trousers (size 30 waist,

Latham noted, wondering if he focused more on ab and oblique training if he could whittle his own waist down from 34 to at least a 32; he would try), and then, for dinner in the main dining room, a traditional blue Oxford button down shirt (16 x 34, like Latham's), a regimental tie that appealed to Jack even though Latham tried to interest him in a flashy one he thought Jack would prefer, a traditional navy blue blazer that fit perfectly right off the rack, a pair of gray flannel dress slacks, ditto, and a pair of Gucci loafers like Latham's (size 11 ½ versus Latham's 10 ½).

They left Jack's clothes for dinner in Latham's locker in the Clubhouse and walked to the Starting Deck to sign in with the Greens Master, who introduced them to their caddy, Franklin.

"We have to give you fair warning," Latham said to Franklin, "right up front. We're just beginners. We have no idea what we're doing, we're—"

Franklin smiled. "Not a problem. Beautiful afternoon." He looked out over the course. "No humidity. Like yesterday." He shook his head at the memory. "This will be like a cake walk in the park. Relax. Enjoy. I'm here for you. You don't worry for nothing."

Latham teed up, hoping to impress Jack with his first drive—he had hit ball after ball a straight 150 yards or more on the driving range last week—but topped the ball and watched it dribble three feet from the tee. Jack swung a mighty blast that hooked sharply left and bounced the ball off the roof of a car speeding down the Shunpike. Onward they marched toward the first green, 458 yards away, a par five, gaining a few feet here, losing a ball there, 13, 14 shots, halfway there when a golf cart came charging toward them and stopped next to Franklin. The driver and Franklin conferred. The cart sped away.

Franklin hoisted the two golf bags onto his shoulders.

"You," he said.

"Me?"

"Yes. You. Pick up your ball. You," he called over to Jack, "pick up your ball. Groups piling up back there. Not happy, man. Not happy at all. We got to gain a hole or two. And fast."

From then on, Franklin pushed them, not bothering to search for out-of-bound balls, handing them new balls, giving them the proper club to use, showing them where to aim, sometimes hitting for them, keeping score in his own fashion which made them feel like they were actually doing pretty well if they weren't counting strokes in their heads, the three of them joking and laughing and placing imaginary bets through the 18 holes, until the Clubhouse re-appeared.

After a couple beers in the Men's Grill, Jack and Latham showered and changed, getting dressed for dinner. When Jack put on his blue blazer and tie from the Pro Shop, he could have passed as the scion of one of the founding members of the Club, home from Princeton, a look he seemed to relish when he checked himself out in the mirror, a role he embraced for the rest of the evening, always making sure his Rolex glistened below the cuff. It was as if he dined in such linen-tabled formal settings every evening: reviewing the menu with a critical eye, ordering Scotch (*Johnny Walker Blue*, of course), a dozen oysters, surf and turf, picking out an expensive bottle of French wine to go with dinner, sampling it for the waiter as if a connoisseur. Latham could tell he was really getting off on being in this setting, to be playing this role, picturing himself not as a gym rat but as part of this scene.

For the next week, he'd be telling his buddies at the gym all about his day at Haverhill. Crème Brule, after dinner drinks, and on the way through the lobby he saw a glass fronted display case with cigars, and asked Latham if he could try one, selecting the most expensive. They walked out to the terrace overlooking the course, now fading in night shadows, Wall Street tycoon, Master of the Universe, taking a puff, deep in contemplation over his next deal which would shake the markets.

Chapter Fifteen

"Any chance I could crash at your place?" Jack said as they drove out past the Golf Club's Gatehouse.

Latham looked at him.

"I think I'm pretty well lit," Jack continued. "Probably had a little more than—"

"You think? I'm surprised you're still standing. I'd be in a coma. Sure, not a problem at all. I've got a guest room. It's all ready and it's got its own bathroom and—"

"Thank you, man. Really 'preciate it. I don't need anything. Really. I can crash on the floor and be a happy—"

Latham showed him the guest wing when they got back to the house. "Bathroom there. Cabinet right above the sink: toothpaste, a couple brands, take your pick, dental floss, a bunch of toothbrushes, things like Aspirin, Advil, Excedrin, Tylenol—"

"I may need them all."

"Ready for anything. All towels clean. More in that closet."

Latham opened it to show him.

"Help yourself. The glasses clean. Anything else you need, look in the cabinet below the sink. Extra pillows in the closet by your bed if you wanna try some others, everyone likes a special feel, and—"

"I'm good, man. All good. When you hittin' the sack?"

"Right now. I'm wiped. Eighteen holes? Advanced cardio."

"Now? It's only like," Jack looked once again at his Rolex, "much too early, dude. It's only a little after ten. Any sports bars you like? Wanna hit one for an hour or two and then—"

"What are you: the Energizer Bunny? How many scoops did you put in your preworkout? Wait a minute— by any chance, did you mouth fuck it?"

"Yeah, you're right. I gotta be back at the Club, 5:30 a.m.. First client 6 a.m. Gotta at least be partially upright."

"That would be a good start."

"So how about just a little porn? Then we'll call it a night?"

"OK," Latham said, relieved he didn't have to go out again and sit in a noisy sports bar and pretend he was interested and understood what was going on and wondering when to cheer and with what degree of vigor.

Latham led Jack into his bedroom with the big TV.

"Here, you take that chair," Latham said, pointing to an easy chair.

"No, that's OK. I don't need it; it's yours, I can just lie on your bed."

"No, no, go on, you'll be more comfortable. See that wooden lever on the side? Just pull back on that, and the chair reclines. All the way back if you want."

Jack sat down and started experimenting with positions. Latham turned on the TV and handed him the remote.

"Here, pick out a good one. Something you'll like. Whatever you're into."

Latham was waiting to find out what Jack's turn-on was.

Jack scrolled through selections, pausing at a few, moving on until he landed on one and started it, fast forwarding past the perfunctory lame set-up to where the action began.

Latham in the chair he pulled next to Jack's watched the screen, feigning interest in the same old routine. He looked over to Jack to joke about it. And stared.

Jack had taken out his dick and was working away at it.

"Come on buddy, join me," Jack said, eyes on the television. "Take the edge off."

"Don't you want some lube?"

"Whadda you have?"

"I think I've got some *Swiss Navy* or *Gun Oil*. Or something like that. Let me go see. I go through about a six pack a week."

Jack smiled as he kept watching and stroking and pulling.

Latham came back from his bathroom and handed him a tube.

"Here, try this. This is a good one. Silicon based."

Jack looked at it, pumped some into his hand and went back to work, his eyes, now with a hazy gaze, staring at the screen.

Latham couldn't take his eyes off the scene.

In his bedroom.

Was this a dream?

Jack in his bedroom.

Jerking off.

How did this even happen? He was afraid the least false move or misspoken word would break the spell.

And end it. That Jack would say "fuck off, perv," and leave. Latham stood up very slowly, quietly left the room, and came back with a flexible clear plastic ruler, sitting next to Jack and getting ready to measure.

"Here, wait a minute," Jack said, taking the ruler from Latham.

Latham was sure that was it, that he was going to say "get outta here", but instead he got to watch as Jack, with apparent experience, pushed the ruler under his penis and placed the head along the plastic.

"How big?" Jack asked, still looking at the screen.

Latham looked. "Holy shit, you're hitting a touch over eight inches. That thing is huge."

Jack smiled, put the ruler aside. "It gets even bigger."

Latham worked up his courage. No second chance. Now. Now.

"Want some help? He asked and braced to hear "no," wondering how he'd make a graceful retreat.

"Sure," Jack said, and handed him the *Gun Oil*, clasped his hands behind his neck, pushed further back in his chair, and closed his eyes.

Latham rubbed his palms together with the lube and then slipped his hand around Jack's cock with an experienced grip. Then, Lathan started working around the head, then began to stroke up and down the shaft, varying his rhythms, tempo, and strength of his grip all while he watched Jack's face to determine what triggered any visible responses.

"It feels real good, doesn't it," Latham said quietly, working on Jack with one hand and cupping his balls with the other, putting increasing pressure on them.

"Mmmmm," Jack mumbled. "Hey, I dare you—" and his voice trailed off.

"You dare me what?"

He hesitated. "I dare you to lick it." He paused. "Just once."

Latham got out of his chair and kneeled in front of Jack, taking one of Jack's legs and putting it over his shoulder, feeling the solid pack of calf muscles, and, hearing no protest, doing the same with his other leg, then pushing Jack's thighs closer around his neck, closer to feel their strength and warmth. Jack squeezed tighter.

Latham leaned in and put the head of Jack's penis into his mouth, slowly circling his tongue around the head, then worked it deep in until his lips touched pubic hair.

Jack settled farther back in his chair, closing his eyes.

* * *

Latham had set his alarm for 4:30 a.m. so that he would have time to shower and shave before waking Jack at 5:00 a.m.as he had requested.

At exactly 5:00 a.m., Latham knocked softly on the guest room door and opened it.

Jack gave a wake-up groan, sat up, rubbed his eyes, ran his hand through his hair, cast aside the duvet and got out of bed, sporting some serious morning wood.

Jack bounced it up and down with his palm.

"Bro, wanna help me with this?"

* * *

"You're more than welcome to live at my place," Latham said as they waited at the traffic light on the way to the gym.

His carefully rehearsed line sounded casual, spontaneous. Just the way he had hoped it would.

Jack looked at him. "What do you mean?"

"You know, if you want to get out of that shit hole where you are? Come stay at my place. You're more than welcome. It would give you some time to save your money. For a place of your own. And get settled here, in town. You could take over the guestroom. And the bath would be yours. And that room next to yours? You could use that. For whatever. So, you'd have your own sort of suite and everything, and—"

"Are you serious, man?" Jack shifted his gym bag on his lap.

"Sure. I mean, my God, right now you're living right next to the tracks and hear those trains rumble through all night, and how do you even sleep, and—"

"Wow. I mean, I can't believe it. You don't think I would get in your way, you'd—"

"No. Are you kidding? You know I'm not even there that much. With the hours I work. And you wouldn't be there that much, either. We both like our independence. Maybe we could grab some dinners together. Sometimes. Hit the driving range?"

"Oh yeah."

"If you wanted to, you could do some stuff to help me around the house, there's always something, and—"

"Hey, no problem. I'm really good at all stuff like that. Really. Man, this would be so great. I mean, I don't even know what to say, you are—"

"You don't have to say anything. You've helped me out at the gym. Like a lot. If this could help give you a head start, it would make me happy and—"

"I mean, wow, no one's ever done anything like this

113

for me. Ever. What if. If you get sick of me? Or if you need those rooms? For guests or anything? Or just need your space? Or—"

"Not going to happen. Way beyond my comprehension."

"I hope you'd tell me to scram, get the hell out of here, dickhead. And I would. I promise. You say the word. And I would vamoose out of there. I'd—"

Latham laughed. The light turned green, and he turned right on to Morris Avenue.

"Somehow, I don't think that will be a problem. I'm pretty easy going. And I think you are, too. We both need our space. And I know we'd each respect that. You can stay there as long as you want, and—"

"Oh man. Thank you. Thank you so much. I don't even know what to—"

"Again, don't say anything. Start today if you want to. After work. We can bring all your stuff over, get you settled in, and—"

"I don't have a lot. Like literally that's an understatement. A couple plastic garbage bags of shit. That's all I left Toms River with. If you're really serious, Austin and I can pack it all into my Jeep and bring it over tonight, or—"

"Tonight's perfect. I'm not working late. I can give you guys a hand, give you your own key, show you how the security system works. All that. You come and go as you please. Make the place yours. We'll get you all settled in and—"

"Bro, I don't even know how to thank you, you can't imagine what this is gonna to do for me. What, I. You're the first person to, really ever to show any faith in me. I—"

"No thanks necessary. This'll be fun for me, too."

114

A driver in the endless line of commuter traffic approaching them stopped and flashed his lights, so that they could turn left into the gym's parking lot. Latham and Jack waved thanks. The lot was already filling up, even as the night clouds were breaking apart with the first light of dawn.

Chapter Sixteen

"Fuck me dry," Ronnie muttered from the cramped back of Jack's new yellow Porsche Carrera.

He was squished in the black leather seat with Todd, as Jack sped along the Atlantic City Expressway. With Austin in the passenger seat. The four Personal Trainers from the Club were taking their day off to go to AC.

"What? Is? Your? Problem?" Austin said.

"I don't have money. I mean, like, literally, none. I didn't bring my fuckin' wallet."

"What are you? A 50% jerk-off? Or a 100 percenter?"

Ronnie thought for a moment. "I guess a 100 percenter?"

"Weren't you ever a Boy Scout?" Jack asked.

"He's probably molested a whole troop of them," Todd said.

Ronnie gave Todd the finger. "What'ya mean, Jacko? Be prepared, all that shit?"

"Fuck that. Make do with what you got. Rub two fuckin sticks together, you get a campfire, right? I got a 10. That's all we need."

They snorted.

"A day in AC?" Ronnie said. "Ten bucks. Right."

"Rub this, pussy boy," Todd said, touching his crotch.

"You'd love that, wouldn't you? You been dreamin' bout that every night. That's gonna cost you a whole lot, big boy."

"What? Your usual rate? A brand-new shiny nickel?"

"You produce it, I'll reduce it."

"Dickhead."

"What are you guys, like third graders?" Austin said. "Unless we hit the jackpot on our first try, we are so fucked. What? You gonna use your 10 big ones to treat us all to a stick of gum, midafternoon? We can rub that. Maybe a genie will appear if we rub hard enough."

"What do you guys want?" Jack said, "A dick in your ass? Don't I always take care of my posse?"

"Fuck, I'm starving already," Todd said. "Think I'm dyin'. Literally."

"And I guess you got gobbledygotz, too?" Jack said, glancing over at Austin.

Austin pulled out a few crumpled dollar bills from his back pocket and spread them on the dashboard.

"OK, so we're up to 14 bucks. Not bad. Todd, tell us you got a couple of beautiful sexy Bens back there?"

Todd took out what he had in his pocket. "Would you settle for: a pair of Abe's?"

"A pair beats a single, any day. At this point, we go for anything. So, if I'm doing my math right, we got, like, what? A grand total of: 24 bucks. For a day in AC. Not bad. We're loaded."

They raced along the Expressway, passing every car in their way with a throaty growl of the German engine.

"This really sucks dick," Todd said. "Twenty-four fuckin' bucks? Now we can't even get some."

"Hey pussy boy," Ronnie said, "if you had 24 grand

117

in your back pocket? You still ain't getting some. No one's gonna touch you. You're probably a carrier. Cooties transmitted with one touch."

"Jerk-off," Todd said. "Speaking of pussy, how you all doing at the Club? In that department."

"All my clients? Horny as hell," Ronnie said. "They all wanna be serviced. Whether they come right out and ask you—beg you—you can just see it. In their eyes. Get them in shape. Good workouts? Gets their juices flowing? A real good fuck. That's all they're thinking bout. And who is right at hand to help them get off?"

They laughed.

"Hey, so how about Miss Perfection?" Todd asked. "Has anyone done her yet?"

"Who?"

"You know, Miss Ponytail Swisher. In the hot sexy spandex."

"Oh, yeah. De-Li-Cious. No, no luck. She really sticks to herself."

"I found out her name," Jack said.

"Man, did she actually talk to you? Details. Spill it."

"Are you kiddin'? I've offered her a towel? Like a million times. And all I get? That perfect smile. And a head nod—no. No, I asked one of the staff guys. Cory. He knows everyone. And for those of you who may have an interest? Her name is Diana."

"Diana," Austin said.

"Diana. Diana," they all said, together.

"Diana," Ronnie said.

"Diana," Todd said. "I'd like to cram my big fat hairy dick into that perfect mouth."

"What do you want?" Ronnie said. "You want her to barf all over it?"

"Fuckin pigs."

"So what else?"

"What else? Are you kiddin' me?" Jack said. "I go out on the front lines? and find out her name? And you're askin' me: what else? So, what the fuck have you guys done?"

"So, no advances from her? No signs of interest? Of what she's dreamin' of doing with you?"

"'Fraid not," Jack said.

"So, what the hell. If she doesn't fall right away for your 18 inch guns and 30 inch waist, she's gonna be one tough fuck."

"Like all the beauty queens: look, but don't touch."

"So, we gotta up our game. Sell her a dream. Like all the others."

Jack roared up in front of *Caesar's* as if he was a regular, handed the keys to the valet who had run over when he saw a new high-end sports car storm in, and the four piled out, stretched, and walked up to the Casino's entrance.

A guard stopped them. "Sorry guys. You can't come in like that."

Jack looked at him, smiled, pulled up his tank top, flexed his abs. "You 'mirin?"

"What?"

"You 'mirin?" Jack did a double bicep flex.

The guard stared at him. "OK, get the hell out of here till you get some proper clothes on."

"They have a store in there where we can get some stuff?"

"What?"

"Do you have a store in there we can buy some clothes? You'll like?"

"Not a matter what I like, guys. House policy. No.

You can't go any farther. Without appropriate attire. There's a place down the street." He pointed.

"Hey man, you can make an exception. Come on. Believe me, your customers aren't gonna mind. At all. You should be paying us to even go in there. Men: show the good man."

They all flexed and posed.

The guard looked at them. "Guys, guys, it's not me. House policy. Zero tolerance. That would be a big fat: zero. So, scram."

"OK, men," Jack said. "Clearly he's not into aesthetics. I guess we ain't gonna blow our 24 g's here after all. Let's hit another casino."

They walked around to the Boardwalk.

"Twenty-four bucks ain't gonna buy us diddley-squat. Not one fuckin T-shirt," Ronnie said. "Or a snack. For even one of us. What now, Einstein?"

"I swear to God I'm dying," Todd said. "Need food. Fast."

"You guys are so lame," Jack said. "When in need? Go gay for pay. Or are you too proud? You got pride? And ready to starve?"

They looked at him.

"Stand back, boys. Gimme room."

With his back to the wide beach and ocean, Jack stripped off his tank top, threw it down, kicked off his sandals, dropped his gym shorts. Underneath, like a lifeguard, he had on neon orange square-cut *Speedos*. He dropped to the Boardwalk, did a quick 50 pushups to get a pump, then picked up his shorts, pulled his 10 dollar bill out of the back pocket, and stuffed it into the front of his trunks so that most of it dangled over. And began a leisurely flexing routine as if in a body building competition.

A group of tourists strolling the Boardwalk paused. And stared. Others walked by, stopped, turned around and came back to join the onlookers. Jack made eye contact and pointed to his flexed bicep, encouraging them with his other hand to come closer and feel it.

A mother and her teenage daughter shyly walked over and asked if they could take a photo with him. Jack took their iPhone, held it out in front of them, with the teenager on one side and her mother on the other and the beach in the background. He chatted them up, asking where they were from, if they'd had any luck at the casinos, the mother, giggling, stuffed a five-dollar bill into his *Speedos*, then bent down for another shot, inserting another bill with her teeth. Her daughter rolled her eyes. The onlookers laughed.

Others came to take a photo with him, young girls, teenage girls, mothers, women old enough to be his grandmother, men who seemed interested in his responses to their fitness questions, each of which he answered as he would a paying client at the gym. Everyone took a photo, felt his biceps, ran their hands down the ridges of his abs, laughed, giggled, grinned, as they pushed bills into his trunks.

He took a break and rejoined his friends as they huddled and counted the take.

"Close to a buck 50," Jack said. "In what? Less than a half hour? Spread out guys. Pick a good spot. Put on a show. Meet back here. Twenty minutes."

After a while, Jack gave the Club's Wooo woo moose mating call and they gathered from their spots along the Boardwalk.

"Jesus H., we got over $300 here," Austin said after he had straightened and sorted the bills and counted.

"Plus, the 24 we started with," Jack said.

"If I don't get food, like real soon?" Todd whined, "my body is consuming itself; I'm gonna disappear. Nothing's gonna be left; whatever's left is gonna blow right out to sea. Tell Harrison what happened to me."

"Little Toddy's out of sorts," Austin said.

"I'm dead already. Spread my ashes in the ocean," Ronnie said.

"I gotta take a wicked leak."

"We've got more than enough for a real good meal and then some," Austin said, "let's go find a restaurant."

"Men, men," Jack said, flicking the bills, "you little girlies are so lame. What we're holding here is, number one, our gambling stake; number two, we can't even gamble if we don't at least each buy a regulation Dad shirt and Dad shorts to get into a casino; number three, where do you think we're gonna spend the night—in my Porsche? Room and board. Let's not blow it all on a fuckin' lunch when the four of us can scrounge a meal. OK?"

They stared at him.

"Come on. This is like taking candy from a baby. All we gotta do is find some outdoor hole in the wall? Which has a waitress who's 'mirin. Or, better yet, a waiter who's 'mirin. Let's just take a little stroll down the Boardwalk and see what we want."

They did a group fist bump explosion and followed him.

"This'll be like way off our training diet, OK," he continued, as they worked their way through the crowds. "So, don't go expecting a teeny tiny portion of perfectly grilled chicken to weigh on your little fuckin pussy scales, OK? Just consider this our bulking phase."

122

Along the way, they caught the eye of a waitress who was bringing out an order to a family at a picnic table and had her laughing as they explained their plight. She returned with a tray piled with a pizza, meatball subs, and overflowing Sloppy Joes. Jack handed her a 20 as thanks and they scarfed down the forbidden foods, as she bought out a stack of ice cream sandwiches and cans of Pepsi.

Afterward, they wandered the crowded summer beach, down where the waves were breaking, Todd jumping high to catch an errant Frisbee and soaring it back to the teenagers tossing it, who then threw it back to include the four Personal Trainers in their game. They tried out impossible show-off shots and catches, leaping and diving into the breakers, emerging with a shake of their heads and contagious grins. A bunch of onlookers followed as the game proceeded down the beach.

A sail on a catamaran for helping haul it down the beach and out past the breakers. Like King Kong, they posed for selfies next to the mast, and stood at the bow like Viking gods. Free board-shorts and T-shirts from the manager of a souvenir shop who found them amusing (they all selected colors he couldn't sell, like bubble gum pink and fluorescent green, all in size small which, when they worked their way into them, accentuated every muscle, bulge and curve). Hot dogs and soft drinks from a friendly Boardwalk vendor who joked with them.

Their nest egg intact, they returned to the Casino, where a different guard opened the door for them in their new tourist attire.

There, their run of luck ran out at the craps table, but they had put aside enough for dinner, the parking garage and the tolls home, reaching the Club to shower, shave and flaunt their new tans, and stories, when the first members arrived at 6:00 a.m.

Chapter Seventeen

It was late that Wednesday night in August when Latham finally got home.

It had been the evening of his law firm's end of the month partnership meeting, which began at 5:00 p.m. and, always, within an hour, had devolved into the same partners—who spoke with such distinction and decorum in the courtroom and in client meetings—telling each other to "go fuck yourself," calling each other "cocksuckers" and "cunts" and "pussies" and "dicks" and "dickwads" and "dickheads" and "douchebags and diddle-dots," and responding with a "suck my cock" to every suggestion for change, until, close to 8:00 p.m., when they began laughing at the ridiculousness of it all and went out together to dinner, ordering endless platters to share, of calamari and clams casino and scungilli and pasta with red sauce and pasta with white sauce, with shots of Sambuca and rounds of grappa and toasts of *sempra dura* which they found even more hilarious the fifth time one of them proposed it.

Latham was wiped. When he walked up the stairs from the garage, he noticed something out of place.

It was a hockey puck.

On the kitchen counter.

Under it, a note Jack had scrawled:

Buddy—
Off to Cape Cod for a few days. I've asked Austin to take over my clients while I'm gone. Be sure to make him work his ass off for his $$$—
Later, Jack

Latham picked it up, reading it again and again. Cape Cod? Where? Why? How long? And with whom?

The house suddenly sounded too quiet. Like it had stopped breathing. The China Trade pieces, the nautical antiques, had lost their meaning, their magic. Now they were just objects with nothing to say to him. He felt as if he was flat-lining—all thoughts, all observations, all plans that always buzzed in his brain? Gone. This type of silence itself was a sound he had never heard before in his house. The enormity of that sound made him uneasy. The sound of eternity in it frightened him.

He heard the grandfather clock ticking the seconds in the hall, which he had never noticed before, now each second as loud as a gunshot.

He picked up the hockey puck. They had gotten it when he and Jack and Austin went into the city to see the Rangers play the Devils.

"I can't believe it," Jack had said when Latham got out of the Town car that had brought them in and had asked them: "so is this Madison Square Garden?"

"I can't believe you've never been here before," Jack said. "Austin, you've been here, right?"

"Sure," Austin said. "Many times. Everyone has."

"OK," Jack said, "so a brand-new experience for our young buddy, Latham. See all the things we're checking off your Bucket List?"

Latham had gotten them seats right behind the

protective plastic barrier around the ice rink, and as the puck and the players slammed into it, it felt like they were in the game. They had so much fun that night that they went to see the Rangers again when they were at the Pru Center in Newark. This was when they all had bought hockey pucks, and T-shirts with their favorite players' names and numbers, which they wore the next day to the gym.

Latham picked up the puck and walked into Jack's room. It looked as it always did. Like a crime scene. He always joked with Jack that there should be yellow police tape stretched across the doorway.

Jack never slept under the covers. He slept with the duvet wrapped around him, on top of the sheets and blanket Maria so carefully made up each Tuesday when she came to clean. The duvet was twisted into a lumpy cocoon, the way he always slept, and for a moment Latham thought Jack was in it. He listened for breathing. And went over to straighten the duvet.

Haphazardly strewn across the floor and chairs—a tangle of T-shirts with undecipherable words and symbols, twisted black boxer briefs and compression shorts, legs of Diesel jeans knotted around a large—still damp—bath towel, a broken-in Frye harness boot, a golf glove from a few evenings ago when they went to Haverhill's driving range after supper, a black Nike sneaker, his gym bag spewing forth his gear, empty Starbucks cups, a True Religion shopping bag from their latest visit to the mall this past weekend, golf shoes they got at the Pro Shop, crumpled receipts for what Latham had charged.

Latham picked up one of the pillows and put it to his face. He could still smell Jack. He looked for an impression where his head would have been, then fluffed it and placed it back on the bed.

On his bureau was the ticket stub from *The Book of Mormon*. This was the one Broadway play Jack had wanted to see. It sounded to Latham like a religious theme, and he tried to interest Jack in another play, maybe *Jersey Boys*; but in their aisle seats, two rows back from the stage in the Eugene O'Neill Theater, they had cracked up from the opening lines to the end. The Town car took them back to the Hotel Carlyle afterwards, where, by chance, they had been reassigned to the Roger Federer Suite for the weekend: a living room and kitchen between two bedrooms and baths. "Didn't you sleep in Roger Federer's bed?" Latham innocently would ask Jack whenever a conversation with Austin, or anyone else, veered anywhere near that weekend.

That was the same weekend in the City when they had dinner at Sparks Steakhouse and had looked at the spot where John Gotti had gunned down the boss of the Gambino crime family, Paul Castellano. That was the night Jack had ordered the four-pound lobster. Latham had snapped a photo when it arrived at the table, and later when it left the table, and printed it out and framed it: Jack had written on it the date and the inscription: "Score: Jack—1. Lobster—0".

It was also after that dinner with too much lobster and wine that Jack had decided he really wanted to get the Diesel jeans they had looked at earlier in the day, and as the Town car approached the Diesel store at one minute before the 10:00 p.m. closing time, they got out of the car and started racing down the street, pounding on the glass door of the store as the clerk was inside, locking up, Jack somehow communicating that it was a life or death matter that he get the jeans right then, the clerk laughing and letting them in to make the sale. Latham at the same time had bought an identical pair for himself. The same size. They wore them every weekend after that, when they went to the mall or tried another local restaurant for dinner.

Latham smiled, remembering the first time a check-out girl at Whole Foods had looked at them and asked if they were brothers ("My life is now complete," he had said to Jack, "I can now die and go the heaven." "See," Jack had responded, "your Personal Trainer is a miracle worker. Knocked a couple decades off your appearance, just like that.") More often clerks in stores would ask Latham—as he pulled out his credit card to pay for whatever Jack had selected—if Jack was his son. Not as good as the brother question, but Latham and Jack would play along and say that Jack was home from college on break, oh yes, a junior, where? University of Miami, his major? and right about here, realizing their answers were not coinciding, would quickly divert the clerk.

On his mirror, Jack had taped a color picture of the Amalfi coast he had clipped from a magazine. That was the first trip they wanted to take together—to Italy, to stay on the Amalfi coast. A close second was the Cayman Islands. Latham had told him they could try both. Their plan was on the spur of the moment to just get on the computer and book seats on a flight and reserve a hotel room for a couple days, and just go. No planning, no big deal. Just go. These ideas felt reasonable when he and Jack discussed them, they felt so right to Latham, who was ready to leave his work and his clients for any new adventure with Jack. He considered it making up time for the days, the months, the years at the office—where had they gone? So fast, so fast. His work had drained decades from his life, in five minute drips and drops, all carefully recorded on time sheets and billed to clients.

Latham walked back to his bedroom, taking off his suit and tie. As he got ready for bed, a line from a poem he had studied in high school English, a poem he hadn't thought about since then, bounced in his brain: "The world beats dead/like a slackened drum".

Tonight, his home felt different, dead. He picked out from a bookshelf in the hall a poetry anthology to look for the poem. There it was. The line he was thinking about was from that Amy Lowell poem, "The Taxi":

> *When I go away from you*
> *The world beats dead*
> *Like a slackened drum.*

Several times that night, as Latham slept, the deep sleep of the bone weary, he thought for a moment he heard the phone ring. But even in his sleep knew he was dreaming. There would be no reason for Jack to call him. He could come and go as he pleased. With whoever he wanted. And there was no way Latham could show how needy he was and call Jack and ask him where he was. And how long would he be gone. And what was he doing. And when was he coming home. And who he was with… And who he was with.

When the clock radio came on at 5 a.m., he felt like shit from the partnership dinner. If Jack was there right now, they'd be chugging Jack's latest favored preworkout, chased with a handful of supplements, and he'd be regaling Jack with stories of last night and the plates of calamari and scungilli and cheeses and clams and red sauce and white sauce, and Jack would be telling him what to do at the gym that morning to work it off.

Just having Jack around the house, he realized now: these had been the most comfortable days, the most relaxing days, the most wonderful days he had known, days that had jolted him out of his life on autopilot, suddenly to see everything again with fresh thoughts, with young eyes, so that each day felt like the first day of summer.

Now, this morning, his world felt flat, weary, old. The same as it had been. Before Jack.

As he sat down in the kitchen to eat Jack's prescribed breakfast of wheat germ and chia seeds and flax seeds and raw pumpkin seeds and sunflower seeds, mixed with *Special* K and topped with blueberries, he remembered his high school dance. The band, the band on the stage at that moment, he saw them again now. Four guys from his class with fantasies of making it as the next hot group. How they had been riffing a song popular then, "Don't Let the Sun Catch You Crying", with its haunting line that Latham now remembered: "It may be hard to discover/that you've been left for another." How that night, at that dance, at the moment, he had discovered how hard it was. And he remembered the song's promise he had clung to the next year, far away at college: "But don't forget that love's a game/and it can always come again."

Chapter Eighteen

Anne fished out the keys and unlocked the front door.

The house smelled musty, in a nice Cape Cod summer place way, a house that had been closed up since she was last there at Thanksgiving, with Richard, Meghan and Walker. Now the summer was almost over. Labor Day was next week. Richard had had meetings in Europe. Meghan was taking extra courses at Georgetown to get science credits. Walker was a counselor at a lacrosse camp in New Hampshire. So fast. The summer had gone so fast.

When she pulled the drapes in the living room and opened windows, a spanking sailing breeze off the bay billowed the drapes into the room, like a spinmaker.

It was only 10 a.m.. They had made it to the Cape in Jack's Porsche in a little over four hours.

"Do you like it?" Anne asked.

"Oh man, this is insane."

Jack looked down to the beach and across the bay to the islands, walked into the sunroom, opened the drapes and looked out the large window all the way to the barrier beach, with blue glimpses of the sea between the white dunes.

"You're kidding me," he said "this is awesome to the max. Let's take a dip."

"Let me show you around real quick and then we can change. I haven't had a chance—yet—to work any magic on the place. It's old, pretty old, 1950s. And could use a facelift. For certain. So, excuse the condition. It was the setting that sold us."

"I can see why. You got water views out every window, your own beach, your—"

They walked room to room, opening drapes, flushing toilets, testing the sinks, lowering the temperature in the refrigerator, changed into swimsuits, and then went outside and walked around the house to the garage.

They carried the *Sunfish* out of the garage and down the sandy path to the beach, hooked on the tiller, hauled up the sail, pushed down the centerboard and were skimming across the bay, poking around the islands and into coves, skirting the sandbars in shoal waters, the warm southwest breeze tearing them along with the lee under, the spray soaking them, the boat heeling so far over it flipped in sudden gusts, the two of them screaming and laughing as they stood on the centerboard to right the boat, only to have it flip over on the other side until they mastered its quirks. They hauled up on that thin sliver of barrier beach that seemed to float between bay and sea and sky. The surf broke playfully on the ocean side, inviting skinny dips and body surfing. As they lay on sand that for eons of time had been shifted and sorted and polished by the surf until it was as fine as flour, as fluid as sugar, the breakers in solemn cadence crashed up and down the empty miles of beach. Back in the dunes, the summer breeze ruffled through the beach grass like a doting parent mussing a child's hair.

Sunny summer days, clear starry nights, day after day, all week long. Time hung suspended.

In the afternoons they sat on the deck chairs under the pines, looking out over the bluff thick with salt spray rose, fragrant with the last white flowers of Summer.

"You really like it?" Anne said.

"It's paradise."

They sat and watched terns hovering over the shallows, diving for silversides.

And gulls flying back and forth to the islands.

And fair-weather clouds out over the bay, with shadows of clouds floating on the water.

There was always a breeze moving through the pines on top of the bluff where they sat, and they could hear the breakers booming up and down the barrier beach, a steady muffled faraway hypnotic roar except when, on occasion, a solitary giant tripped and crashed and for a moment shook the world.

"We could live here," Anne said.

Jack looked at her.

"I mean, I would try to get this in the divorce settlement. In New Jersey divorce is no-fault, 50/50 I would ask for this. I don't think Richard would care. We could live here. It's real quiet, cozy off season— November through April? into May. But they're a bunch of gyms where you could work. We could travel a little. Everyone escapes a little in the winter, you have to, but I think it would be so good to live here. With you."

"Anne?"

"I know, I know. I'm hitting you all of a sudden. With a lot and— You could start a fitness YouTube channel. Right here. You've seen those. Some of those guys get hundreds of thousands of subscribers. Millions. And are making good money. Really good. Sponsorships. You—"

"Anne? What the—? This is crazy talk. You can't leave Richard and—"

"Walker and Meghan are grown-ups, now. They're OK. Richard wouldn't care. He'd be free. The magic's long gone for us. We—you and I— could start a line of fashion underwear. We could. You're always talking about your quest for The Perfect Underwear. We could design them. To your specs. Who better to model them?"

"Anne?"

"And Richard would be so—"

"Anne—you can't just leave—your life. This is crazy talk. We've only known each other for what? Like a month? A little over a month? Your home. And family. And—"

"Jackson." She reached over and held his hand in hers, interlocking fingers. "A month. Almost two. Magic months. And in these months, you have become my life. You now *are* my life. Literally, as you would say. Literally. You *are* my home. You *are* my family. We are so meant to have found each other. Now. At this moment. Now. Us. We are so meant to be with—"

"Anne, this is so… this is nutso. I didn't—I mean, don't get me wrong. OK? This is fun. A lot of fun."

"You've flown me to the moon."

Jack wasn't sure what to say. He thought of all he'd learned from her. "Anne, Anne, you've taken me on, like, a crash college course in—in everything. I feel like I'm learning so much about, about, you know, everything I've missed, I—"

"You are so sweet. You're my best student." Anne swung his hand up and down. "You're this teacher's special beautiful pet. You're Phi Beta Kappa, summa cum—"

134

"We're great together. That's for sure. Believe me, it's a lot of fun. But that's what I thought it was for you, too. Fun."

"Oh, believe me, it is."

"But I'm just freakin 24. I'm—I'm a kid, for God's sake. I only just started making some money. I couldn't support you like—"

Anne waved her other hand, dismissing everything around her.

"I don't need all this. I've had everything—and I mean everything—I ever thought I wanted. And like they say, it really is all… nothing. I mean it. When you get it, really, it means? Nothing. You find that out. You'll find out. You'll learn that, too. You find out what is really real. What is really important. In life, in our fleeting, sorry little lives. That last a nanosecond. Believe me. So fast. So fast."

Anne looked out over the Bay. "I can guarantee you:" she said, "it is not granite countertops. And it is not wine cellars. And it is not—"

"Not even a home theater? You gotta admit, that's sick."

"Come on. Be serious. Will you please be serious? Just for one minute? No, not even our home theater. Not even with those plush seats."

"That recline?"

Anne laughed. "I have to admit. We initiated that one pretty well."

"Real well."

"I'm serious. Everything I want, all I want, ever, everything—is: you. Just being with… you. Forever."

Jack held her. "Why don't you see if you feel the same way after having me around a little bit more? You'll be so sick of me by then you'll—"

135

"No. Never. Never my love. That, my love, is way, way beyond my human comprehension."

"You oughta talk to my brothers to see how sick of me they got."

"You have a brother?"

"Two. Oh yeah. Two older brothers. Real beauts."

"Do they look like you?"

Jack laughed. "No fucking way. They're lazy pieces of shit. Couch potatoes. Sitting in tiny office cubicles. In a building. In an office park. In Toms River. Part of the 'work-force.' The most iron they've ever pumped is like, I don't know, like lifting a paperweight? Twice. That's a rep for them. They think I'm crazy, doing what I do. Living a fitness lifestyle."

"Jackson. We have to live together. I have to get you out of that perv's home. Before it's too late."

Jack groaned and shook his head.

"Come on, Latham's not a—. What do you think, he's some kind of a child molester? Slipping a date rape drug into my dinner each night? Sneaking into my room? When I'm sound asleep? And climbing into bed with me? And having his—"

"I—"

"Latham's got a big heart. He's let me take over his guest wing. He took me in when I had nothing. And I mean no-thing."

Anne brushed his words aside as if flicking off a pesky greenhead fly.

"I think you'd actually like him," Jack continued, "a lot if you just got to know him. To give him a chance. He's a good guy. And where would we live, anyways? I doubt Richard would let me rent a room or two. In your house. And I don't think Latham would be interested in having you live there with us—"

136

"He may not be a child molester, but he's definitely trying to convert you, and—"

"Oh, come on. Stop that. That's crazy talk. You do know that, right? That there's no such thing as conversion, right? I mean that's been—"

"That's what they say, but I bet he's thought a lot about it, about giving it the old college try. I mean, my god, the way he looks at you? During his sessions with you? Everyone's seen it. It is such a joke. I'm surprised the Club doesn't provide him with a bib. So that he doesn't drip drool all over the equipment, and slop—"

"So, he likes me—"

"Likes you? That, my dear young man, is the understatement of the year. The century. He wants to be you, he wants to…Patti saw you guys walking through the mall and—"

"Hand in hand?"

"No. Of course not hand in hand. But she was asking if I thought you two were, you know, an item."

Jack rolled his eyes. "Tell me, what year is this, any ways? And you gals are still gossiping, clacking away, when you see two guys together? I mean come—"

"Oh, come on yourself. Get real. It is not just two guys. He could be your father and—How much older is he?"

Jack thought. "I think like, 20 years?"

"See?"

"See what? We're like about 20 years apart too, right?"

Anne was quiet.

"Come to think of it," Jack continued, "you and Latham must be just about the same age, right?"

Anne started to say something and then stopped.

"So, I'm filling something in his life right now," Jack continued. "He enjoys having me around. Having a buddy. The poor guy's—"

"Poor guy, my ass. He buys you any little thing you look at. Twice. It is so sick."

"The poor guy's having some fun. Doing stuff, things he's never done before. It's like he's pals with Austin and me, getting a chance to do things he missed out on. Come on, give him a—"

"You sweet innocent young man, you have no—"

"Believe me, he's harmless. He's got a beautiful heart. I have to get you two together. You probably have a lot in common."

"Yes, we do. And that would be: You. That, my dear young boy, is called a *menage a trois*. And believe me, that's about the only thing I'm not—"

"Hmmm. You never know till—"

Anne ignored him.

"We must find somewhere in town to live," she said "We have to get a place that is… ours. Just ours. Let's at least look when we get back. Will you at least go that far? To look? For me?"

Jack was quiet for a while, watching a catboat tack back and forth to pass through the channel between Anne's beach and the island. Anne squeezed his hand.

"Sure," he said, "why not. One step at a time. We can see how long it takes before you kick me out and I'm on the streets and sleeping in one of the Spa rooms. At the Gym. At night."

Anne got up from her chair and climbed onto him.

"Hey, I sort of like that idea."

"What?"

"You and I. Let's spend the night in one of the Club's spa rooms."

"Hmmm. A little kinky. I'm always up for a little kink. We could hide out till they close and—"

"I know this. For certain," Anne said. "Even if you do have any kinks or quirks—and you certainly don't have any discernible ones, you're perfect—"

"Yeah right."

"Even—even if you did have a quirk or two it would, to me, it would be so adorable. I would worship any quirk. And love every kink."

Those nights were soft with summer sounds as they lay on the big bed in the room under the eaves, all the windows open, the lap of water on the sand, the peepers in the wetlands discussing the day's events, the seals moaning on the flats across the bay. There were a few lights scattered here and there along the west shore, way back beyond Pochet. Far away, the lights of a dune buggy swayed along the barrier beach, while closer, it seemed, much closer, the Milky Way shimmered, bridging sea and sky. And all night long, as they fucked and dozed and cuddled and laughed and talked, the steady southwest wind sighed through the screens, while breakers boomed along the coast.

Chapter Nineteen

"OK," Jack said, "so you and Austin? Were you guys just jerkin' each other while I was away? So, are you like literally back to square one? Like the sorry specimen I found before I even became your Personal Trainer? Or are we ready—right now—to kick it up a notch? And become a real man?"

"Let's do it."

Latham sat on the rowing bench next to the lat pull down station, watching as Jack rummaged through the bin next to it filled with a curious collection of miscellaneous apparatus no one ever seemed to use. He pulled out a leather collar and fastened it around Latham's ankle, testing different holes before securing it with the buckle.

"How does that feel?" Jack asked.

"Good," Latham said, grinning, "real good. Could you make it even tighter? Sir?"

"Fucking perv. No, not unless you take me out to dinner first."

As Jack poked around in the bin for the other collar, Latham looked at him.

"Man, you know you are so fucking pussy whipped, right? It's pathetic."

"What the fuck are you talking about?" Jack said, squatting, looking up at him.

"Oh, come on. Have you even seen yourself? She's as much as leading you around like a little lap dog. On a pretty pink leash. I mean, my God, did she take your balls? Do you even know where she keeps them? The next time we watch some porn I'm gonna have to check and see if I can still count two. One. Two. I doubt they're still there. Just a gaping hole where they used to be. Before she cut them off."

"You're nuts."

"It's your nuts I worry about. Can't you see yourself? Everyone else does. You're like some Teddy Bear she carries around. And props up next to her. And pats on the head. And coos to. I mean, it's disgusting. She's old enough to be your mother. You're about the same age, you probably are the same age, as her kids. Can't you see she just wants someone new to mother?"

"See, you think that," Jack said, straightening out the collar on Latham's other ankle. "And Anne thinks you're trying to turn me gay."

Latham stared at him.

"Oh. Good. Lord. She does know that's impossible, right? What does she think: I'm the director of some special conversion camp? Over at my house? Like a reverse conversion camp. Turns straights gay?"

"No. But she's sure you're thinking about it."

"Give me a break. She is one sick bitch."

"I really gotta get the two of you together, to talk, to get to know each other. She's really nice and I think—"

"A little afternoon tea? Some scones? How special. A little social. But you're never around anymore. Where the fuck have you been?"

Jack tightened the other leather collar.

"OK, now stand up."

141

"So, where the fuck were you? Last week?"

"What?"

"Don't what me. I missed—" Latham paused, then started again. "I missed a whole week of sessions with you. Look what's happened to me, look at—"

"What? You look the same to—"

"No man. I lost my pump. I'm losing definition, look how—"

"Didn't Austin help you? I asked him to cover for me."

"Fuck Austin. Yeah, but it's not the same. He doesn't motivate his clients the same way you do. He doesn't inspire them. He wouldn't even go to dinner with me. Look, I'm wasting away. Living on disgusting *Lean Cuisines*. Were you with that skank grandma? Grandma Skank."

"What?"

"Strange coincidence: she was gone all week, too. In court, you know, prosecutors always say there's no such thing as a coincidence. Did she, what? chain you to a radiator or something? You better watch it. When her husband finds out she's drooling all over a cute kid, he's gonna—"

"Man, can't a guy even take a few days off? At the end of the summer? For Christ's sake. For vacation? I'm entitled."

"I'm just giving a little friendly advice. Cause no one else will. Hey, they got a leather chest harness in there? I'd really like a leather hood, too. If you got one of those. Lace it up real tight. Just slits for the eyes so I can see you. To make sure you don't try to run away from home again."

"If you don't shut the fuck up, I swear to God I'm gonna look for a rubber ball mouth gag in there. I think we keep some in the back room. For when clients start acting up."

Jack shook his head and clipped an elastic cord to each ankle collar and the other ends to the lat station.

"I'm likin this exercise," Latham said. "A lot. Master, you now have me just where you want me: in bondage. I am now your slave. Sir. Do with me what you will. Please abuse me. Real hard. I bet she's into that too. Does she have you whip her?"

"Would you shut the fuck up? People are watching." Jack looked around. "We're both gonna get kicked outta here if you're not careful. And, FYI? When you finish with this new routine? you're gonna be so sore. When you wake up, tomorrow? You're not even gonna be able to walk up, or down, stairs. You'll have to find someone to push you around. In a wheelchair."

"Sounds real good, Sir."

"Dickhead. OK. Hands on hips. Extend your right leg to the right. Far as you can. Farther. Make it hurt. Ten times. Come on. Twelve times. I want to see 10 perfect sets."

"Ten?"

"You heard me. Ten sets. Twelve reps each. Balls to the wall. No more pussy boy routines."

Jack led him through a new leg routine to mix up the muscles.

"Man, I feel it already," Latham said as he worked through the sixth set.

"I bet you do. You'll be lucky if you can even crawl tomorrow. On your hands and knees. I keep telling you, if you keep doing the exact same routines? Like what you were doing before we met? You're never gonna progress. Your muscles won't grow. Like mine."

Latham looked at Jack's biceps.

"We have to mix it up," Jack continued. All the time. No more autopilot."

Jack stopped counting as Latham was in midway position.

"Whoa. Whoa," Jack said. Jack was staring at him. "Wait just one friggin fucking bullshit minute."

"What? What's the matter?"

"What the fuck? That's my tank," Jack said, fingering the bottom edge of Latham's tank top.

Latham looked down. It was the gray one with the black figure of a skeleton riding a motorcycle, and above, the logo: "Good Times". The sleeves were bound in black, as was the neck.

"Uh oh," Latham said.

"Is that mine?"

"Oops."

"That was my favorite. How did you get it?"

"You can have it back. Here. Do you want it back?" Latham said, lifting up the bottom of the tank.

Jack jumped back in mock horror. "Yech. Gross. Get that crusty cum rag away from me."

"You sure?"

"Yes. I'm sure, you little klepto. Haven't seen that all summer. How'd you get it?"

Latham looked at him. And paused. "I hope this is not too weird for you…"

"Oh, this is gonna be good. Spill your guts, klepto. Confession time."

"OK." Latham looked embarrassed. "Well, do you remember the first time we talked in the locker room?"

"No. But OK."

"Yes, you do. It was that day you did the rope climb.

144

When you came back to our alcove, from the shower and everything? I was gone. And so was all your workout gear?"

Jack looked at him.

"You fuckin' little thief. Yeah, everything. I do remember. I had to go commando the rest of the day. Ever try 40 minutes on the treadmill, commando?"

Latham shook his head no.

"No? Well guess what? You will tomorrow. See how you like that."

"I'm sorry. I, I just—"

"So, looks like the law finally caught up with you, doesn't it? Is this the first time you've been caught? Red handed?"

Latham nodded his head yes.

"Is it the first time you've done it here?"

Latham looked down.

"Come on, boy. Come clean. Was this the first time?"

Latham shook his head "no".

"So, it looks like we've just caught ourselves a habitual offender, doesn't it? Sure looks like your run of luck ended, doesn't it? Your photo should be in the post office. Three to five in the slammer should straighten you out real nice, shouldn't it? And you know what the prison doctors do to habituals like you, don't you?"

Latham looked at him.

"Castration. That's right." Jack playfully smacked him in the crotch. "That would straighten you out once and for all. Wouldn't it?"

"Sorry. I'll get you another."

"No, I'm just joshing you, you fuckin felon. That actually happens to me. All the time."

"It does? So, I'm not the only perv in here?"

Latham resumed the count on his leg extensions.

"Far from it. But to me, you'll always be king of the pervs. Of course. And—"

"Thank you. Thank you very much. I'm touched." Latham touched his heart.

"Stop," Jack said. "Start that set all over again. You lost the count."

"Again?"

"Yes again. Better get used to it. That's how it's gonna be when the prison guards are in charge of you."

Latham started counting again.

"No man," Jack said, "I can't even begin to tell you how many of my underwear have mysteriously disappeared since I started working here and—"

"Really?"

"Oh yeah. Really. But actually? It is sort of flattering. I guess."

Latham stared at him.

"Yeah. No, I mean, to think there are guys out there? Who think of you? In that way? I mean, that's good stuff. The day I can leave my undies on the floor in there? Outside my locker? Unattended? And they're still there when I get back from a steam and shower?"

"Yeah?"

"It's over. Or O-V-E-R as you would say. That would be the day I know I've lost it. That's when I better start looking for another job. At a desk. In a cubicle. In a friggin' office park."

"So, it doesn't bother you?"

"No. Not at all. And I can usually figure out who took them and—"

"You can? How? How can you do that?" Latham

146

stopped. "Are there cameras in the Locker Room? I've wondered about that and—"

"What do you think, are you like crazy? I bet that would violate a whole lot of laws, Mr. Criminal Attorney. But you can usually pretty much pick up on who out there is interested in you. In that way. And—"

"How?"

"Wait. First, time to make you climb the risers."

"Come on, man. I don't wanna do that."

"I know you don't. And that's why you're gonna do them, Dildo."

Jack unclipped the ankle collars and led him to the back of the gym with the stacked pile of risers.

"This'll get your butt real nice, ready for your time in the pen. So, all your cellmates can enjoy it."

Jack pulled out one from the stack and put it on the floor in front of the mirror.

"Ok, con, climb that mother—up, down—20 times. Give me perfect form or you go back to count one. And start all over. And all the way down on the squat position. Your usual whining bullshit is over."

Latham began, watching Jack in the mirror.

"And let me hear you do the count. Out loud. So you don't cheat. Like felons do."

"OK. OK. One. So how do you know? Who stole your stuff?"

"Man, it's really not that hard. You pretty quickly see who's always staring at, whose eyes are like? radar-locked on you? or who's looking at you in the mirrors, and then they quickly look away if you catch them?"

"Three. Did you ever catch me?"

Jack snorted. "You really have to perfect your technique, felon boy. You always looked like you were visually undressing me."

147

"Four. Sorry about that."

"No, it's OK. It was sort of endearing. I guess."

"Really? Five."

"And they'll sort of follow you around the gym so they can be in the best position to look at you, no matter what you're doing. Or they'll watch what equipment you're using? And as soon as you finish, take your place, so that they can feel the warmth of where you were sitting, or the sweaty handles or something like that. Sit in your sweat. Pretty sick, isn't it sicko?"

"Guilty, Your Honor. Twelve."

"That's pretty sick, bro."

"What?"

"Getting off by sitting in a puddle of someone's ass sweat. I mean, my God—And if that's 12—start from scratch."

Latham stopped and got off the riser. "Come on, man, that was 12."

"If that was 12? So's my dick. Start again, ass-sweat sitter."

Latham laughed and started again. "One. Hey, don't knock it till—I mean, if you isolate anything about sex, right? It's pretty disgusting. I mean it's not like we're lapping up the puddle or anything."

"OK, stop. I'm still digesting breakfast. I bet if no one was looking, you'd at least doggy woof the seat."

"Three. You got that right. And maybe put a few drops behind our ears as the day's cologne. *Man Sweat.* That should be a new brand."

"Gross."

"Seven. So, Mr. Ned Normal: don't tell me you wouldn't doggy woof the cycling seat, say, of Miss Ponytail Swisher? I've seen the way all you Trainers have locked your radar on her."

"Is it that obvious?"

"That would be, a yes. Nine. You all are trying so hard not to directly look, and that makes it even worse. Every mirror angle is utilized by you horn dogs."

Jack sighed. "A lot of guys ahead of me. I'd have to get at the back of the line for that delightful little doggy woof."

"See. Same difference. Humans? Fourteen. We're really nothing but sick, perverted, disgusting little animals."

Jack laughed. "Well, when you put it that way. But I'm not letting you slip by this so fast, Mr. Slippery Attorney. So let me get this straight. You're saying you're getting off sitting in a puddle of someone's ass sweat, squishing all around in it and—"

"Seventeen. Well, it's gotta be the right someone to make it—"

"Blah, blah, blah. Let me tell you something, boy: You're just lucky you're not right now in the correctional institution for the criminally insane. Yet. Better watch it."

"Maybe we'll end up as cellmates there?"

"I'd tunnel out real fast."

"So, what else? What else are the giveaways that some guy's got the hots for you? Twenty."

"I doubt that was 20, but I'll give you a pass on that one." Jack placed another riser on top of the first one. "Twenty more. And don't fuck up the count this time."

"Shit. One," said Latham, stepping up to the higher level.

"Oh, it's so easy," Jack continued. "So, when you go into the Locker Room? Those sicko guys, like you, they'll be trailing you in. And stand next to you at the urinal and—"

"Hmm. Four. Good idea."

"Don't try it, dickhead. Or they pop into the Steam Room a minute after you go in, or just happen to be passing, back and forth, when you're shaving. And wander by your alcove as you're stripping, and all that."

"Guilty as charged. Eight. I've done all that."

"I'm sure you have. See? People come to the gym for a whole bunch of reasons. But I guess whatever gets you in here is good, right?"

"Yeah. I guess so. Thirteen."

"And when I put two and two together and figure out who feels that way about me? Who the thief is? Bingo. Paydirt. Another live prospect for a paying client."

"Like me? Fourteen."

"Like you, Dildo. Low hanging fruit. Ready for plucking."

"Fifteen. So other guys have done it? With you. Interesting."

"As long as this is confession time?"

Latham looked at him. "Oh this should be good. Sixteen. So, you've done it, too? Let me guess—with Harrison?"

"Fuck you, jerk-off. No, I was gonna say I've been known to leave my sweaty workout gear, there on the floor, unattended, as bait—"

"O.M.F.G. Seventeen."

"Oh yes. To stir up a new client or two—"

"Your Honor, a classic case of entrapment. Case closed. Eighteen."

"Hey, whatever it takes to stir up new business, right? Don't tell me you lawyer boys wouldn't bend the rules a bit to do whatever it takes to land a new client?"

"Guilty as charged. Twenty. Done."

"Not so fast."

Jack put on a fourth riser. Latham groaned.

"And by the way," Jack said, as Latham started the climb, "what do you guys even do with all the priceless treasure you steal?"

"What?"

"You know," Jack said. "You steal the sweaty gear. You take it out of here. Then what? No," Jack quickly added, and held his hands over his ears and started singing "Old McDonald had a Farm". "Don't' tell me, I don't want to know. 'And on his farm he had a goat,'" Jack sang loud. "Ee I ee I oh.' I don't—"

Latham laughed. "Let's just say: they're well taken care of. And are in good hands. You never have to worry about them. Again."

Latham patted his tank top. And pulled it up and kissed it.

"I'll tell you this," Latham continued. "Four. They're never washed."

"Disgusting. Thanks for that visual. Come on, man, ass to the grass."

"I'm trying. Nine."

"Well fucking try harder. Do you want a flat lawyer ass? Is that what you want? As flat as your attaché case? Is that what you want, Billy Briefcase? Or do you want a smokin' hot ass like this" Jack slapped his butt. "An ass that's gonna fill out your jeans? So people do a double take when they pass you on the street? Or you notice people are following you, staring?"

Latham squatted lower and groaned as he came back up.

"Now you're cooking," Jack said "Ass to the grass. Go so low it hurts coming back up. Push up so you feel it in your legs."

151

"I feel it, I feel it," Latham said, staggering. "Fifteen".

"This is good. One minute rest. Then I wanna see 20 more perfect ones."

"Fuck me hard."

After 45 minutes of the new routines, Jack tossed Latham a hand towel from the pile above the sink. Latham rubbed it over his head.

"After all that, I need 20 minutes on the table," Latham said, pointing over to the Stretching Tables. "One of your real good stretchings. A real serious one."

"OK, but listen, you gotta promise me something."

"Anything. You know that."

"For God's sake, I'm beggin' you: please don't get a boner on the table this time. Your gym shorts are tenting up so everyone can see it a mile away. Everyone's looking."

Latham laughed. "I can't help it, man. It just pops up like that. I can't control it. When you climb aboard with me and I open my eyes and you're—"

"Fuck. Think about something really disgusting."

"I know what: I'll think about your skank grandmother. There. That did it. That's a real buzz killer. Dick's ascended. And gone into hiding."

"Listen, lawyer boy. Just make sure 'it' behaves." Jack made air quotes. "Otherwise, I swear to God, you're gonna be wearing a hockey cup in here. That's gonna keep that horny dick where it belongs."

"Sir, yes Sir. This horny dick needs to be disciplined. Sir."

Latham lay on his back on the Stretching Table and got comfortable. He put a rolled-up towel under his head. Jack got one of the moist eucalyptus-scented towels from the small refrigerator outside the Pilates Room and laid it over Latham's eyes.

152

"OK dickhead," Jack said. "Just start thinkin' about baseball or something."

"Roger," Latham said. He paused for a moment. "This is so weird: everyone on the team looks, they look like you. Every last one of them. Their uniforms are skin tight and really show off their…"

"Shut the fuck up. I swear to God: keep that fuckin' boner under control. Or else."

"Or else what?"

"I'm gonna assign Blaine as your Personal Trainer."

"Oh man, anything but that. I'm gonna be good. From now on. I'm thinking of that skanky ancient cunt whose stinky drool dribbles all over you. There, that did it. No tent, see? Uh oh. Maybe killed it for good. Hey, how about dinner tonight, Harley Tavern, 7 p.m.? We'll get caught up."

"Count me in. But don't even try tempting me this time to split that side with you, you know, that twice baked potato thing?"

"Not even to celebrate your homecoming?"

"No deviations from our clean diet. Got it? All the bull shit is O.V.E.R.. Our Mr. Olympian regime diet starts now. For real."

"OK. New beginning. Hey man, it feels so good to have you back. I—"

Jack held Latham by the ankles and yanked them. Hard.

Latham sighed.

Chapter Twenty

"Yo girlfriend," Patti called to Anne when she saw her walking back from the showers, holding a towel below her neck. "So, how was the Cape?"

"O.M.F.G. Paradise."

"I bet it was. Look at you girl: you got yourself a real nice... tan."

"Oh. Thank you." Anne held out her arm and studied it. "Every day, perfect summer weather. Glorious, glorious days. Enchanting."

"Lucky girl. I don't even see any tan lines." Patti scanned her from head to toe. "Are you telling me a refined, suburban, monthly book club regular, country club matron like you was, could it be, running around the dunes? Au naturel?"

"Maybe. Just a little. Don't you just abhor bikini lines?"

"I do. Such a problem. By the way, have you seen Jack? He's got a really sexy tan, too. Wonder if he has any tan lines?"

Anne kept drying herself and patting her hair with a smaller towel.

"We should check him out," Patti continued. "See for ourselves. Hey, I know. Let's sneak up from behind and yank down his tiny nylon shorts."

"Sicko."

"I guess he and his buddies must have gone to AC again?"

"I guess."

"Jack was gone all last week, I think. I don't think I noticed if Austin or Ronnie were away. In fact, I'm pretty sure Todd was here. Come to think of it, Ronnie, too. And Austin. Now that I think about it, I remember seeing them all here. Each day. Except Jack. I don't think I saw him."

Anne looked up at her.

"Girlfriend," Patti said, "do we need a little chat?"

"About what? What's up?"

"Just between us girls, right?"

"Of course. What happened?"

"OK. We've known each other for, how long? Forever, right?

Anne nodded.

"So, I'm just gonna just come right out and cut to the chase, OK?"

"Sure."

Anne stopped drying and looked at Patti, who was rubbing lotion into her arms.

"And then determine if you need, OK, maybe an intervention?"

"What? What do—"

"OK. Here goes." Patti cleared her throat. "Did you, by any chance, did you take your Personal Trainer to the Cape? With you?"

Anne looked at her, then quickly peered into her locker, straightening her clothes.

"Oh, good Lord," Patti said, throwing her arms into the air. "Coo coo ca choo, Mrs. Robinson."

"Patti, we have to talk."

"Jesus loves you more than you will know."

"Is this confidential, cross your heart, may your boobs descend to your belly button confidential? Right?"

"Oh, good Lord, you're doing him."

"Patti," Anne said, looking right at her friend, "I love Jackson. So much."

Patti stared at her. And gave her an exaggerated eye roll.

"Oh, good Lord." Patti laid the lotion on the bench next to her. "Lordy Lord. Girl: No. You. Do. Not. You merely lust him so much."

Anne shook her head.

"I've never felt this way about anyone. Ever. Never."

Anne sat down on the bench next to Patti, her towel around her shoulders.

"This is so, so different," she continued. "I feel like my life has just begun. It's just started. I've just begun to really, truly live. Be alive. See. Feel. In a whole new way. I don't even know how to explain it. It's the most—Being with him, it's—I—"

Patti stuck her index finger into her open mouth and made noises like she was gagging, about to heave.

"Oh, good Lord, girlfriend, he is 24. Read my lips. Twenty-freakin-four. You're what? With vials of Botox? a 50 gallon drum's worth? Injected into your pretty little face? Every three months? To even be able to—sort of pass, sort of—for the age you fantasize you are? In flattering lighting?"

"So?"

"So? So, the sex is great, I'm sure. But he's a kid. A beautiful, gorgeous, kid."

Anne sighed. "Patti. Patti."

Patti shook her head. "You do know that men's brains don't even fully gel? At least for a few more years? It's all still all liquidy in there. Molteny. Mush. Liquidy. Molten mush. He has no idea what he's even doing."

Anne shook her head no.

"Patti, I love him, he is so… like I've…"

Patti continued.

"He's having a great old time, isn't he? Having Mrs. Robinson, a real live, grown up, an honest to goodness adult, desire him. What kid wouldn't? I mean, what a kick for him. You're—"

Patti paused and slapped her forehead.

"Girlfriend, please tell me, oh please, please tell me: you didn't buy him that Porsche? Did you? Jesus, Mary and Joseph, are you completely out of your—"

Anne laughed. "No. Cross my heart, I did not give him his Carrera."

"Yeah right"

"No, I swear."

"So let me get this straight. So, he's got a rundown beat up heap of a Jeep? That sounds like it's held together by, by I don't know what, loose screws and paperclips?"

Patti made the sound she imagined. And pretended she was driving a car, hands on the wheel.

"And all of a sudden, Ba Boom, in he roars, in a brand new hot yellow Porsche? Vroom. Vroom."

"I know."

"My, my. Either he's saving all his personal training nickels, is that it? Or maybe, I don't know, did he get himself a paper route? For after school?"

"You're so mean."

"Or maybe, just maybe? He found himself a—"

"No, I swear to God, I didn't buy him that. He told me

all about it. You've seen that good-looking lawyer guy, the one Jackson works with? Before me? Every morning? That time? Right before me? That Latham guy?"

"Ah yes, deary, everyone knows who that Latham guy is. The middle-aged rich guy. Also infatuated with Jack. Hmmm. Sort of like—"

"He gave it to him. Latham. He felt sorry for Jackson and worried about him in that old Jeep and—"

"Oh, I bet he was just worried sick. And I guess a sexy yellow Porsche would be just about the safest car for Jack? Didn't A.J. Powers just report that? Tops for family safety?"

Anne shrugged. "What can I say?"

"Can you say Chevy? Can you say Ford? Pretty safe cars in those lines, you think? If Latham is so—worried—"

She made air quotes and rolled her eyes again.

Anne didn't respond.

"Oh Lord. So, your sweet young innocent Personal Trainer is also doing Latham, too? That's the only reason, girlfriend, the one and only reason, a Porsche would suddenly appear. Out of the blue."

"Man, you are so cynical. Can't you see how maybe—"

"I'd say you got yourself some stiff competition, girlfriend. Looks like your man-boy is doing anything, everything, that has two legs. And a healthy bank account. Figures. At that age. That's normal. At that age, they would do a piece of fruit. A nice slice of meat. A vacuum cleaner. Perchance, as you would say, perchance, a cute electric toothbrush. If it had enough bucks. Or someone old enough to be his—"

Patti stopped talking. Diana was walking by their alcove, heading out toward the gym. She stopped.

"Hey girlfriends," Diana said. "You finished?"

"Done for the day," Anne said. "How about you?"

"I'm a little late today. Running late. My bad. How is it out there?"

"Not that crowded," Patti said. What are you working on today?"

"I'd be very happy to burn off 1,000 calories on the treadmill. Realistically? If I can hit 200? Without someone bringing out the paddles? And calling 9-1-1? I'll call it a day. Come to think of it, you think our Trainers here are trained in mouth-to-mouth? What if, you know. To revive us?"

Patti looked at Anne. "That's got to be part of their certification, right?"

Anne nodded. "Got to be."

"In that case," Diana said, walking on, "I may try to push beyond 200. And hope, if need be... to be resuscitated."

"Enjoy your workout," Anne said.

"And the resuscitation part, especially," Patti called after her.

They gave her time to get out of earshot.

"Why do I think they'll all rush to resuscitate her?"

"Even before she even hits the floor."

"I wonder."

"So where were we?" Patti said.

"You were in the midst of one of your cynical flights of a suburban housewife's, repressed fantasy. Patti, just so your overheated brain can take a little rest: Jackson is not *doing* Latham, as you so delicately put it. Jackson's helping him around his house."

Patti guffawed. "I bet he is. And just for the record? If you call him Jackson one more time? I swear to God, I'm gonna hurl."

"Jackson is such a beautiful name that—"

Patti kneeled down in front of the bench and pretended she was vomiting over the side. She wiped her mouth with her towel.

"Pig," Anne said.

"I've seen him, I've watched Latham, everyone has. He's obsessed with Jack. Just like you. It's so sick. That's all this is, you know. For both of you goobers. A stupid puppy love infatuation. You're both like two goofy, love-sick, 13 year-olds. He's even starting to look like Jack."

Anne looked at Patti.

"Can't you see it?" Patti continued. "I wonder how much he pays to get his hair dyed? To precisely match Jack's?"

"What?"

"Oh, come on. You know that guy's hair was never that sexy honey color. All of a sudden? A perfect match. The exact *exact* same color. The exact same cut. Every single strand: identical. Come on. Case closed. I bet he drags Jack to the hair salon he goes to so that his stylist can make the match perfect. Listen girlfriend, if I ever see you walk in here with that same color—"

"Hmmm. That's actually not a bad idea. Not bad at all, I—"

"I swear to God, if I—"

"Interesting. Very interesting."

Anne stood up and walked to the mirror in the hall and lifted up her hair. She looked at it from every angle.

"Jackson and I would be like, we'd be twins. I want his beautiful, luscious color. Brother and sister. I could pretend I was Jackson. Dress like—"

"Gag me. Stop. I'm making this worse. Reel it in, girl."

"Loving it. I bet I could wear his clothes and—"

"Oh I'm sure that would look so good considering he's about ten times your size. Maybe you could start a new trend: Scarecrow Chic."

Anne rummaged around in her gym bag. And pulled out a pair of black Under Armour compressions shorts. She held the underwear in both hands and cradled it between her shoulder and chin, cooing to it, as if to a baby, smothering it with kisses.

"Bloody Jesus. Are those his?"

"Aren't they beautiful?"

Anne extended them out toward Patti.

Patti recoiled as if Anne was waving a dead mouse in front of her face.

"Get that filthy thing out of here."

Anne brought it back under her chin and started stroking it.

"She didn't mean it" she cooed to the underwear. "You are not filthy. Don't even listen to her. She just doesn't appreciate the finer things in life. She—"

"Good Lord. Girl, I'm going to have to have you committed. I think a few sessions of e-lec-tro-therapy will do wonders for you. I'm serious. Get that disgusting rag away from here."

Anne hugged the underwear, gave the pair a final kiss then slipped them on, smoothing them out, caressing them with her hand, the front, the sides, the back.

"See? Perfect fit."

"Did he give you those? Perhaps as a special gift? Or did you just steal them from him?"

"They were with his pile to be washed. But they weren't even dirty. They smelled so good. And fresh. Here, see? So why not—"

Patti stood up, moving away from Anne.

"What?"

"What?"

"No, it's just you're so quiet all of a sudden. Have you finally run out of your Psych 101 drivel?"

"No. I was just wondering."

"Wondering what?"

"Exactly how many volts the doctors are going to have to pass through your besotted little brain to bring you back to normal."

"Hey: love, girl, is a wonderful thing. Love is a many splendored thing".

"I swear to God you're gonna make me puke, stop."

"It doesn't all have to be just the Nancy Normal sweet little Rodgers and Hammerstein world you and most of your little plain vanilla friends live in," Anne continued. "True love: it's always something to be celebrated and…"

Patti smirked.

"What? What is your problem? Can't you—"

"No, I'm just imagining the song Rodgers and Hammerstein would have written about your love: 'I Could Have Danced all Night (in my boyfriend's underwear),' that would be a good one. Or how about—"

"That wasn't even Rodgers and Hammerstein, you—. That was Lerner and Lowe. Didn't you learn anything at Vassar? Except how to pack groceries in your station wagon. Without showing too much leg."

"Very funny. Rodgers and Hammerstein. Lerner and Lowe. Same difference."

Patti paused and stared at Anne.

"Wait a minute. Wait. Just. A. Bleepin minute. Did you, by any chance, did you—"

"Did I what?"

"Did you buy him that… Rolex?"

Anne grinned and giggled and sat down again, drying her feet.

"Guilty. As charged. Isn't it a beaut? It was my idea. So, we're in the mall and I made him go into the Rolex store with—"

"Oh yes. I'm picturing it now. I'm sure you had to drag him in. Kicking and screaming. 'No. No. Please don't make me go into that Rolex store', he must have begged you—"

"Bitch."

"And pick out my favorite," Patti continued. "Please. I'll do anything. Anything but that. Not the Rolex Store. Please, I beg of you."

"Are you finished yet?"

"No, no, anything but the Rolex—"

"Shut up." Anne smiled. "I had him try on that one. First one we tried. The deep blue face made it, made that blue of his eyes pop and—"

"I bet his eyes popped. Probably fell out of their sockets. And dangled there. At his good fortune. What did he have before? A Mickey Mouse Club watch?"

"And the gold? Next to his skin? It was so meant to be. It was something that just had to be done."

Anne got up again and walked out to the hall to the station by their alcove. She picked up each pump bottle of lotion and read the labels, then selected one and put the others back on the counter.

She held it up for Patti to see.

"Is this one any good?" she asked Patti.

Patti held it and read the label.

"Probably just as good as all the others. What's your

goal? To keep your skin looking like you're what? Like your boyfriend's?"

"If only. I would bathe in it."

"So, ka-ching-a-roo for a nice new Rolex. And I suppose that very thin, very gold, new chain he sports around his beautiful young neck? You gave him that as a two-day anniversary present?"

"Bitch. Gold against Jackson's skin is—it's pure magic."

Patti did another eye roll and a head shake.

"Stop. Full stop. You're worshiping the kid. This is so sick. He's not some young innocent personal trainer. You, and his other goofball sugar daddy, you've turned him into a—a gigolo. He's now got two fairy godmothers. You two are turning him into nothing more than a spoiled rotten kid. If nothing else, think what you're doing to him. You're ruining him. You—"

"Patti, you don't understand. At all."

"Oh, I think I do. Can't you see that Jack was born with these incredible looks. Yes, he's worked to perfect his body—"

Anne sighed.

"Stop that. This instant. If I hear that lovesick cow sigh one more… Girl, sweetheart, it's all genetics. He was born with that. And probably since the day he popped out of his mother's womb, everyone's been fawning all over him and treating him like he's someone special. And that shaped who he became, who he is. But he's not special. Repeat after me: He. Is. Not. Special."

Anne said nothing.

"He is not a god," Patti continued. "Repeat. OK, at least repeat in your besotted brain. He just looks like one. He's just a little boy, in a god's skin. He's a regular goofball kid in a very pretty package. I'll grant you that."

"And that, my friend, is exactly where you are wrong. So wrong. In so many ways. Jackson is so much more than a pretty package. So much more than—"

Patti stood up and stroked where her package would be if she were a man and made the motion men make to simulate playing with it.

"Pig. I'm trying to be serious. Jackson is so much more than his beauty. He is the most caring, the most loving, the most intelligent—"

"Good lord. Is he also a hypnotist? Cause Anne, darling, you are so under his spell. Yes. He's entertaining. Yes, he's a lot of fun. My God, he can even entertain you with all his magic tricks. Whenever—"

Anne sighed again, pumped some more of the skin lotion into her hand and spread it the length of her leg.

"It's like you've bought your own home entertainment system," Patti continued. "That you can drag around wherever you go. I'm sure it's a boatload of fun. But do you realize how old all that's going to get when you're both a year or two older? Let alone, 10 years—"

"See, that's where I think—"

"And what about—have you even stopped to consider, even for a moment, just what Richard—oh yes, remember him? Remember Richard? Think real hard. Remember? Yes. That Richard. You know, the one whose ring you wear."

Patti took Anne's hand and cupped her hand over the large square-cut diamond surrounded by sapphires. "Your husband. Have you even stopped to think about just what Richard has done for you?"

"I know. Believe me, I know. And I'm so grateful and—"

"Grateful? Grateful. I feel a big 'but' coming.

Grateful? He's given you every single thing your tiny little heart ever thought it desired. And along comes Mr. Abs six pack"

"Eight, but who's counting."

"Oh, good Lord. Have you named each one? So, Mr. Abs. Mr. Smokin Hot Ass. Here he comes, right into your amazing, wonderful life. And boom. Richard who? Meghan who? Walker who?"

"Don't."

"Who are these people living in your house, you must be saying to yourself each morning. This is where Jack—excuse me. Jackson. This is where Jackson and I play house. Jackson, my brand new Ken doll boy toy. Who can do everything." Patti pretended she was playing with a Ken doll, hop scotching it through the air. "And even fucks me real, real good."

"Patti, I know. I know. I know. I do know. Don't think I haven't wrestled with all that. Every day. But Jackson is my—"

"Stop. Hard stop."

Anne looked over at her.

"If you even start," Patti continued, "to even say *that* word."

"What word?"

"Soulmate, soulmate. Soulmate. I swear to God if you do? I'm gonna chuck all over all your pretty little pedicured toes."

"OK. I won't say 'soulmate.' But I will say this: he completes me in a way—in a way I now know, I now realize, I see this for the very first time, I never have been complete before. Ever."

"Anne. Darling. Sweetheart. My precious one. You are so textbook."

"And just what now are you babble wabbling about, dearie?"

"You, young lady. you have gone doty. What you are suffering from, my dear young lady, is so simple. So easy to cure. Straight out of every elementary textbook. Under the midlife crisis chapter."

"Give me a break. I mean—"

"If you were a man, you'd what? You'd be buying yourself a Ferrari. Convertible. Fire engine red, right? And so, tooling around town. With a sporty cap to cover your bald spot."

"Give me a break. You don't—"

"Just look at it, girlfriend: Walker leaves in what, two weeks? Off to Duke. Bye-bye. Meghan's gone. Poor, poor Richard—you know I pray for that poor man every night? Poor Richard is out there, right now, busting his butt trying to make you more money. To what? To satisfy all your insatiable desires an—"

"Oh please—"

"Don't interrupt, missy; not polite. And you, poor little you, ah yes, all alone in your, your palace. Which you have made so perfect there's nothing left for any workmen to do. So, you wander its 50 rooms with nary a soul to boss around. So instead, what do you do? You don't buy a Ferrari cause you're not into cars."

"Do they have a stick? I still can't do a stick shift."

"Of course, you can't. Richard's always done all the hard stuff for you. So, you go out and buy yourself a cute young personal trainer, instead of a rite-of-passage Ferrari. All for your own. And pretend you're his age. And that you're going to live your youth all over again. With him. Just the way you dreamed it would be. Happily ever after. This is so basic textbook. It's not even a challenge to figure out what's going on here."

Patti closed her locker door with finality.

"OK," Anne said, "have you finished with your bogus pop psychology class? And ready to be a real friend? Patti: I need you to understand. I need you now. I really do."

"Sweetheart, I am so here for you. You know that. Always. But not until I pull you back to the real world. Please, please come back. Get out of this fantasy world you're swirling around in. This is what a good friend does. Girl, you are so far gone. Are you on something? Something's fucked up your usual crystalline powers of reasoning."

Patti stopped. Then continued.

"You're not swallowing, are you? Exactly how much of Jack's jizz is in you, girlfriend? Ahha. This must be why you're becoming him, that's—"

"You are getting so gross, it—"

"Hey, listen, girlfriend; someone has to stop you before you ruin your life. May I make an immodest suggestion?"

Anne heaved an immense sigh. "I don't see that I have any choice at this point."

"Clearly you don't. I would suggest you and your Jackson boy-toy. Just go ahead. Rent a room. Twenty-four hours. And go right ahead. Just go for it. Fuck your little brains right out. And just get it out of your system. Once and for all. So that then you can go back to resuming the life you really love."

"Patti, you just don't get this at all, you—"

"Oh, I think I do. What I know is this. I know you, young lady, cannot, simply cannot, be really happy, unless: you're knee deep in some new construction project, right? Am I right?"

Anne looked at her.

"Unless you're creating something. Unless you're bringing home your precious books of swatches and tile samples and lavishing hours on them. Unless you're bossing around your squadron of helpers and decorators, seeing whatever is in your mind come to life. All the amazing, beautiful, wonderful things you create. That is your passion. That is where you are truly fulfilled."

"So?"

"So that's fine. That's good. But tell me this. OK? How long will you be satisfied playing house with this Jackson boy, checking out samples of linoleum. For you two lovebirds to lay together on your kitchenette's floor? In your mobile home. On cinderblocks."

"Is it a double wide?"

"Knock yourself out. Go for it. There it is, your double wide on cinder blocks. In a trailer park."

Anne laughed. "Is that really what you see?"

"Frankly? Yes. It is. How long would you be satisfied not going to any of those galas with Richard, you know? The ones where you don all the jewels he's lavished upon you. And you in your latest slinky chic black *Issey Miyak.* And you pretend you're oblivious to all the oohs and aahs when the two of you walk in. Like movie stars. Like royalty. Hmmmmm? How long? Remember all that stuff?"

Anne walked out to the hall and tossed her towel in the hamper and put the lotion back on the shelf under the mirror and came back. Anne pulled her slacks over Jack's black compressions shorts. Patti was still talking.

"Why can't you just have a regular old plain Jane affair like everyone else? Buy him some baubles. If you get off on that. Mother him. Go ahead. Bathe him. Give him a bubble bath. Dress him up. Change his clothes. Burp him. Powder his darling behind. He'll have some fun. That's all men really want, you know. Someone to take care of them. To mother them. You'll have a lot of fun nurse-maiding him. And then, once you get that all out of your system, you both go your own merry ways. And get on with your real lives. Not your teenaged pimply fantasy lives."

Anne stood up and took her blouse out of her locker.

"You just don't get it. Jackson *is* my real life. I want to be with him. I need to be with him. So badly. In every way. Twenty-four seven. I have to be with him. Every day. Of every year. Forever. I want to be with him the rest of my life."

Patti let out a mournful groan and rolled her head.

Anne looked down and pulled a sneaker from her locker and put it on.

"OK. So just tell me this," Patti said. "I just have to know one thing."

Anne looked at her, warily, and raised her eyebrows.

"How is it? You know. With him?"

Anne thought for a moment and looked into the distance.

"You have no idea. When you feel this way about someone? And someone looks so, so like that? Remember when you told me they were all like—like a different species? The Personal Trainers?"

"Yeah?"

"You were so right."

"Momma mia. You are possessed. By an alien. The time for an intervention has long since passed. A long time ago. We're so way beyond an intervention. You, girlfriend, need an exorcism. Now."

Chapter Twenty-One

While staring into the mirror across the corridor, Latham shoved the Brooks Brothers raincoat deeper into his locker so the door would close.

He had zipped in the liner that morning. The seasons had changed overnight. Autumn already was in the air.

He continued to look, transfixed.

"Like what you see?"

Latham startled, as if someone had caught him touching himself.

He hadn't realized he was obviously staring at the new guy in the next alcove. Latham had been watching the stranger in the mirror as he peeled off his gym gear as if doing a strip tease—the tank top (he raised his arms over his head, stretched, then ran a lazy hand down his side from his armpit to his obliques), the black running shorts, each sneaker, socks, his black Under Armour boxers, revealing, stage by stage, the body of a hunk.

He was a little over six feet, probably weighed around 210, and was so cut that each curve was perfect, as if he had descended from the ceiling of the Sistine Chapel, deep dimples, meaty lips that revealed sparkling white teeth when he grinned at Latham, short, perfectly groomed dark hair. The dick and balls, commensurate. Latham had been staring at him in growing amazement.

Here, right across from him: the gulp-inducing perfect man.

"What?" Latham fiddled with his locker.

"I said, like what you see?"

Latham felt himself sweating. And turning red.

"I'm sorry," Latham said, "I guess I was daydreaming and—"

"Hey, no worries, man, that's why we're all here, isn't it? To be admired? I'm flattered. Thank you for noticing. It'd be a bummer if no one looked. And liked what they saw."

He fastened a white towel around his waist and walked over to Latham, hand extended, walking right into Latham's personal space, shaking his hand, then putting an arm around his shoulder.

"I'm Dylan," he said. "First day here. Great to finally meet someone."

Latham stared at him, not sure if he was supposed to put his arm around Dylan or what. An exploding fist bump was the most intimate male greeting in the Club. He shook his hand.

"I'm Latham."

"Sorry?"

"Latham."

"So, there's a name you don't hear that often. In fact, I think you're the very first Latham I ever met. Latham: cool. So, how'd you get that name?"

"Oh, it was my grandfather's middle name. And I guess my parents liked it and—"

"Cool. Latham. So how long have you been a member here, Latham?"

He had dropped his arm from around Latham's shoulder, but still stood right next to him, in his space.

The way he did seemed natural, not at all objectionable as it would have with anyone else. Latham noticed that the man smelled good. Clean. And that he was as perfect close up as he had appeared at first sight. Not even a pore.

"Oh, man. I was probably, like, the first member here. I literally joined while the gym was still under construction—sight unseen."

"Then this is my lucky day. You can tell me everything I need to know to get me up to speed. Real quick. Let's take a steam and you can fill me in."

Latham looked at him and stammered. "I don't know, I have to—"

"Come on," Dylan said, "we're gym buddies now. Here," he said pulling his towel from around his waist and handing it to Latham. "I'll grab another. Let's do it."

Dylan returned, fastening around him another large white towel, putting his arm around Latham's shoulder and herding him out to the corridor and toward the Showers and Steam Room.

"So, tell me, how is the Steam Room here? Scale of one to ten. You use it every day?"

"No, not that often, actually. Sometimes. When I have, it's pretty good. They went through this period where it kept breaking down? Clogging up or something, and it would be closed off. For repairs. But it's been working for a good long stretch now, so hopefully—"

"Nice. After a real intense workout? Nothing better than a good steam. How long do you stay in? When you use it?"

"Oh, I don't know. Not that long. Maybe 10 minutes, max? Before I get fricasseed."

Dylan laughed. "Let's try 20 minutes today, OK? I like 20. You got a watch?"

"Yeah." Latham held up his wrist.

"Mmm. Very, very nice," Dylan said. "Piguet."

"Very good," Latham said. "I'm impressed. You called that at 50 paces."

"I'm pretty much a watch-aholic. The best seems to always call to me. Maybe someday…"

Latham liked the way it felt, walking through the Locker Room, talking to this god as if they were good friends.

"OK, Mr. Latham Piguet. So, your job is: time us. From the time we get seated. On the 20 minute mark? We're outta there, into the showers."

"That's not too long? Aren't there some cautionary things about—"

"Hey, no problem. I'll keep an eye on you, OK, and if I see you fading? I'll get you outta there real quick. Promise. A little mouth to mouth if needed, and you'll be a new man. I'm certified." He gave Latham's shoulders a shake. "Hey, you ever try an ice-cold shower as soon as you get out?"

Latham was thinking how it would feel to be revived, to open his eyes and see Dylan right over him, breathing into his mouth, those delicious lips pressing into his.

"No fucking way. Heart attack city. Just a regular shower to get back to—"

"Oh, man. This you gotta try: Steam Room? Twenty minutes to open up all those pores and drain out all the bad shit. The toxins. OK? Then right into the shower, pounding on you. Ice cold. Like a glacier. When you get outta there? You're gonna be more awake, more alert, more ready to go, than like? ever in your life. Guaranteed. You're gonna feel truly alive. For the first time in your life. That's what gyms are for, right? I'm going to show you. Just stick with me, Latham; you are in for a rare experience."

"You trying to kill me? To get my locker or something? Why am I experiencing shrinkage already?"

Dylan laughed. "After the Steam? After the Shower? After you rub dry? I guarantee. OK? Guarantee: shrinkage is not n. o. t.—going to be a problemo."

"If you say so."

"Oh, I say so. Just stick with me for this first session, and trust me, you're gonna be thanking me. From now on, you're going to be coming to the gym each day, every single day, not really to work out. That's OK. We gotta do that. But you'll really be coming to do the Steam Room and ice plunge challenge."

They walked through the Shower Room and Latham pulled open the fogged-up door at the end.

"So here it is."

The door closed behind them.

"Man," Dylan said, "this is thick. Can't see a thing. HELLO? Hello? Anyone in here?"

The steam kept hissing, swirling around the hot damp room, bursts of it, clouds of it, drifting, impenetrable walls of it.

"Guess not," Latham said. "Usually there's at least a few guys in here. Probably we hit it right between crunch times—after the early birds leave for work, that's always busy, so this is probably the momentary lull before the classes are over and—"

"Here, up here," Dylan said. "Let's sit on this upper level. The higher you are, the more intense the steam."

He felt along the wall, then put his hand on Latham's back and guided him the one seat up to the higher level, where Latham untied the towel, positioned it in the corner and sat down. Dylan climbed up and sat right next to him, his thigh along Latham's. Latham was squished as far in the corner as he could get. He couldn't see Dylan right next to him, just knew he was there by the slight pressure of Dylan's leg against his. Which felt natural, comfortable, good.

They sat quietly for a while.

"Mmmmmmmm," Dylan sighed. "This is soooo good. You sweating yet?"

"Am I sweating? I'm drenched."

Dylan reached over and whisked his hand down Latham's chest.

"Excellent. Your pores are opening up. Flooding out all the toxins. Keep it going."

Latham thought for a moment, then brushed the sweat off the back of Dylan's neck and down his shoulder. "You've got it coming too, man. Big time."

"Oh yeah. This is good. So, you're a lawyer?"

Latham looked over toward him. "Guilty as charged. How'd you know? Do I look like one?"

"No, I don't know. When that guy whose locker was near yours, when he was leaving? I heard him say to you to go bill a lot of hours. So, I just assumed. But also, could have been a lucky guess; everyone here seems to be either a lawyer, or involved in some sort of financial scheme. Fifty-fifty chance of getting it right."

"So true. Which are you?"

"Actually? neither."

"Thank God. What do you do?"

"I'm sort of, you know, between jobs right now? I had been in my dad's plumbing business. So, if you ever need a drain unclogged, or if your toilet keeps running?

and you can't catch it? That's an old plumber joke. You know who to call."

"Good. Always good to know. And I'm pretty sure higher hourly rates than any lawyer here. So, what kind of job are you looking for now?"

"I don't know. Everyone tells me I'm sort of wasting my life. Doing that. Dead end. That I could be more. Do much better. I don't know. I'm looking around here this morning? and wouldn't mind being one of those Personal Trainers out there. Is it hard to get one of those jobs?"

"I don't know. I think you need to take some courses. Get some certificates, different levels, all that. Get certified. I do know one Trainer pretty well and can try to find out for you. Or introduce you to him. He could fill you in."

"That'd be great. Thanks. Which one?"

"You know Jack?"

"No. I don't know any of them. By name. I just sort of saw a bunch of them out there. Helping people. So assumed they're quite a few."

"Yeah, there are. And they come and go during the day. Different shifts. Jack is that really good looking one? The really ripped one?"

"Yeah, I don't know. They all look pretty fit. Maybe you could show me? When we're out there."

"Sure. Any time. He's a nice guy, easy to talk to. He's one of the new ones, but built up a book of business. Real fast. And I think he's doing really well. Financially."

"Sweet. I'd definitely like to talk with him."

Latham felt his eyeballs burning in the moist heat so that it was almost painful to keep his eyes open; he wondered if the steam mechanism was malfunctioning.

"Isn't the steam supposed to take a pause every once in a while?"

"What do you mean?"

"When I've been in here before? It would always seem to go through cycles. The steam would come up, then it would pause for a few minutes and the room would sort of clear, a little, then start up again? This just keeps coming up. And up. Non-stop. No rest period."

"Oh yeah. It feels real good."

"Yeah, but it feels like my eyes are frying."

"I know. Mine, too. Just keep them shut. And enjoy. Nothing to see anyway. So how long we've been in here, so far?"

Latham checked his watch, holding his wrist close to his face. "So far? Eight minutes. Can we make it?"

"You're gonna get the steam of your life. Sit back and relax."

Dylan reached over and patted Latham's thigh, running his hand down to brush off the sweat, then clasped his hands behind his neck and sighed.

"So, you live around here, Latham?" Dylan asked after a few minutes of quiet.

"I do. I'm just about a half mile up from town. So, this is really convenient. That's why when the Club first opened, I jumped at a membership. How about you?"

"I actually just found a place here last week. You know Harley Tavern?"

"Sure. Over on Prospect?"

"Yeah. I was able to get a room right above it."

"Sweet."

"Sort of interim. I hope. But talk about a convenient location. And I've gotten to know the owner a little so he'll sometimes comp me a drink or two if I stop in. Hey, you wanna go there for dinner? Tonight?"

Latham looked over and couldn't see him through

the steam. It was only the feel of his leg against Dylan's that made him realize he wasn't dreaming. And made him rationalize blowing off the dinner meeting scheduled that evening with a prospective client.

"Sure. Sounds good. What time's good for you?"

"You name it. Whenever Larry Lawyer here stops billing hours for the day, I'll be ready."

Latham laughed. "A real lawyer never stops billing, but I usually call it a day by six. That's all I can take. Want to say 7:00 so I can get home and cleaned up?"

"You got it. Speaking of time, how long have we logged in here now? I'm starting to prune up."

Latham wiped off the face of his watch and brought it close to his eyes. "We've been in... for... 18 minutes. Do we go the distance?"

"Fuck yeah. Of course we do. One Mississippi, two... "

It felt to Latham that at least five more minutes had passed before Dylan said "OK, you think you're ready for the ice challenge?"

"No. But if you make me, I'll give it the old college try."

"That's the spirit. No first timer is ever ready, and no first timer in their right mind is going to even attempt it. Alone. They'd run out of there? Two seconds flat. Squealing like a little girl. That's why you need a partner-assisted first time."

"OK man, OK I guess, if you say so."

"I insist. I'm gonna be like your Navy Seal leader. So, we're on this mission together. Got it?"

"Why do I have the feeling you're going to trap me in the shower?"

"Because I am. I'm going to block your exit and shower with you. You OK with that?"

"Why not."

"OK, open those pores up wide cause on the count of ten? We're making a break for it. Straight to the Niagara Falls of the Arctic Circle. Nine. Ten. GO."

Dylan helped him down from the ledge, opened the door, and herded him into the first unoccupied shower stall, closed the door, and turned on the water. Full blast. Ice cold.

"Fuck fuck fuck."

Latham struggled to break free of Dylan's hold and get out the door.

Dylan held him under the jets, pushing up under his chin to raise his head that he was trying to bury into Dylan's chest to avoid the blast.

"Come on, come on, don't be such a big wuss pussy. You need it on the head. Great for the scalp. The hair. All over. Take it like a man. This beautiful mountain fresh water!"

He fought to hold Latham under it, keeping his own back to the door, with one hand grabbing the container with the Club's special liquid soap with the peppery smell, and started rubbing it over any part of Latham's body he could reach.

"You may as well just stand there and take it. We ain't goin' nowhere till we're both done. So, we got a ways to go."

Latham was making moaning noises and kept trying to merge into Dylan to get away from the cold and find any warmth.

It never began to feel any better; every splash like a paper cut hit by lemon juice, the only thought was to get it done and get out of there. Latham never stopped struggling as Dylan spread the soap over him and rinsed it out of his hair, rubbed it in again, rinsed again, making sure every inch of his body was hit by the glacial blast, again and again.

At last Dylan turned the knob, the water stopped to a trickle, he opened the door of the stall and led Latham out, grabbing from the stack on the counter outside the showers a bunch of large white towels, still warm from the laundry's dryers, and tossing some to him.

Latham covered his head with one, draped another around his shoulders.

"You like that?" Dylan asked.

Latham kept rubbing, throwing his towels into the bin, grabbing fresh ones still holding the dryer's warmth.

"Not sure if it's something you ever would like," he finally said, "but I'm glad we did it. I have to admit, I do feel energized. But that may be the last gasp of life before an aortic aneurism."

"I'm proud of you. You went in there and took it as well as any newbie I've ever seen. You took it like a man. Dinner's on me. Your reward for bravery on the front lines. Come on, let's head back to our lockers."

As they dried off in their alcoves, Jack walked in.

"Hey bro, you finished?" Jack said. "Heading to the old gulag?"

"Yeah," Latham said, "that's it for the day. The fun's over. All downhill after this."

"That's the spirit. Nothing beats the Temple of the Gods. Wanna grab some dinner this evening? When I get home? I'm off at six."

Latham looked at him, then looked into his locker and pulled out his dress shirt.

"Man, wish I could. Booked. Rain check?"

"Not a problem."

Jack walked down toward the sinks.

"So, what kind of supplements do you use?" Latham asked Dylan.

Dylan stopped drying his back and looked over at Latham.

"I mean," Latham continued, "what would you recommend. For me?"

"Well, it depends."

Dylan did a double bicep flex and grinned.

"You want this sort of result? Or what are you thinking of?"

Latham looked.

"Yeah. That would be a good start."

"OK, bro. Let's get you started. Come on over here and I'll show you exactly what I have."

Chapter Twenty-Two

Anne walked into the Locker Room, peeling off her scarf and ski jacket, as Patti was rubbing her hair with a towel.

"Ohhh, it feels soooo good in here," Anne said. "Nice and warm. I am fro-zen. Have you used the Steam Room yet? I have to defrost."

"Yup. All done for the day. I'm out of here. Errand time. So, you just dropped your son off? At Daycare?"

"Ha, ha, very funny. Do you have like an endless supply of those?"

"No, I just wanted to make sure: did you clip his mittens to his sleeves before you dropped him off? So, he won't lose them? On the playground?"

Anne heaved a dramatic sigh. "Why can't you just be happy for us?"

Patti looked at her in the mirror.

"Because I'm responsible. I broke up your family."

Anne stared at her. "No, you didn't."

"No? You left Richard. And Meghan. And Walker. No one is talking to you. All our friends think you've lost it. Everyone—"

"Patti. No. Can't you see? You, of all my friends?" Anne pulled out a hanger from her locker and hung her black ski jacket on it and put it in her locker. "I'm with the man I love. We're creating a business, shaping it, watching it grow, we're—"

183

"Anne, you're my best friend. You know that. Always will be. But this is like, it's like watching a train speeding around a corner? Going much too fast. And you know for sure it's about to jump the tracks. De-rail. And there's not a blessed thing you can do to stop it. All you can do is stare. With your mouth hanging open."

"Well at least close your mouth, sweetheart. Not becoming. And this particular train? Happens to be doing very well, thank you very much."

Patti was quiet as she pulled on a boot. Then took the other from her locker.

"Well, I don't know if you guys are making any money, but I guess I have to admit: it sure looks like you two at least, I guess at least you're having a lot of fun."

"Indeed."

"Man, if you would have taken me to Hawaii? For a stay at the *Mauna Kea*? While I'm stuck here? Freezing my titties off. I'd have given you the best sex you've ever had. If that's all it takes."

"Girlfriend, is your mind always in the gutter?"

"Pretty much, yeah."

"And just for your information, FYI as they say: Hawaii was a business trip. Not a vacation. That was a photo shoot for Jackson. For our *Voyeur* sportswear line."

Patti put on her other boot. Then folded her gym gear and put it in her gym bag on the bench next to her.

"Oh, I see. And the photographer you now seem to be supporting? And his cute young assistant? Who I'm sure is also now on your payroll?"

"It does take a village."

"They just happened to suggest Hawaii? As the very best location to get the perfect photographs of Jack... son? Like, they couldn't be taken right here? In the parking lot? In the gym? In the Locker Room?"

Anne snorted and smirked.

"Wouldn't he look just as good here," Patti continued, "as he did out there? On the golden ka-ching beaches of *Mauna Kea*?"

Anne shook her head, as she sat down and pulled off her boots.

"Girl, you just don't get it, do you? We're selling a product. A lifestyle. We are selling what Jackson is modeling. If we can catch our audience's attention? With great locations? exotic places they fantasize about? that's half the battle, right? Jackson's their fantasy—"

"Clearly, he's your fantasy. And, young lady, a word to the wise? You are *buying* into your own fantasy. Never such a good idea?"

Anne ignored her and continued.

"In a fantasy location. Doesn't get any better than that, does it?"

"OK. Hmmmm. I see. But may I ask this?"

"Oh Lord. Sure. Why not?"

Patti stood up, scuffling into her boots.

"Just this: have you ever stopped to calculate exactly how many pairs of undies you will have to sell to pay just for that one trip? First class both ways, I'm sure. For you. And your Personal Trainer. And your mooch photographer. And his hanger-on boy toy, and who knows who else?"

"We—"

"Beachfront rooms at the most expensive resort out there. And I'm sure you fed your group well. And maybe kept them happy with occasional luaus? And outrigger canoe rides? So, exactly how many undies does this equal?"

Anne smiled and looked into the distance.

"One paddle, two paddle, three paddle, four—"

"Say what?"

"Our outrigger canoe song."

"Bloody bunions."

"I have to say, that shoot? Some trip. That place is? How to describe? Beyond beautiful. Idyllic. Truly an honest to goodness tropical paradise. Those words don't even begin—I wish you could have joined us and—j"

"Join you? If it takes a village, I want to be a resident of that village. But just the airfare? One way. And by the way, girl, you need to stay focused. I don't know what you're using for money?"

Patti looked at Anne, but she didn't answer.

"But really," Patti continued, "you ought to be like really, really, careful how you manage it? That's got to last—I mean, Bermuda, too?"

"Ahhh. *Cambridge Beaches*. I remember it well." Anne stood one of her boots in the bottom of her locker. "That's one of our marketing strategies. Showing Jackson in different settings so that—"

"I know, I know. Hey, here's an idea. Put me on the Village payroll."

Anne looked at her. "Send me your resume, dearie. We are, of course, an Equal Opportunity Employer. So, what position would you like, young lady?"

"I don't know. Maybe—maybe you could hire me... as the official fluffer?"

Anne stared at her.

"Excuse me? The what-er?"

"You know. Every real professional photo shoot has one. I've read about it. The guy who adjusts the model's junk so that, you know, it's... they're, everything's properly positioned inside the garment? Showing to their, shall we say, best advantage?"

186

"Oh, good Lord. Girlfriend, you are so sick. You do know that don't you? And that's why I love you. But no way in hell would I let you anywhere near Jackson's jewels. Let alone touch them with your filthy strumpet hands."

"Strumpet. That's another one of your quaint English words I love. Strumpet. No, no, fear not, fair maiden. As cute as they are, I'm really not aroused by prepubescent boys. Wait," Patti said, putting her finger to her lips.

"What?"

Patti was quiet for a minute. "No," she said, "it was just the gobble gobble gang passing. Coast clear."

"Ahhh," Anne said quietly. You have no idea what you're missing, my dear friend. Never too late. Never too late. Lots more of them out there. Just as you once told me. Remember? Take your pick, you said. By the way, I think that new one, that Dylan one, is dreamy. Perfect for you. Just to sample."

Patti laughed. "I love it. Love your idea of 'sampling'. You moved pretty quickly from sampling Jack—son to spreading the poor lad on a cracker to enjoy with your afternoon jam and tea. It sure seems you and Latham have identical tastes. In cute men. You do know that Latham's doing him, right?"

Anne stared at her.

Patti continued. "Oh yes. Come on girl. Are you under a rock? Or maybe just globetrotting too much? Sometime go take a look out the windows. Behind the Stairmasters. Right next to Jack's yellow Porsche? Dylan's new black Aston Martin. Convertible."

"Sweet chicken."

"Sweet chicken indeed. That should officially now be called: Latham's Parking Section. Have you heard it?"

"What?"

187

"Dylan's car."

"No. What?"

"When he starts it up? And guns it? The deep throated growl of the engine." Patti made the noise. "It sounds like he's about to launch into interplanetary space."

"So, an Aston Martin? Love it. You have to give it to Latham. That man does have exquisite taste."

"Yeah. In beautiful cars. And beautiful men. So, what's his next friend going to get? We ought to place bets. A Bentley? Ahh, to be cute. And young. And buff. Where did we go wrong? We've had to work hard for our money."

"Tell me about it. So, fluffer? OK. I still have a few openings. Maybe I can fit you in."

"Thank you. Thank you very much. I'll practice. To get ready."

"I would have loved to have had you join us on our photo shoots. Can you imagine how much fun we, you and I, would have had?"

"I've certainly imagined it. In my dreams."

"But see, I truly was saving money, the project's official fluffer, as you call it, that apparently was part of Ron's assistant's job description. He just assumed that responsibility. Without even being asked. Or billing for it."

"Oh, I bet he did. And I bet you could have saved even more money if you had him pay *you* to be the official shoot fluffer. Believe me, he gladly would have."

Anne rolled her eyes and wrapped a towel around her chest.

"Oh yes," Patti said, "I'm sure he would have paid good money to be able to get his hands in Jack's— Jackson's—undies. Throughout the day."

"Speaking of Jackson's undies: as a worldly young

lady. Who seems to know just, shall we say, just a tad too much about fluffers? OK? Ready? Tuesday's pop quiz: Do you also know all about model samples?"

"No, but I hope you will enlighten me. I'm a real quick study."

"I, too, am learning a lot, my friend. So, the products Jackson is wearing when we do a shoot? We're finding that there's a real market for them and —"

Patti stopped putting on her coat and sat down on the bench. And put her hands in the T—time-out—position.

"Oh no. Stop. Full stop, girlfriend. You're not going to tell me that—"

"Ah, Little Miss Muffet, my sweet young friend: you really must tune into one of Jackson's internet chatturbates. With his fans."

"Chatturbate. Love that. Probably pretty descriptive of what goes on."

"Yes, apt indeed. You must see one to understand. It's like if you or I were having a bad hair day? And we could push a key on our desktop? And thousands of guys would appear instantly telling us we're the most beautiful thing they had ever beholden. And that we are all they wanted to devote their lives to?

Patti looked up at her.

"Worshiping us."

"Really?"

"Oh yes. Really. Worshipping. And bidding against each other to buy our dirty, or I should say worn, under-wear."

"No."

"Take a look sometime. See what you think."

"OK, I will."

"Let me know if you bid on any."

Chapter Twenty-Three

"All ready, Jackson?" Anne said.

"Yup. Just got a real good pump. Ready to go. Look: my bicep vein is popping."

"Let me see."

He did a double flex and bounced his pecs under his tight T shirt.

"Oh yes, it's working. Really well. OK, here we go. Another opening, another show. Try to seduce your fans."

"No problemo."

Anne made some adjustments to the camera on the tripod in the corner of their bedroom in the apartment. Jack pushed a couple keys on the computer on top of the desk in front of him.

And around the world, several million computers pinged to alert their users that Jack was online, ready to have another chatturbate with his fans.

Jack looked straight into the camera and gave his deep dimpled grin.

"What up, guys?"

He glanced at the computer screen to see how many were watching. It was a Tuesday morning. Some fans would be at work. Some at school. Others would be in the dentist chair. Maybe someone would be on jury duty. Or doing a sing-along at a senior center. But as he watched, the number of viewers was jumping, from 75 to several thousand in a couple seconds, to 6,078 viewers in less than half a minute. Enough to start up, then watch as more came aboard.

"Hey guys, thank you all for coming. We've got a real good crowd today. Let's have some fun."

He looked at the screen again. The first message was already there. Jack replied.

"Hey Andy, good morning. You're number one again. Always my first viewer. Most loyal fan. Really 'preciate it, man. You're terrific. Love you, bro."

Anne did a close up of Jack's face so that it would seem he was talking directly to Andy. Jack smiled and blew him a kiss.

Jack and Anne discussed Andy often. Who was he? Was he on his computer 24/7, waiting for Jack's dog whistle? He couldn't have a job. Or maybe he worked at home? If he did, how could he always put aside whatever he was doing as soon as Jack came online? Exactly what was it that Jack did for him? That, of course, was the big question. What did he feel about Jack? They wondered if they should do something for him, could they send him something, like an autographed photograph? Something of Jack's? Or would that be encouraging someone who might turn out to be a sicko stalker, who was having trouble separating reality from whatever fantasy life he was living?

Andy had typed in: "You look so hot, honey; wish I could wake up next to you. Maybe someday…? "

"Aw shucks, man," Jack said into the camera. "You're so sweet. Just back from the gym. An hour on the treadmill. I probably look like I'll drop any minute."

The usual softball questions began to be thrown in:

191

how to gain weight; how to bulk; the best way to get shredded; when did he start working out; what sports did he play in high school.

Foreplay, Anne always called these initial parts of the chat, as Jack slowly worked his magic, which worked his viewers into a slow, simmering frenzy.

That opened up the floodgates. The flattering emails jammed in, one on top of the other.

"Hey sexy. You're looking better each day; how do you do that?"

"Hey cutie."

"Any chance I can sleep on your chest? After that, my life will be complete. Please."

"Can I taste your nipples?"

"I want to bury my face in your sweaty armpits after you work out. And live there."

"How do you get that ass to look so delicious?"

At last, one that Jack could address.

"Any of you guys who want to develop your glutes? There are a couple great routines I would recommend." He half turned so that Anne could zero in on his butt, which he flexed under his tight gym shorts. "Of course, the best are squats. Like I tell you, just keep doing them, guys. Ten reps, sets of three. Next time, or maybe after you can do that with perfect form, add a little more weight to the bar. Five pounds? Can you add ten more? Same thing, every day, three sets of ten reps. You're gonna be surprised how soon results will be visible. Wait till you see how you fill out your jeans. It's gonna be like they were painted on you."

He smacked his ass a couple times.

"Your friends are gonna be able to use your butt as a shelf. Hack squats too. The leg press. Lunges. You know, with maybe a 15 pound dumbbell in each hand? Just keep doing those. All around your gym. Go sideways. Go backward. Work those butt muscles from every angle to get this look."

Anne panned around to his other buttock.

"Hey, and guess what, guys? Added benefit here. A little trade secret: you keep doing squats, leg presses, all that? You're gonna start producing more testosterone than you know what to do with. That's gonna help you build more muscle, even faster. Squats are the number one exercise secret to building that body you want."

Anne got all of Jack's body in the shot. He clasped his hands behind his back and tensed his arms, twisting his triceps to show them off from every angle.

"By the way, with enough man juice left over to have as much fun as you wanna have. You're gonna be able to shoot, I don't know, six feet?"

He winked at the camera and laughed.

"Hey, I know a lot of you guys want to hear more of my personal routine. I do read your comments. Wish I could respond to all, but hey, I gotta work all day." He paused. "To keep this look."

He struck a body builder pose in front of Anne's camera.

"Maybe someday we can film at the gym. And I can take you through my own personal routines. Let me know in the comments below if that's something you'd like to see. I'm here for you guys. Let me know what's on your minds."

The focus on Jack's butt and his references to testosterone was producing the inevitable result. Messages flooding the computer screen, one on top of the other, most of them with the same request.

"Come on, Jack. We can't take it anymore. Take off your shirt."

Jack grinned at the screen as he scanned the messages.

"Guys, guys, you're embarrassing me. Is something wrong with this shirt? Don't you like it?"

Anne came in for a close up of his skintight black T shirt.

"This is one of my favorites. You're giving me a complex. That it doesn't look good on me."

He flexed a little, stared at his biceps, kissed his right bicep and stopped.

"Wow, I don't wanna rip this shirt. This is one of my favorites. I slept in this one last night. It's so comfortable. Should I cut back on my bicep curls so I don't get any bigger? And tight? I guess I gotta start cutting back on the reps before this thing ends up in shreds."

"Take it OFF," the messages kept demanding, sometimes with the same viewer sending his plea repeatedly.

"Take it off?" Jack said. "Well, you know the drill. Your super chat button is gonna help me decide how serious you are about this. It's a little chilly in this room."

He pretended he was shivering.

"But I'll take it off if you guys are really serious. Show me just how serious you are. Oh, and by the way guys, whoever makes the highest donation, in one minute, 60 seconds from when I say GO, will also get this T. I'll take it off and mail it out to you today. In a Ziploc bag. Overnight postage. Anyone want it? Maybe you'd rather go out and buy a new one, rather than one I've slept in all night?"

Jack watched as the size of the donations and the name of the donors popped onto the screen. He did a close-up call-out to each:

"Hey, Blue Ridge Trucker, thanks man."

Jack looked at his Rolex: "Exactly 35 seconds more guys. Blue Ridge, let's see how you do."

Anne panned in to Jack staring at his Rolex so his fans could see his watch, as he lifted up the bottom of the T to reveal each ab, one by one.

"Final 20 seconds guys, going nine, going eight, seven, six, five, four, three, two… ONE."

He pulled the T over his head and swung it around on one finger, as he flexed his abs and turned so that Anne would get the best shots.

"And the winner is… Peter A, from Brockton, Massachusetts. At $575. Congratulations, Peter. You got a real nice one. This was my all-time favorite. Got a lot of miles on it. Hope you enjoy it."

Jack laid the T shirt on the desk and neatly folded it, then opened a drawer of the desk, pulled out a Ziploc bag and placed the T shirt carefully into the bag, sealing it.

"Peter, my man, email me your mailing address, and I'll get this off to you so that you have it tomorrow morning. May still be warm when you open it. These bags seal in the freshness real good. Hope that's OK. If not, you can always return. Full refund."

"If he returns it," the next message read, "I'm bidding. Even higher."

"Thank you, Travelin Man, but there are always more. Or email me a special request, if you want anything customized before I mail it. You know the drill."

Jack went through his upper body flexing routine, biceps, triceps, abs and obliques, traps, back. He glanced over at the computer screen. He was up to over 700,000 viewers right now, with all the usual questions tumbling in. He did an alternating pec bounce as he answered each question:

Age?

"Twenty-four. And a couple months."

Weight?

"185 pretty consistently, except when I'm prepping for a photo shoot and have to get super shredded."

How many days a week do you work out?

"Pretty much every day now. A couple hours a day."

Straight or gay?

"How about bi? I'm pretty open to everyone." (Anne repeatedly reminded him that was the only correct answer so he wouldn't lose part of his audience.)

The floodgates opened again.

"You are so sexy."

"I love you so much."

"Please sleep with me, just once."

"I wanna fuck you so bad."

"Where do you live?"

"So, guys," Jack said, trying to regain control and cool it off a bit, who's got some more fitness questions?"

A regular always wrote in asking Jack to "poke your hot belly button", another wanted to lick his pits and "yummy nipples", one always requested, "please just run your hand across your crotch, just once please." Another always the same: "I have to see just a tiny bit of your pubes, lower your undies just so we can see a wee bit."

Their requests sounded like the most important thing in their lives, which at the moment, for them, they were. One viewer wanted to put his head "between Jack's muscular thighs" and beg him to "squeeze hard, harder." Another said he would kill his mother for the chance to spend a half hour alone with one of Jack's sneakers.

"You need a good spanking," Jack responded to those whose requests started to cross the line, which then would be good for 10 minutes of S & M banter.

At just about this point, every session moved on to focus on Jack's dick. How big is it? When can they see it? Cut or uncut? How many times a day does he do it? A grower or a show-er? When can they see it? Please now.

Jack then explained once again the YouTube rules, how he couldn't go as far as he would like without being de-monetized. He re-directed the focus of the audience.

The demands for him to remove his gym shorts started.

"OK, OK, if any of you guys want to make a superchat donation for these really great workout shorts, I'll send them to you. And then we can get down to business: going over my personal leg routines at the gym. Same rules on the shorts: 60 seconds from the time I say start. These are really nice ones, by the way. *Gym Shark*. Nylon. Light fabric. Love this color. Look at it. Liner to hold the goods in place. Really moves with you. Breathable. I've been wearing this pair for my workouts. All week. So, if you want me to wash them before sending them to you? Just let me know. OK? Ready, set, start."

Steve of Grass Valley, with a bid of $900, was the winner.

"Steve, you want me to wash these before I send them off to you? No? You sure? OK." He pulled them down and sealed them in another Ziploc bag, then smoothed down his snug gray boxer briefs.

Anne zoomed in for a close up as he flexed his thighs and went through a posing routine, focusing on his bulge and the head of his penis, which the tight fabric highlighted as much as if he was naked, veins and all.

"So, I've had this idea guys; this may be fun. So, you know I've been working on designing The Perfect

Underwear. This is going to be my *Voyeur* brand. I've told you all about it. We're almost there. I've gotten the design perfected. I just ordered the fabric, which I know you're gonna love. Feels so good." He ran his hand down his underwear. "The contrasting band around the waist, and around the hem of the legs. The *Voyeur* label, which will be hand sewn on each pair. Hey, and these are all being made in the good old U.S. of A. Right here. I found a place in Philadelphia that does it. We've gotten the box designed. This was a full day photo shoot to get the picture of me you're going to have on your box."

Jack picked up a box on the desk and held it to the camera, which focused in on the front. "Here. Here's the front," he said, touching his hand over his bulge to demonstrate. "And here, look, you turn the box around," he dramatically turned it, "and look at this. Here I am from the back. On the golden beaches of *Mauna Kea*. On the big Island of Hawaii."

The camera focused in to show the background.

"That was some trip. Let me tell you. You ever get the chance to go there? Jump on it."

Smiling, Jack scrolled through the pages of comments tumbling on to the screen.

"Wow. You guys really want to go with me? Together? Maybe we could get up some sort of contest; whoever wins, gets to accompany me on a three day stay at *Mauna Kea*. Is that something that may interest you?" Jack looked at the screen and grinned. "Sure looks like it."

"Hey, look at this," Jack said, pulling a bureau drawer open all the way, as Anne panned in to show it stuffed with underwear of every color, style and fabric. He pulled out a handful and tossed them onto the bed, then grabbed some more, spreading them around the bed, picking up a pair here and there and holding them in front of the camera.

"Just look at all these. This is what I did when I set out to design the perfect *Voyeur* underwear. For you. I bought a pair of everything that was on the market. Everything. Then took each of these bad boys out for a test drive. How did I like the cut? What about the fabric? The color. The design. How did they make my boys feel? That's the most important, of course." He absent-mindedly touched his crotch. "And not just for a couple minutes. How do they do all day long?" His hand adjusted his junk. "How are your boys doing when you take them off at the end of the day? How do the undies look? How did I look in them? Guys, look at all the research that went into *Voyeur*. Look at what I've been doing for you. A couple weeks more—I'll keep you up to date—and you'll be able to order your own pair. The best undies ever created."

He tossed a handful from the drawer up in the air.

"But let's have a little fun now. If you'd like, I can model any of these you'd like to see on me. I can tell you the pros and cons of each. Let me know if…"

He looked at the computer screen and laughed.

"Looks like you guys wanna do this? OK, so let me know what you'd like me to try on first."

Jack took more from the drawer and added them to the colorful leaf pile of underwear on the bed. Then looked at the computer screen.

"Oh man, I see the style that's winning. Hands down. A thong. You wanna see me model a thong? And close second? A jock strap. I don't know, guys. You know YouTube might smack my knuckles if I show you what a thong can do. Maybe a little later we could do just a front view of a thong, or a side view. Why don't we start with a trunk and then sort of work our way back to something a little, shall we say, tinier?"

He sorted through the pile on the bed.

"Do I see any superchat donations for this trunk?"

He held up a slinky charcoal fabric and let it hang down to show the length.

"As I recall, this one fit real nice and really showed the goods. It pops them. Any superchat to encourage me to try it on? Hey, and for all these I model for you today, I'll send them to the winner in a Ziploc bag. And you can of course let me know in your email if you'd like them customized."

Anne focused the camera on Jack's face as he changed right there into the next pair of underwear, and then came back into focus on his torso as he smoothed down the sides of the gray *Unico* trunks.

Chapter Twenty-Four

"W.T.F." Patti said, as Anne boarded the treadmill next to her, laying her towel over the top bar.

"What?"

"You know - W.T.F., what the fuck?"

"I know what it means. Duh. But is that the same way you greet the refined ladies of your book club? As they come in, clutching their precious assigned required reading for the meeting?"

"That none of them, by the way, have actually read, and—"

"You know your members well."

"Yes, I do. A suburban ritual. Then they all look around, ready to chow down. On teeny tiny finger sandwiches. Right?"

"Stuffed with one micro-thin cucumber slice."

"Hey. There's a kale leaf in there, too. Which they munch as they're looking *frantically* for the wine. Clearly, they only waste their time with this nonsense 'cause they don't' know about Jack's chatturbates."

Anne laughed. "Ahh, so you tuned in. At last. Good girl. Which one? Not that they're all that different."

"I saw most of yesterdays. And so, I'm watching. And listening. And reading the comments. And saying to myself: W.T.F."

Anne pushed the left button to raise the incline, then the right button to increase the speed of the treadmill, to work up to Patti's speed.

"So? Did you do as Jackson instructed?" Anne said. "And go below and hit comment, like, subscribe?"

"Well, to help you guys? Of course I did. But it sure doesn't seem like you need any help from little old me. I mean, my God, the number of poor souls who were tuning in? I saw the numbers going over—"

"Well yesterday was a fairly typical day. We can get them over that on occasion. If we announce ahead that Jackson is going to do something special and—"

"Like? Dare I ask what?"

"You know. If he announces a day before he's going to speak on, on you know, some weighty important topic?"

Anne increased her speed again as she worked up to her rhythm.

"Such as?"

"Like, just as one example: 'Shave Your Balls? Pros and Cons.'"

Patti laughed. "I think even I would tune in for that one."

"You and everyone else hoping for some, shall we say, helpful visuals."

"You do need visuals on these how-to's. I mean, I really would not have believed it." Patti increased the speed of her treadmill. "I know," she paused and began again, "I know, I know I'm going to regret—"

"What?"

"Regret even saying this. But… I think maybe you've got it. I think you guys really may be on to something. I wouldn't have believed any of this stuff even happens and—"

"Say what? I can't hear you," Anne said, cupping her ear. "So noisy in here. Please repeat that?"

"Ha, ha, very funny. You heard me. Loud and clear."

"Coming from you? This is high praise. Indeed. So maybe I'm not just some suburban bitch? Going through a very difficult change of life?"

"Come on. Be fair. I never thought that. I just—"

"I know. I know. I'm just jazzing you. So… what did you like the most? Of all?"

Patti pushed the treadmill incline up again, from 14 to 15. Running flat out.

"Jeeze Louise," Anne said. "Are you competing with the Swisher? I can't go that fast and —"

Patti cut back her speed so she could talk.

"Well, first of all. I gotta hand it to you. I thought it was just you—and Latham—obsessed with Jack. Clearly you are not alone. He must have that 'something' that"

"Ahh. Am I hearing this correctly? Are you telling me what, that you think there may be something to Jackson beyond his gorgeous, dreamy looks?"

"Well yes. I have to admit: there is clearly something there. Intelligence? Charm? Whatever it is. I found myself, I don't know, captivated? Swept in?"

"That's so sweet. See?"

"Though maybe you do share your obsession with? I don't know. Like, thousands of gay men and—"

"Tens of thousands."

"OK, tens of thousands. Who jump when Jack… son whistles. I assume they're all guys?"

"I'd say mostly. Probably over 90 percent? Ninety-five? That's one of the questions they're most interested in, the one they keep typing in, asking him: are you straight? Or, gay?" Anne looked over at Patti. "I keep reminding him always, always to say 'bi.'"

203

"Good idea."

"Well, when he's in the chat room, I tell him, he's a performer. He's an actor. He's weaving a fantasy for his viewers. And a central part of that fantasy is that he's available. To them. That they could have him. They don't want to hear that I'm in the picture."

"Yeah. Gross."

"They don't want to know he's in a relationship. Or good god, that he's doing a woman. Icky poo."

Patti laughed. "If only they knew."

"We'd lose half our followers with one click. And the other half the next day." Anne looked out over the gym. "Believe it or not, we actually do get some sweet, refined gentle ladies watching. Not a whole lot, I grant you, but some. Maybe even some of your book club ladies?"

"That would indeed be something. What is it? What do all these guys want? What are they, like looking for? I—"

"What do you mean?"

"Like exactly what is it these guys are feeling? Why are they all tuning in? This stuff has got to be so, so, I don't know? Affirming? For Jack."

"You got that right, girl. What adulation. What validation for him."

"It's unbelievable," Patti said. "To them, he's like some sort of, I don't know what? A star? A god. A celebrity?"

"No doubt about it. Same thing. What makes certain people—"

"I mean, come on, girl. Picture if we were having a really bad hair day? Or something? Yeah. Like today."

Anne looked over at Patti. "Stop that. You're looking good. But what if we could push a button on our computers? And suddenly there would thousands of guys telling us how beautiful we are, and drooling all over us, and essentially telling us how much they'd like to do us and—"

"There are many days I could use that. That's for sure."

"You kidding? Me, too. As I film Jackson doing these chatturbates, I—"

Tiffany walked in front of their treadmills with a pile of folded towels cradled in her arm, holding one out to offer each of them.

Patti and Anne both smiled and shook their heads 'no' and continued talking.

"I'm thinking to myself: both sides are getting a whole lot of 'bating' during his fireside chats."

"I like that," Patti said. "Bating. Clearly, his fans are getting off."

"For sure. But Jackson, too. Each viewer, each subscriber, each 'like' comment he gets is like, I don't know what? Like another drop of dopamine? Shot right into Jackson's main vein. It's like he's hooked up to some intravenous dopamine drip."

"Me. Me. Me next. How can I get hooked up to that? Just for an hour?"

Anne laughed. "We could go together to get hooked up. Like we go together to our Botox appointments."

"Count me in."

"But seriously," Anne said, "I always want to make sure all this doesn't go to his beautiful young head; I try to keep him grounded. We talk a lot about his fans, what they want, what they are looking for."

Patti took her towel and wiped around her hairline, then put it back over the treadmill bar.

"I think what they're looking for?" Patti said.

"When you get right down to it? Maybe an online strip show?"

"Maybe. A virtual strip show. I guess you could call it that. That certainly is part of it. He's teasing them. It's a flirt fest."

"Extended foreplay."

Anne nodded. "He's a big tease, for sure. Amen to that. He's out there getting them worked up, but street smart enough to be careful not to go too far. The minute they get off? And some of the guys will type in that he's giving them boners and they're about to blow, as they say, 'I'm gonna bust, you're making me cum', they type in all that fun stuff, the minute they blow? The End. The party's over."

"Time to call it a day."

"They're going to shut down their computer".

"And take their pretty balloons and—"

"And the last thing on their minds? At that point? Bidding on a pair of Jackson's undies, and—"

"Oh yeah. I loved all that. That was my favorite part. How he took all his underwear out of that drawer in your bedroom? And asks them which pair to try on next and—"

"Oh my, yes. And did you note how predictable the requests are? Thong. Jockstrap. Bikinis. In that order. Thong always, always first."

"Loved how they keep typing in 'show us your butt', again and again."

"They all want a chance to oogle Jackson's beautiful behind. Which a jock strap can display nicely."

"Yummy."

"But we really have to be careful just how much we show. So that the YouTube police don't come down on us and try to kick us off."

Anne looked up and surveyed the gym, looking for Jack.

There he was, outside the yoga classroom, demonstrating a deadlift for a client. He let the weighted bar drop to the floor and saw Anne waving. He waved back. Patti took both hands off the treadmill and gave him a two-handed salute. Jack laughed, shook his head and returned to his client.

"I never thought at Bryn Mawr I'd be majoring in: Men's Underwear," Anne said. "Art? Renaissance History? OK. But Men's Underwear? I think I now just may be the national expert. I can tell you anything you need to know about Calvin Kleins, 2(x)st, C-IN2. Our big competitors. The Big Three."

"A college degree in men's undies. Knowing you, you'd be awarded summa cum laude. No doubt about it. So, I have to ask you this, Miss Phi Beta Kappa."

"Shoot."

"What was all that chitter chatter about Jack customizing the underwear someone buys? For some exorbitant amount of money. For dirty underwear."

"Excuse me, missy, what? How many times do I have to tell you this? Jackson isn't selling dirty underwear. To anyone. What he is kindly offering to his fans are model samples."

"Oh yes. Sorry about that. I knew there was a nice, polite name for them. Just forgot for a moment. Model sample. Excuse me. So, when he customizes them, is he like writing his name on them? Autographing them? In Magic Marker?"

Anne looked over at Patti.

"You sweet little lamb," she said. "So pure. So innocent. So lost in the woods. Sooo virginal."

Patti looked at her, taking her towel and wiping her face.

"What? Are you sewing his name tag in them?"

Anne laughed. "No, you dear, sweet, thing. If a customer wants the model sample he just paid, say $400 for? to be—"customized"—shall we say, Jackson is happy to oblige by, you know—j"

"What? No. I don't know. I don't get it."

"OK. To be blunt? Cumming on them."

Patti gasped.

"Then sealing them in a Ziploc bag—fresh to market, from farm to table as restaurants say—and overnighting them, all for an additional charge of—"

Patti had covered her ears and was staring straight ahead, singing the chorus to "American Pie": "Drove my Chevy to the levy, but the levy—'"

"Oh, for heaven's sake, missy: have you been living under some mossy rock? In the forest primeval? With all the murmuring pines and the hemlock? Jackson gets at least 200 bucks more for personalizing a pair. Doing what comes naturally. He's selling out. All he can, shall we say, handle."

Patti stared at her as she ran, pushing up her speed again.

"You just may be," Patti said, "the marketing genius of the Western World. You're developing a market for what used to be thrown in the dirty laundry hamper. Yes?"

"Well. OK. Yes. Yes. I guess you could say that."

Patti shook her head in wonder.

They pedaled quietly for a few minutes. Staring at their counters.

"Whoop de doo," Patti said. I've just burned off

enough calories to have, I don't' know, two kale leaves on a wheat-less cracker? That'll be what? Twenty bucks at the café?"

"Miles to go, sweetheart. Miles to go. And I think those go for 20 bucks for two crackers. So just 10 bucks for one."

Anne pushed up her speed and for a moment assumed the perfect posture and form of the Ponytail Swisher.

"Show off," Patti said.

"Man, that's hard to sustain that," Anne said, dialing back her speed and degree of incline. "Got to hand it to her. She'll do an hour like that. Hear that?"

"What?"

"Listen. Hear it? The other worldly machine like pounding of little Miss Swisher on her treadmill."

"God, it's like a piston."

"In overdrive."

"Ah, to be young and fit. If we had started about 10 years—"

"Fifteen?"

"OK, 15 years ago? I bet we could be doing that now."

"I doubt it."

They pressed on, only glancing occasionally at the row of TV screens above them. Someone came out of the Spinning Class in the room next to them, the music in that darkened room blaring before the door closed again.

"I'm glad you could watch Jackson's chatturbate."

"A whole new world for me. He is good at it. I'll give him that."

"Somehow, he's a natural. His YouTube numbers keep moving up. And up. Companies are starting to see him as what they call, an Influencer. They're sending him all sorts of stuff. For free. Hoping he'll endorse it on one of his chatturbate sessions."

Patti shook her head. "Must be nice. An Influencer. I can't even influence what book my book club ladies select. What does he, what kind of stuff does he get? Anything any good?"

"I don't know. Between the gifts his fans send him? And all this other stuff? We're getting boxes every day."

"Must be nice. Anything any good?"

"Oh, it may be a bundle from a new sportswear company, developing its own line of stringers, gym shorts, all that. Or underwear brands, that's for sure. He'll get a box with 50 pairs of different styles and colors. Colognes. Razors. Skin care products. Hair products. Clothes. Shoes. Sneakers. Necklaces. Bracelets. You name it. Anything they think would benefit from a tip of the hat from Jackson."

Patti kept jogging for a while. "OK. OK," she finally said. "I know I'm going to regret conceding even this. You may truly be on to something. If you can somehow tie all this into *Voyeur* and—"

"I can't hear you, sweetheart. Would you please speak up?"

Chapter Twenty-Five

As the waiter led them through the choreographed chaos of the steakhouse, past the packed, deafening bar, into the crowded back room, with servers bustling in every direction, putting down and lifting up plates and glasses and utensils and refolding napkins, Anne felt as she had the first time she sported the huge square-cut diamond ring Richard had given her a few years ago on their 25th anniversary: as proud to show it off as she was now, walking in with her magnificent young god. She loved the way he strode in as a crown prince, never noticing or acknowledging the stares and double takes of his subjects as he passed each table.

"Will this be satisfactory?" the waiter asked, stopping at the only empty booth, half-way down the aisle.

"Perfect," Jack said, as they slid in.

Anne liked the way it felt: as if they were enclosed in a cocoon, just the two of them, the black padded walls on three sides, the two benches so close to the table their faces almost were touching. She sometimes fantasized about being locked in a tiny prison cell, with Jack as her cell mate, and was looking for the right moment to suggest playing out that scene with him: 24 hours locked away together.

"My name is Stefan. I will be your server this evening. May I offer you bottled water? sparkling? tap?"

"Tap is fine," Anne said.

Jack looked at her and mouthed "*Evian*?"

"It's probably not going to kill you, just this once," Anne stage whispered.

"I'll leave you with menus," Stefan said, handing one to each. "And our wine list. By the bottle. Or glass. If you have any questions, I'll be right back with your water."

Anne studied the menu.

"What do you feel like?" Jack asked

She put down the menu and looked at him, searching for his sneaker under the table and squeezing it between her feet. She still loved the feel of his foot in a sneaker, the squishy feel of it. His sneakers still fascinated her. She loved the smell of them. She loved buying him any new pair that caught his eye at the mall.

"I feel like some more protein," she said, daintily wiping around her mouth with her napkin. "A good way to celebrate that haul you made today with your chatturbate. If we knew we could do that every day? We wouldn't even need to start a company."

Jack smiled and returned the pressure on her feet.

"How many shots?" he asked.

"I don't know; a lot, that's for sure. Fifty grams? Like the whey protein shakes you make? Maybe a little extra tonight?"

"Well, I have this feeling? That maybe a brand-new shipment? Is coming in. Real soon. So, we may be able to get you a double or triple helping. Right after dinner."

"Let's skip the dinner part."

Jack shook his head.

"No can do. As your Personal Trainer, you know I

believe you need a balanced diet. In addition to pure, high test protein."

"Damn. Oh, OK."

"So, let's see what you want from the menu. Then later, maybe, we can stop at our special all-night restaurant and see what it might have to offer. Maybe, as a special treat, cause we're doing so well with our workouts—"

"And getting *Voyeur* off the ground," Anne added.

Jack looked at her and raised his empty water glass in toast.

"To ripped bods and booming business."

"Here, here," Anne said raising her glass.

"You're doing so well," Jack said, "you might like some whipped cream on top of your dessert?"

"Yes, please."

"Or maybe some sprinkles?"

"Yes, please."

"Both?"

"Yes, please."

"So, what looks good?"

Anne stared at him, and again wiped her mouth with her napkin. She had slipped off her shoes, and under the table was pushing her toes into his crotch, varying the pressure. She watched his eyes as they began to lose focus.

"Man, you're as much of a horn dog as I am," Jack said, staring into his menu. "And I gotta be literally like at the criminally insane level. Are women supposed to be this horny?"

"Only if they're slutty. And—properly aroused."

"Before the restaurant for our special dessert starts to sell out of inventory? What do you want to order?"

Anne looked back at the menu.

213

"What do you think about the halibut?"

Jack scanned the menu and found it.

"Eleven," he said.

"What? On a scale one to ten? Have you had it here?"

"No. Eleven grams of protein. Not bad. But you should ask for it without that sauce. Plain is better. What about for starters?"

"Should we split a dozen oysters?"

"Man, you tryin' to trigger the launch mechanism? Right here? Neither one of us needs any help in that department, that's for sure. They should be real good here, though. Love oysters. Let's do it. Gotta make sure we get horseradish."

"I'll ask for it."

"So, what about a side?"

"That twice baked potato is calling me but forget about that. I know, I know. I've learned enough from you not to even dare talk about that. In your presence. Want to split the grilled asparagus?"

"Sold America."

"What do you feel like?" Anne said.

She looked at him, and just as he was about to speak said: "Stop. Wait just a minute. I swear to God. If you start telling Steven—Stefan—whatever his real name is—just how many ounces of lean grilled chicken you want, and the exact size of your broccoli florets, steamed, you know what I'm going to do to you, don't you?"

"No. But I am curious."

"I'm going to tie you down real good and—"

"Oh yeah."

"I do know how to hog-tie a man, you—"

"You do?"

"Oh yes. I'm going to hog tie you and force feed you that red velvet butter cake they always have here, warm. With vanilla ice cream. And spread it—very neatly, OK?—all over your abs and down those beautiful oblique muscles to—"

Jack laughed. "The hog-tying part sounds kind of interesting. Kinky. But interesting. We may want to try that sometime. A whole new world could—"

"Don't tempt me. You don't even want to peek past that door. Hey, you're the one who told me everyone needs a cheat day. This is yours. When you sold that first pair of your undies in this morning's chatturbate, you covered the cost of a whole bunch of dinners. Talk about amazing profit margins."

"And that guy even wanted his customized."

"Ka-ching. I hope you're at least thinking of me when you, you know, customize?"

Jack laughed and looked at her. "Sure. Whatever you say."

"OK, so you've got to eat like a regular human now and then." Anne closed her menu. "Hey, let's plot out where *Voyeur* is going. While we wait. And how we can get it there."

She found a pen in her purse and flattened her napkin to write on.

"I know. But now I have to eat clean," Jack said. "This is my job. This look? This is my livelihood."

Anne looked up at him. "I know, but—"

"And I'm just getting into a new transformation. I'm nine days into it and—"

"Good Lord, and what, pray tell, is *this* transformation? You just finished one of your programs. Remember? That crazy 72 hour fast? You ended up looking like,

I don't know what, one of those ads of a child starving in Haiti. It was sad."

"I know. I know. That didn't work so well."

"So, what is it this time?"

Another server walked up behind Jack, and, with tongs, extracted a piping hot pop-over from his basket and placed it on Jack's butter plate. The server had put one on Anne's plate and walked off before Jack noticed it and pushed his plate aside as if a fresh, wet turd covered it.

Anne put her hand over hers to feel the warmth. With her hand still on it, she was able to slip a finger deep into it and extract a small piece from the soft center. She enclosed it in her palm. For later. When Jack wasn't looking.

"Oh man, don't even mention *that* transformation," Jack said. That was a world class failure."

"Why? What happened?"

"Everything. I was doing that with Austin. You need a buddy for these things. Seventy-two hours: no food. To see how shredded we could get? We were like dying, literally, dying when we reached 50 hours. And called it quits. I think my fat percentage is so low to begin with that my body had nothing to feed on but my internal organs. The vital ones. I was probably literally like dying."

Jack closed his menu and put it aside.

Anne saw the Clarkes, her neighbors, walk by the booth, each staring at their iPhones. She thought how they looked like most of her friends. Worn out. After 25, 30 years of marriage. Of suburban life. Their eyes blank. Lifeless. Their step plodding. Together, but not even talking or noticing each other. How sad. "There but for the grace of God go I," she thought to herself. She again put her foot on top of Jack's sneakers and rubbed it.

"Fasting is supposed to sharpen your senses," Jack continued. "And give you a hard reset. But I was literally dyin'. That, and I don't think Austin and I got enough potassium. Or water. We should've been using those electrolyte salts to get the sodium and magnesium we needed. Now I know. And we both had just been through that bulking phase? Where we were just cramming food in for gains, a lot of processed food, we weren't focusing on our health back then, and when you eat processed food you can't cut it off, just like that, cold turkey." He snapped his fingers. "That's what happens. This time's gonna be different. This is going to be transformational. I'm a week and a half into the transformation."

"Congratulations?"

"But I'm frustrated."

"Why? What's the matter?"

"Well, cause I'm bustin' my butt. I'm training at complete insanity level. It's like the most intense it's ever been. I'm trying to take it to the next level. But I guess I'm impatient, I'm not feeling any difference in training, nothing different in how I carry myself, nothing different in the visual. The visual is the same. I mean, I can't see any difference. Can you?"

Anne looked at him.

"Jackson, are you bat shit crazy? You cannot improve upon perfection."

"No, no. This is not perfect." He held out his arm to look at it, as if it belonged to someone else. He looked down at his chest. He began to bounce his pecs underneath his tight T-shirt, first the left one, then right, left, right, Anne as fixated as a mongoose watching King Cobra's hypnotizing dance.

Anne took Jack's hand and pulled his arm across the table.

"This is, without a doubt," she said, "beyond any reasonable doubt—" she paused dramatically: "The Most Perfect forearm ever created."

Jack looked up at her. "Thanks? But do I feel a big 'but' coming?"

"No, really. No but." She held onto his hand and pulled his arm and turned it over.

Jack clenched his fist and his forearm muscles appeared.

"See," Anne said, "look how that muscle pops. That one." She traced it with her index finger. And pressed on it. "And look how all those adorable veins are popping up. All over the place. How do you do that?" She paused as she traced the pattern of veins. "So does that come from like, a whole lot of fapping?"

"Very funny."

"I never asked Richard this, but seriously, I've always wondered. Been curious. About men. What it is, exactly, they're even thinking. I don't have a clue what goes on in their brains. I don't think any woman does. So, before we met, like, how often did you, as you would put it, rub one out? Each day? A lot, I bet."

"I mean: Ma'am. Isn't this a little personal?"

Anne glared at him.

"Did you just call me ma'am? Fuckin dickface. So how many?"

"Hey, it took me 10 years, 10 years of really, of hard work, of dedication, to get this look," Jack said, admiring his forearm. "That doesn't happen overnight. And FYI, if fapping did it? You'd see forearms like this all over the place. Have you ever seen one this good? Before? I mean really?"

"I'm just kidding. It's gorgeous," Anne stroked her

218

hand back and forth over his forearm, patting it. "Man, 10 years? That's sick. It took Michelangelo just two years, I think it was two, to sculpt, out of marble, chipping it out of hard marble, chip, chip, chip, all of *The David*. Forearms, ankles, genitalia, huge balls, weenie, the works. That was in the early 1500s. He was just a kid. In his 20's. I think. I think he was 25 or 26 when he started."

"So maybe, like in a few more years? I could do something like that?"

"Jackson, you can do, you can accomplish whatever you set your mind to. You've already done it. With your own creation, your own *David*. You've already created a masterpiece."

Anne lifted his hand to her mouth and kissed it. She put a couple of his fingers into her mouth and started nibbling on them, sucking them, looking up at him as she did.

"Hey, don't spoil your appetite," he said. "Before the oysters."

Anne took his fingers out and held his hand, interlocking her fingers with his.

"A delicious starter. And on top of what you've already created? On your own? I think in two years? We'll have developed *Voyeur* into a going business with, some stores like *Vineyard Vines,* what do you—"

"So how do you know all about this stuff? About David and everything."

Anne looked at him, still holding his hand. "That was in my Art History course. At Bryn Mawr."

"No kidding? You learned stuff like that?"

"Sure. That's when we got to—that was my favorite class, by the way; I took it as a gut to get some credits I needed but—"

"A gut? What the hell is that, what, like a stomach with no abs?"

Anne laughed. "No. You know, an easy course? One you don't have to work too hard at to get a decent grade? That's what we used to call them. Guts. One you can, you know, coast through? That was my plan. But that ended up being my favorite class and maybe the one most important to—"

"Why? Why that—"

Anne brushed the closed fist of her other hand across her mouth and got the soft popover piece in without Jack noticing. She savored. Swallowed.

"You know. In opening my eyes to see the world in a different way?" She ran her tongue around her teeth to destroy any evidence, then put her left hand over her popover again, to feel the remaining warmth, and dug the same finger in, deeper, pulling out another piece without leaving a tell-tale hole on the top.

"It was when we came to the Italian Renaissance," she continued, "that our professor told us all about Michelangelo, Leonardo da Vinci, the *Mona Lisa*, all that—"

"That's neat. So, two years? To make that David statue?"

"Two years. And don't forget Michelangelo's—he's the one who painted the ceiling of the Sistine Chapel. Lying on his back. On scaffolding. For five years. I still have my Art History book at home if you want to read more about—"

Jack looked at her. "No, I'm good," he said, and felt the outlines of his forearm muscle.

"We could go to a museum to see some of the art in real life. If you'd like. An adventure. Have you been to the Met?" Jack shook his head no.

Anne looked at him. "OK then, it's a date. Metropolitan Museum of Art? Here we come. Someone could spend a year in there, so we should pick out a starting place. And take it in bite size portions. How about the Frick?"

"Is that another museum?"

"A really nice small one. We'll go there, too…"

"The only one I've seen is the one with the dinosaurs and—"

"The Museum of Natural History."

"That's it. A sixth-grade field trip. Those things were huge and—"

"That's a must see. There's so much. The Egyptian room at the Met. This'll be so—"

Jack looked at his forearm. "Deadlifts really help."

"What? Help what?"

"Develop the forearm."

"Oh."

"Just this morning I did five by two deadlifts, with a seven by three deficit, I was a little stiff, I mean, I actually felt a little lethargic, but had a pretty decent workout with the first set at 565, bumped it up to 585, which is six wheels, the last three sets were 600 so I was really excited about that, each seemed to get easier and easier, I was using a slightly wider stance which I think made it a little easier, I failed the third set. Three times. Which I wasn't happy about. Then I decided to stop being a bitch and just picked it up, adding five-pound progressives. I'm going to repeat that first thing tomorrow."

Anne looked up as two waiters rolled a cart past them, plates steaming with lobsters and steaks. She inhaled. And held it.

"Sounds good," she said, breathing again and

looking at Jack. "Can you still squeeze my workout time in? Hey, and don't forget, we've got Ron coming in tomorrow to do your *Voyeur* boxer brief photo shoot. You OK with that timing?"

"Sure. Lucky I'm into this program, right? I'm pretty fucking shredded now. I could be better if you give me two more weeks and—"

"Jackson, we have to keep this thing moving. Time is money and—"

"No, I know. This time I want to see how far I can go. You only get really one shot at it, that's it. That's my philosophy. My training is going to be more intense than it's ever been. I'm doing three-hour workouts. Minimum. I'm trying to take it to the next level. I've started training twice a day. Three hours morning. Later if I feel like it, two hours more. I'm going to join a gym in the Township and—"

"What?" Anne stared at him. "You're leaving the Club? You—"

"No, no, no. I should have said I'm joining another gym. This one's in the Township. To get a second membership. I need two gyms. The new one? Open 24 hours a day. It's only a few miles away. So, I can always go. It's got like 10 times the equipment. No wait. Actually, don't tell anyone, but better equipment than our Club. A little older stuff, but that's OK. Four, count em, four bicep curl machines. To hit the guns from slightly different angles."

"Wow," Anne said. "Four?"

"Yeah. Awesome, right? Each different. I want to get in there and just do it. It's always good to try another gym, new equipment, a new environment, new people, literally a new experience, all that good stuff. It's motivating. Spurs you on to try new-"

"Ron's going to be set up by 9:30 tomorrow. Is that—"

"Excuse me," Stefan said "have we decided? Or would we like a few more minutes?"

"No, no, we're good," Anne said. "We're going to split a dozen oysters."

"Very good ma'am. Excellent choice."

"And I'd like the halibut, but plain, nothing on it. Can they do that?"

Stefan looked up at her. "Certainly, ma'am, I'll make a note. Any sides?"

"Yes. We'd like to split the grilled asparagus."

"Certainly. And sir?"

"I'd like two roasted chickens."

Stefan and Anne looked at him.

"Excuse me?" Stefan said.

"You know, a roasted chicken? Two."

"A whole chicken?"

"Yes, please. Two. It's not on the menu but I'm sure they have them. Back there."

Stefan looked confused.

"Two entire chickens? Anything on it? Them?"

"No thank you. Just the chickens."

"You have to excuse him, Stefan. He's on a very special diet."

Stefan looked at her. Then back to Jack.

Jack looked at him. "I'm sure it won't be a problem. It's just a roasted chicken. No bells, no whistles. Just two of them."

"Yes, sir." Stefan looked again at his pad and turned to leave. "May I get you more water?"

Both Anne and Jack nodded yes and placed their glasses to the side.

"Got to stay hydrated," they said in unison, and smiled at each other and hooked their pinkies together.

The waiter left to place the order.

Anne was quiet for a while.

"So, tell me this: someday when we're out with friends," she said, "or perchance—"

Jack laughed. "Perchance," he said, imitating Anne's accent.

"Perchance we're at some award ceremony. For *Voyeur*. You're going to order a couple of chickens? Not chicken francaise. Not chicken marsala. Not chicken a la king. Not even... chicken parm? But... *two* chickens?"

Jack was holding out his arm, turning the palm up, then down, tracing his forearm's vascularity with his index finger.

"You don't see any changes?"

Anne looked at him. "I see great beauty, Jackson. I see the hand of Michelangelo in creating man. I see... what am I supposed to see?"

"It's frustrating. I'm just not seeing the visual. Maybe a little more vascularity? I need to see more lines. More veins. I want to get my neck veins visible." He felt along the side of his neck. "Like Todd's. You ever notice his?"

Anne looked at him.

"Right along here, Jack said, running his fingers down the sides of his neck. "I've got to get serious about shrugs."

Anne put her hand along his neck.

"A little more hardness? I'm weighing myself like after every time I eat? It's stuck on 183. I—"

"Good Lord, Jackson. This arm already looks like a road map. It looks like Leonardo's drawing of the perfect

Man. I'll show you. In my Art History book. You can't expect instant results. I'm sure it takes a while. Just like developing our business. You—"

"No, I know. This is like nine days in, and hey, I was waiting to tell you. I wanted to surprise you."

Anne looked at him. And wondered if he was about to propose.

"I think today may be the breakthrough day."

"What? Why? What happened?"

"I don't know, I just feel different today. I feel like, like I'm carrying myself differently. You know. It feels like that. It felt like I was crushing out reps, no problem, this morning. It felt like my endurance was, like, nonstop? Like literally I could go on and on. It even feels like there's some chaffing along my inner thighs. They're rubbing together. I see a rash developing there. It's a little raw on my left inner thigh and—"

"And that would be a good thing because…?"

"No, I've been targeting my inner quads. To get them bigger. To get more of that curve in there. If you get that chafing, if you see that, that would mean they're growing".

Jack slid out of the booth and stood next to Anne.

"Here," he said, "this is what I mean," pulling up the bottom of his workout shorts, grabbing his underwear on the way up, yanking the handful as far up around his crotch as he could.

"See?" he said, "see that?" Flexing his thigh till the muscles popped, twisting his leg back and forth, pointing to a spot where he thought there was chaffing. He pulled the fabric down and slid back into the booth.

"You know," Jack continued, "usually everyone does maybe three or four sets of maybe eight to 10 reps on the leg press? I've been going for as many sets as it takes to get 200 reps. With perfect form. My feet positioned out. To target the inner quads. I want to get more of that curved look along here."

He raised up in the seat and ran his hand underneath his leg.

"Today is the first day I think it's working. All the reps? They're bringing more blood, more nutrients, in there. You can see it happening. I was training legs today, going from one exercise to the next, to the next. Crushing out reps. Burning sets. Crushing them. No rest between sets. I felt invincible. I felt like I could go on forever. I'm working the calves and abs twice a day now. Maybe three times. I'm training heavy. Now that I can go to the new gym at night. I'm going for quality. And detail. Not just mass any more. I'm going for additional detail in several areas. I'm willing to live in the gym. I'm dedicating myself to this experiment. I'm ready to sacrifice. I'm going to destroy myself. Then let the muscles recuperate. And grow. And destroy them again. And again. I haven't seen the visuals yet."

He looked over at Anne to see, once again, if she had noticed a difference.

"But it will come," he continued. "I want to get things to the next level. Eating. I'm ready to eat clean. I'm going for five to eight meals a day. Food every three hours. Once as soon as I wake up. One meal, maybe a protein shake, some almonds, cottage cheese right before bed."

Anne slipped another popover piece into her mouth and mouthed it like a communion wafer.

"All high protein," he continued. "The rest spread out so I'm getting fuel every three hours. I'm going to focus on getting my compounds up. Squats getting up there. Deadlifting consistently. Benching. My butt came off the bench today. That's not smooth. I've got to work on perfecting my leg drive."

Anne looked at him and nodded.

"Training. Eating. Sleeping. That's my job," Jack said. "That's my livelihood. So, I can show others how to do it. Train them. At the gym. And on YouTube. I'm ready to live in the gym."

Anne looked at him as she swallowed the popover particles, eyeing the lovely pats of daffodil-yellow butter, softening on the plate between them.

Chapter Twenty-Six

It was dark after dinner when Latham drove Dylan to his house to show him where he lived. When they went inside, they could hear the cold wet wind blowing through the pines and spruce and hitting the windows. A wintry mix was expected by morning.

Latham closed the drapes and put on some lights and turned up the heat. When he got back to the living room, Dylan was sprawled on the sofa, sneakers off, his eyes heavy.

"You got a really sick place here," Dylan said.

"Thanks. I like it. Let me show you around."

"Here, sit down first," he said, patting next to him. "Let's relax, for a minute. That was some steak. That may have been the best I ever had. No shit."

"No, they always do a great job there. It's packed every night. Sometimes you even see cars from New York; they come in from the city just for dinner there."

"So good," Dylan mumbled, putting his arm around Latham and resting his head drowsily on Latham's shoulder. "I can see why."

Latham could sense Dylan was falling asleep and sat there quietly. His breathing had slowed. It felt good just to be sitting there with him, in his home, on a coming of winter night, as he slept.

Latham closed his eyes.

For a long time, it was quiet but for the windy rain.

Latham was dozing off when Dylan reached over with his free hand as if moving in his sleep, and undid the top buttons of Latham's shirt, slid his hand inside, cupping his pec, absentmindedly massaging a nipple. Latham wondered if Dylan had had too much to drink, but sat there, eyes closed, not wanting to break the mood.

Neither moved.

Neither spoke.

Latham wondered if he himself was asleep now, dreaming this fantasy scene.

Dylan slid his hand back and pulled his own shirt over his head, then finished unbuttoning Latham's and helped him out of it, leaning over and kissing Latham's navel, poking his tongue in it.

Latham put his hands around Dylan's head, pressing him in, as Dylan's hands circled Latham's back, holding him. Dylan swung his body in closer to Latham, straddling him, kissing each nipple, nibbling them, biting them, sucking at them.

Latham was one of those guys whose nipples have a direct connection to the dick, which already was responding. Dylan felt the change and grabbed Latham's erection through his jeans, giving it a vigorous shake, then, returning to his work, moved up to his neck, under his chin, until all of his mouth covered Latham's as they began hungrily kissing, sucking, trying to enter all the way into each other through their mouths.

As he worked, Dylan's hand had unbuckled Latham's belt and pulled it through the loops, dropping it on the floor.

He pushed Latham back on the sofa so that he was

reclining, as he squiggled out of his own jeans and tossed them aside—he was commando—then pulled off Latham's loafers and socks and pulled his Diesel jeans down his legs and over his feet and off and then yanked off his boxer briefs, all the while his tongue and mouth exploring all of Latham's mouth and face, his eyes, his ears, his nose.

Still holding Latham around the back, Dylan stood up with him.

"Where's your bedroom?"

"Upstairs."

The two moved as one up the stairs, flopping down on Latham's king size bed, rolling over and over, exploring every part of each other, finding what felt best, until it was over.

They lay quietly, wrapped around each other, cuddling, listening to the sigh of the wet winter wind through the trees.

As they lay there, Latham thought how Dylan was so different from Jack. Latham had been happy to worship Jack; Jack had been happy to have someone worshipping him. But even after they got to know each other, were comfortable with each other, there had always been limits. Latham had tried ways to sleep with Jack, even suggesting they just take a nap together; Jack wouldn't even go that far. Latham could kiss and nibble any part of Jack's body he wanted, except his face, which had always been out of bounds. Jack was very happy to be loved but there had never been any attempt at reciprocity. That was OK. Jack was fun. Jack was funny. Just to be with Jack, to have him as a buddy, had been all that mattered. Just to be close to him.

Dylan was different. Dylan seemed ready to give it all.

"Any chance you could stay here tonight?" Latham said.

"A very good chance," Dylan whispered into Latham's ear, licking around the edges. "I'm not going out there. Into that."

They lay quietly, listening to the wind waves surging against the house, the first attacks of sleet pinging against the window.

Latham pulled the covers around them.

"You'll find I'm very quiet when I'm sleeping," Dylan said. "You won't even know I'm in your bed. Promise. You'll get the best night's sleep ever. And be ready to hit the gym and then be Mr. Lawyer. Bright and early tomorrow morning."

The wind pounded the north corner of the house, whiffling around the window frame.

"This was just Act One," Dylan said. "Let's get cleaned up during intermission and resume where we left off."

"Hold that thought."

Chapter Twenty-Seven

"My God: You look like shit."

Anne was sitting, texting, her car door open, when Patti pulled in next to her. They always parked against the building, near Jack's Porsche and Dylan's Aston Martin.

Anne's head jerked up and she looked at Patti.

"Well, and a top of the morning to you, too. You make me feel so good about myself. On a dreary winter's morning."

"Sorry. I just—"

"No, it's OK. I'm sure I do look like shit. Because that is exactly how I feel."

Anne climbed down from the front seat with her gym bag and closed the door. She clicked the fob, the horn sounded once, and the side mirrors retracted.

Patti walked over. "Anne, what's the matter?"

"I didn't know it was so obvious, you know, how I look? But I guess—"

"Well, my bad. Shit was clearly not the right word. It's just, it's not the usual 'Anne just walked out from a fashion shoot look' and—"

"You're being very charitable. I'm sure it's more of the Anne just crawled out of a cesspool look. Because that's how I feel, and—"

"Girlfriend. Come on. Nothing's that bad. What's the—"

Anne looked down. "I don't know, I don't know, I don't know, I don't know, I—"

Anne was speaking in just above a whisper, in zombie-like cadence, repeating again and again "I don't know, I don't know," walking over to Patti, dropping her gym bag and hugging her, whispering into the shoulder of her ski jacket: "I don't know, I don't know, I don't—"

"Anne, you're scaring me." Patti stroked her back. "Anne, honey, come on, talk to me."

Anne said nothing.

"Why don't we go get a cup of coffee or something," Patti said, "rather than go in *there*". She pointed toward the big glass doors. "What do you say? Up to you."

Anne held on tight, her body shaking, not saying a word.

"Oh yeah," Patti said, "Command decision. Let's go. I'll drive."

It was after the commuter rush hour and Patti found a parking spot right across from the train station, in front of Starbucks where the snow had been cleared.

"Grab that table," Patti said, "and I'll give them our order. I've been craving a Grande Latte with an extra shot of whip. I'm thinking a blueberry scone. What do you say?"

Anne stared at her. "Are you planning on spending the rest of your day, of your life, on the treadmill?"

"Hey, we're a couple miles from the Club. We're over the Wall. The wardens will never find us here. We can do whatever we please."

"I think just a cup of tea. For me. Please."

"If you say so. Can I get you a scone? A bagel?"

"No, no thanks."

"Well, at least you can share mine. I don't want

233

crumbs all over my mouth when we walk back into the Gulag."

Patti came back a few minutes later, juggling the order.

"So here you go, Flopsy, Mopsy, Cottontail Peter. I even got you chamomile tea, just like Peter's mommy gave him when she took off his adorable little blue coat and tucked him under the covers."

"Thanks. Just tuck me in and leave me here."

"OK. Listen up, girl." Patti took a long sip of her drink and set it down on the table. "Nothing is so bad that two - count them: two—Seven Sister gals can't figure it out. I mean, come on, am I right? Speak to me. Give me a clue at least so…"

Anne wrapped the string of her tea bag around a plastic spoon and squeezed the bag tight, staring at it. At last, she spoke.

"It's just not working. Nothing's working. I—"

"What? What isn't working?"

"Everything—"

"Everything? OK. Now there's at least a start. Progress toward a solution. One step at a time. Could you be just a touch more specific?"

Anne was silent, staring at her tea.

"*Voyeur,*" she finally said.

"*Voyeur*? Why? What are you talking about? The last time we talked you guys had it going gangbusters, you were pulling in 20 g's every couple weeks. Every month. That's not such a bad haul for a startup. Any entrepreneur would—"

"No more. Dead. Dead. In the water."

Anne squeezed the lemon slice into her tea, holding her hand over it so it wouldn't squirt on Patti.

"How? How could that be? Why?" Patti said. "What happened?"

"I think it's that stupid new tariff thing that just kicked in. Everything stopped dead in the water. Overnight. Just like that. No transition. Ba-boom."

Anne slapped the table. Hard. Patti startled. Anne looked at her hand as if wondering what caused it to hit the table.

"Sorry about that." She put her hand in her lap. "We had been getting in stores, all over the country, opening accounts with—"

"I know. Don't forget, I've seen that map in your office room. With all those cute little colored pins in each location and—"

"They'd re-order. Again and again. The independents?"

"Sweet. So, all good?"

"We were close, so close to, with mom and pop stores and internet sales? So close to breaking even. So close to landing accounts with some of the big box stores. That would have made us. So close… "

Anne stared at her tea.

"Which was amazing for a start-up," Patti said, trying to pull Anne back into focus. "So? All good at that point, at least. Yes?"

"No. And then? Nothing, just… Everything dropped over the edge of a cliff. Just like that. Sixty miles an hour straight over."

"Well, that's gotta pick up again. Right? That won't last forever, just give—"

Anne was quiet again. "Neither can I."

"Have you—" Patti said.

"I've tried everything. Just to, you know, get a cash

flow. I've discounted our products, again and again. No bites. Nada. I've tried offering them at below cost. Just to get some cash in the door. Not even a nibble. I've had poor Jackson do even more provocative internet ads, he's all but using the undies as cum rags in our ads. Nothing. It's like that world shut down and—"

"So, is there any way you could get like, I don't know, a bridge loan or something, just to tide you over?"

Anne stared at her tea. She watched a couple walk to the counter and order. Several times she seemed about to speak, but just sighed.

"I'm already so maxed out on loans; TDB, Discover, Amex, if I tried another? I'd only go deeper into the quicksand. I somehow have to stop loss, somehow pull the plug on the whole fricken thing, each day the expenses go on, with no cash flow in the door." Anne took a sip of tea and set her cup down with her hands around the cup. "And then there are the clones."

"The clones?"

"Oh yes. Troll around the internet sometime. All of a sudden? There are like hundreds of Jackson-wannabes. We're the victims of his amazing success, his—"

"What do you mean?"

"His numbers. His numbers on the internet. You know. Subscribers. Number of clicks. All that. He drew so much attention that now? Any kid? Any kid between the ages of 16 and 26, with even the hint of nascent abs? And a barely perceptible bicep bump? They got to have a nice smile, and of course, most important?"

Patti shrugged her shoulders. "You got me."

"Really great hair?"

"Of course. Of course. The hair that always falls exactly the right way. And that always seems to come hand in hand with those pillowy lips, doesn't it?"

"Of course. It all seems to be part of the package: the sharp jawline. Those cheekbones."

"The dimples."

"Flawless skin. It's disgusting, isn't it? All the gifts to one undeserving kid. Nice going, God. Don't distribute them around fairly. Give them all to one person. Well," Anne said, "they've all started their own and—"

"What? Their own what?"

"You know. Like Jackson's. Their own channel. Their platform."

"Oh."

"And it's so obvious they're copying him. They all start off each video the same way, looking at their watches, really seriously, and announcing to their fans 'it is now... exactly... 7:18', and we can watch the pups make their healthy breakfast and consume their shakes and supplements, and head to the gym for their routines and poses, which lets the camera worship each curve and—"

"There really are a lot of them?"

"Are there ever. Coming out of the woodwork. Go sample a few. They're doing all the things Jackson's done: play with his drone, his cameras, his hoverboard, open boxes merchants send to them, hoping they'll promote their wares. We can watch them go shopping, buying all their healthy things. And they all have things like 'My Morning Routine'? where we see them waking up, already looking god-like perfect, and telling their panting viewers how to look even more perfecter. It makes me puke."

Anne squeezed the lemon again into her tea, stirred, and took another sip.

"If only there was a way to copyright or something Jackson's routines," she continued. "But there isn't.

Every start up underwear brand grabs one of these puppies as their spokesman slash spokesboy. They are just flat out imitating him. And each clone cuts into our audience. And sales. Death by a thousand cute guys."

Patti broke off a piece of her scone and held it out to Anne. Anne shook her head.

"Are there new things Jackson could do?" Patti said. "You know, to distinguish himself from the pack?"

"Believe me, I'm pushing him in that direction. Not that he needs much pushing. He loves it all. He is such an exhibitionist. But short of turning it into a porn site, we've pressed the envelope just about as far as we dare without being de-monitized and thrown off YouTube altogether".

"Ok. We have to think," Patti said.

They sat there quietly as a customer came in, got the orders for her office, and left. Outside, a determined snow had started to fall.

"Now, when I really think about it?" Anne said, "I don't think Jackson has ever really been that interested in *Voyeur*. He doesn't get it at all, that I'm doing this for—"

"He's young."

"I know. But none of these guys have any comprehension. Zero. That what they have, what they're selling now, has a shelf life of, I don't know. What do you think? Of a perfect yellow, ripe banana? How about that? A banana sitting on the kitchen counter. Just at that stage of peak perfection."

Patti chuckled. "How true."

"And tomorrow? Don't they get it? How does that fine looking banana look tomorrow?"

"Oh man, if they're the least bit brown? And spotted? And squishy? In my house? Out they go. Into the trash. No one of my prima donnas will touch them."

"Exactly. *Voyeur* is, it was always, for him. For Jackson. I'm doing this for him. This could have been such a great future for him. But I don't think he sees that at all. I can't get him to do anything to help. Beyond the modeling stuff. He's got like zero interest in the business side of the business."

The friends sat there. They watched the snow hit the sidewalk and disappear.

"It's not sticking," Anne said. "We'll be OK."

"No, I think no accumulation predicted for today. Can I get you a refill, Cottontail Peter?"

"No, I'm good. Thanks."

"I guess this poor scone didn't last very long," Patti said, wiping the last piece across her plate to gather up any crumbs. "So, what does Jack see himself doing? When he's, say, our advanced ages? Do you ever ask him that?"

"Yeah. Every once in a while. I don't think someone that age can even think of that. The gap between 24 and 40? Incomprehensible to these kids. He jokes that he'll probably have to be selling his dirty underwear. Door to door and—"

"Yuck. Good luck with that. I have a hard time wrapping my head around why anyone would want to buy anyone's dirty underwear, but a 40 year old man's? Gag me."

Anne laughed. "Who would want our husband's underwear? No market there."

"I only touch Fletcher's with tongs."

"Richard's? I used to use rubber gloves."

"Man, we are so bad."

"These guys just don't get it, though," Anne said "they have no perception that, that these human-gods

239

they're creating? With all their workouts and everything? That once they stop all that? It's not very long before the pump is gone. The abs are gone. The hair is gone. And flash? All of a sudden? They are a faceless nobody, one of the masses of indistinguishable, middle-aged men you see pouring out of the trains each evening. With zombie eyes, and, and—"

"Sloth-like gait," Patti said.

"Goodbye gods. And what then? What then? They simply do not see this. As they perform their fourth set of 35 reps, and mix up another Blue Lightening post workout drink, and—"

"When you look at it in those terms? It is, it's sad."

"It is. And it's inevitable. And I've been trying so hard to protect Jackson from that, the abyss he doesn't even see. Right ahead of him."

Chapter Twenty-Eight

"I don't know, I don't know, I don't —" Anne looked down. "Jacks —"

Her voice broke before she could get out the "son." She stared at her tea and stopped talking.

Patti looked up at her. "Jack? What about Jack?"

Anne tried to get out a word but didn't trust her voice and stopped.

"What?" Patti reached over and held her hand. "Whatever it is, I can help you. Please. Come on. Let me at least try to help."

Anne's face was working in different contortions as she tried to maintain her composure. "I think—I know—he's been with another and—"

"Anne." Patti pulled Anne's hand closer toward her. "Are you sure? Why do you think—?"

Anne struggled again to compose herself.

"The other day?" She paused.

"Yes? The other day? What happened?"

Anne looked out the window, across to the train station. The road now was white, but she could see black pavement where cars had passed.

"The other day, he left his phone at home. When he left for the Club. I know I shouldn't have, but believe me, my intentions were good. I think—"

"I'm sure they were."

"Well, it's just that I wanted to see what kind of porn he watched. You know? So, whatever he's into, I could maybe adapt a little to that?"

"OK, so big deal. Noble intentions. And the results were…?"

"So rather than hitting the key to see what his viewing history was? I hit—I swear to God it was a mistake, and—"

"Honey, I believe you. I still can't work mine right. I'm so old I can hardly even see the keys."

"So, what came up was the history of his phone calls, and—"

"That's OK."

"Well, no it's not. It would be. Except I saw this same number coming up again and again. A 20 minute call. A 40 minute call. Maybe six a day. Seven. Eight. All times of the day. I didn't recognize the number, so I wrote it down. And… I'm such a bad person I—"

"No, you're not."

"Well, I called that number."

"I would have. Anyone would have. And?"

"The Linda Lewis Real Estate Agency. You know, that one on Maple Street?"

"Sure. So big deal. He's looking for a house for you guys."

"I wish. No. That's where little Miss Pony Tail Swisher works, remember?"

Patti looked at her and thought.

"Diana?"

"You got it."

"Still, who knows—?"

"Well, I think I do. I put on my Nancy Drew hat and

called the phone company and somehow convinced them to send me his records going back 12 months and—"

"Uh oh."

"Uh oh, yes. It's been going on for a long time. Patti. Even when we were in Hawaii. Even when we were at the *Mauna Kea*? Patti. Bermuda. I'm busting my ass to build *Voyeur*, a company for him. His future. And he's…"

"I know, I know."

"I don't even know what to think any more. Someone, somehow, who is your life. Who you adore? Worship? And what are they even thinking? I thought I knew. But I don't even have a clue now. I have no idea. I don't know what to think. I—"

They both were quiet for a while and watched the snow.

"Maybe you can't—" Patti stopped, shifted in her chair, started again. "No, I don't mean you, you, I mean maybe anyone—"

"No, I know."

"Maybe no one could ever possess someone, you know, someone like Jack. I don't know."

Anne looked at her.

"No, you know what I mean?" Patti continued. "Guys like that? They're sort of wispy, you know what I mean? A will-o-the wisp."

"I never got that. What's a willow wisp even supposed to mean?"

"Will-o-the-wisp? I don't know. It refers to something, you know, ephemeral, that—"

"Jackson's not effeminate. At all, I mean, just the—"

"No, no, ephemeral. You know, fleeting? A fantasy, something maybe not even really there, something we think we—"

Anne looked confused.

"I mean, when you get right down to it?" Patti said. "What the hell are we all even doing at the Club? Any of us. I mean, it's one thing to try to stay healthy, all that good stuff, right?"

Anne nodded.

"But what about trying to get a certain look? Isn't that, that's nothing but a fantasy. Those guys? All of them? like Jack? Who are trying to sculpt their bodies to look a certain way? I mean, come on, how real is all that?"

Anne smiled.

"When you come right down to it?" Patti continued "It's a complete bullshit fantasy. I mean you know what happens. You've seen it. That's what we were talking about. The day they stop pumping and pull upping and all of that? Say goodbye to the Greek god, say hello to every regular man we see around town. Those guys at the gym? all busting ass to try to be someone else, someone they really can't be. Can never be. Or, at least forever. Right?"

"No, I know."

"And for that split second—split second in the big picture?—that tiny nano second that some of them, like Jack, may achieve it? We all want to fall for it so—"

"I sure did."

"Hook, line and sinker, all of us. And worship it. And think to ourselves: look at what I discovered. Right here. Right in front of me. A living breathing man-god. For me to worship. And adore. And take care of. Forever. But—?"

Anne looked at her tea, and said under her breath, "Ah, but I may as well try to catch the wind."

Patti looked up at her, then down at her latte. She stirred it. "That was maybe my favorite song. From our day."

Anne looked at her and smiled.

244

"Mine, too. There was this guy in our class in high school who played the guitar. And sang it at an assembly. That song. He didn't realize it, or maybe he did; no, I doubt he did; but when he finished? He was singing it in this quiet, shy voice? That was so full of? I don't know. Longing? Full of sadness, maybe? He could have fucked the brains out of every girl in that auditorium. We were all instantly in love with him. We would have stood in line to wait our turn."

Patti laughed. "All you horny little whores-in-training. If only men had a clue how easy it is to get us to put out."

She took a last sip of her latte, put the cup down, and sang-hummed softly, to herself. She didn't even think Anne could hear her across the table, "In the chilly hours and minutes, of uncertainty, I wanna be—"

"In the warm hold of, of his loving arms," Anne sang back. She had changed the words a little. "To feel him, all around me—"

Her voice cracked and she suddenly stopped, looking down.

Patti saw the tears. Falling onto the table. And reached over to Anne.

"And to take his hand—" Anne paused again, and then resumed, even softer, "along the sand—"

Patti could feel her trembling and clasped Anne's hand with both of hers, squeezing it.

"Ah, but I may as well try to catch—"

Anne was looking down at her place, weeping. "I'm so sorry," she whispered. "I am such a mess. I am a total mess."

"Hey, no, you're not. It's OK. You guys had something. Something so special, so real. So rare. I'm right here for you, Anne. I hope you always know that. We can figure this out. We'll figure it out."

Anne tried to say something but couldn't, putting her other hand on top of Patti's, holding tight.

They didn't care who was there, who walked in, who left. They were alone together in there, in Starbucks, alone together in those chilly hours and minutes of uncertainty, trying to, hoping to kill their fears, to leave all their blues somewhere behind them.

It was a long time before either spoke.

"I still love him," Anne said. "I always will. The underneath Jackson. Always, the real Jackson. Who he really is. But I wonder if, I know he doesn't, right now at least; he doesn't see, doesn't have a clue how—"

Patti looked at her, and smiled sympathetically.

"We'll figure everything out. We need some time. Don't' worry now. The Seven Sister gals will handle this. What do ya say? Let's go back there and put our time in. It'll help us zone out. And think. Clearer. Fuck the Personal Trainers."

"I don't know, Patti. I don't know—if I can ever go back there. At least yet. Not yet at least. Now."

"Whoa girlfriend. You know what they say, right?"

"What?"

"When you fall off your stationary bike? The best thing to do is? Just climb right back on board to show you're not scared of it."

"Well… I am scared."

"Hey, my little tit willow, that's—"

Anne smiled. "Tit willow. Tell me again: where were you born?"

"Thought you'd like that one. So, where's the Anne I know? She 'fraid of nothing. No. Thing. And besides,

I'm gonna be right next to you the whole time. Making sure you're OK. And that you don't fall off again."

"Patti, I don't know. I feel so fragile, so—"

"Tell you what: we go back there? We put in a solid 45 minute workout? Like one of our regular days? This'll be good for us. Both of us. And I will personally—personally—line up a session in the Spa. For you. With… Gonzola."

Anne looked at her. "Fuck the treadmill."

"That's my good girl," Patti said, as if talking to her dog. "Who's a good girl? You're my good girl. And you know what Gonzola does for good little girls?"

The friends smiled and got up to leave.

"Can we spend some time in the Steam Room, too?" Anne said.

"Are you kidding me? I'll stay all day in the Steam Room with you. We've got a lot to figure out. Best place to brainstorm. As a matter of fact, how about straight to the Steam Room. Then the showers. And then, da dah, into Gonzola's darkened back room?"

Chapter Twenty-Nine

Latham stared at the counter on his treadmill.

It seemed barely to register each passing second.

Was it even working?

Was the calibration off?

Dylan insisted he do 20 minutes at the maximum incline—15—and at a fairly moderate speed—three—before each workout session with him. Today was leg day—Latham's favorite—and he was counting down the minutes until he could find out what Dylan had in store for him, and train with him, before heading to the office.

He glanced up once again from the treadmill counter to see Dylan come out of the Locker Room, not in his Personal Trainer gear, but rather only in short black workout shorts. No tank top. No socks. No sneakers.

Latham watched, riveted, as he walked over to the deadlift area, bent down to the chalk box to cup a handful which he spread on his hands, and then look over at the two ropes dangling from the ceiling.

In an instant, Dylan dashed toward the ropes, took a running leap at them, and caught them between his legs, swinging back and forth, leaning back, his arms stretched straight out behind him.

Those who caught this improbable move gasped.

Those around stopped whatever they were doing.

And watched.

As the ropes swung back and forth in an arc, Dylan alighted, grabbed them with his hands, and circled around them several times, twisting them together into one, then jumped at them, holding on, spinning with them, executing a perfect flag pole as the ropes continued to spin like a top.

He let go with one hand and continued the flagpole position, then pulled in, opening the ropes up with his feet, twisting one around one leg, the other rope around his other leg, arms outstretched.

The onlookers were clapping.

He performed a handstand between the ropes.

Cheering.

He crunched up and caught the ropes, releasing his legs, performing somersaults and splits, holding sometimes with both hands, sometimes with one, sometimes between his ankles, sometimes behind his knees, soaring around and around with an effortless grace, as limber as if he was weightless, every muscle popping and glistening.

He seemed to be flying. He was out somewhere soaring, beyond the field of gravity.

Jack came out of the Personal Trainers' Lounge at exactly 7:28 to look for Roger, his 7:30 client.

Roger wasn't on the treadmill doing his required time before his session with Jack.

In fact, no one now was on the treadmills.

No one on the stationery bikes.

No one on the Stairmasters.

Jack looked and saw the mob around the ropes, watching Dylan's performance.

Jack walked over, spotted Roger and walked up to him, grabbing his arm, pulling him out of the crowd.

"Roger, my main man, you're not gonna make any gains by watching someone else."

"Shit. That guy is awesome. Have you ever seen him do this? He's incredible."

They watched for a moment as Dylan seemed to fly through the air around the ropes.

"I mean, he's literally just a gymnast," Jack said. "He's really not a fitness person. To tell you the truth, I'm not even sure why he chose this gym. Let's get going so we can get you your money's worth."

Jack led him into the empty room where the next yoga class would take place.

"Here," he said, handing him the jump rope. "You did three perfect minutes yesterday. I want you to go for at least four minutes today. Deal? OK? Are you ready?"

"I guess so," Roger said, looking back toward the gym as again it burst into applause and whistles.

"Here, let me set the tempo again," Jack said, watching Roger in the mirror:

Five little monkeys.

Jumping on the bed.

One fell off

And bumped his head…"

Chapter Thirty

Steamed.

Showered.

Shaved.

Spritzed.

Suited up.

Latham adjusts his tie in the mirror, pulls down his cuffs and checks out his gold cufflinks, straightening them.

He takes the cologne from Dylan's locker next to his, sprays it in front of him, then walks through the mist, the same way Dylan does.

That same fragrance—Creed Aventus, at $400 for three ounces—always lingers throughout the Locker Room now that more members, and Personal Trainers, have switched to Dylan's favorite.

He takes the gym bag from his locker, closes the locker door, picks up his towels from the bench, and leaves the alcove, tossing the towels in the hamper on the way out of the Locker Room.

He pauses.

Latham takes a quick look in the mirror over the hamper, stops, studies himself more intently, turning his head side to side.

Too much gray popping into his sideburns and around the edges. As soon as he gets to the office, he'll call to get an appointment with Joseph for after work. Get his hair colored to match Dylan's and get it cut more like Dylan's, tighter along the sides and back this time, with a hard part cut in with a razor.

He pushes his hair back to see how that will look. Then looks again, leaning in closer to the mirror. The gray hairs are coming in just the right way. The gray gives a distinguished look to his face. It's sort of working. Maybe he should keep it. At least for a while. That would be a good look when he leads the tax panel at the conference out in Chicago next Thursday. At least keep it through that. And then re-evaluate. Maybe, actually, it would help in getting more clients—the look of a distinguished seasoned senior partner.

He looks again, straightens the knot of his tie just a fraction, and tries setting his mouth and eyes to project a mastery of the intricacies of the Tax Code. Not a bad look. Not bad at all.

He leaves the Locker Room.

The gym is in motion. The music throbbing, weight plates banging, treadmills grinding. The Screamer has just let out a bellow as he extends the Ab Wheel to full extension and struggles to wheel it back toward him. Latham smiles. No one else notices.

Those splayed on the stretching floor still look like they were caught in mid-motion by the sudden eruption of Vesuvius, their expressions seem to reflect the sudden perception of the horror befallen them.

Latham spots the guy who looks like the before photo in the old Charles Atlas advertisements. There he is. Same time. Same Personal Trainer—Georgina—who today has him standing on two risers, feet spread, one on each riser, lowering a 30 pound dumbbell between his legs, as far as he can. Latham is impressed with his form. And the fact that he can rise back up after dipping that low. Without something snapping. Or cracking. He again wonders why, with the otherworldly devotion the guy shows toward his daily workouts, month after month, year after year, why does he look exactly the same as the day Latham first noticed him?

As Latham is walking out, he catches Jack's reflection in the mirrored wall behind the chest press; he's working with a client back in the Pilates Room. Latham pauses. And stares. Jack's in the exact same stance as he was that summer day when he had shot his golf ball over the pond and stood by the flag after he sunk the hole with three improbable shots. In that reflection, in that stance, is, suddenly, everything about how it had felt to be out there with him that July afternoon. Latham's stomach tightens for that split second when that image, and everything it carries with it, recedes, as all such fleeting images must, with the sudden inevitable realization that that moment of his life, like so many others, now has drifted forever beyond his reach.

Jack spots Latham looking at him in the mirror, grins and waves. Latham gives him a thumbs up in the mirror and moves into the hall and toward the door out.

He glances at the back of the gym. All the treadmills are being used. Above the music, a drill sergeant instructor is barking orders to his class: "Incline: to eleven. Now! Speed: to ten. Now! Give me five minutes. Flat out. Get set… Go!"

Latham passes the Café, the Child Care Room, the Rehab Center.

Anne is behind the front counter, checking in those arriving.

She glances up as Latham opens the big glass door. Her job, which she's had since the winter, is to greet everyone, check them in and say goodbye to each as they leave.

"Latham."

"Anne."

"Latham."

"Anne. How are you doing?"

"I don't know. OK, I guess. You?"

"We should have dinner sometime. Exchange notes."

Anne looks at him. "I would like that. I really would. Very much. Any night. I'm yours."

"When I get here tomorrow, let's check our calendars and see what day looks good for you."

"You name it."

Latham waves as he walks through the first glass door.

The music muffles.

As the second glass door closes behind him, it is quiet, save for the birds peeping around the ivy that has grown up the side of the building, and that, during the last few weeks, has turned green again.

About the Author

A graduate of Wesleyan University and University of Virginia School of Law, Arthur Vanderbilt is the author of many books of history, biography, memoirs, and essays. His books have been selections of the Book-of-the-Month Club, Reader's Digest's "Today's Best Nonfiction," the Easton Press series, and other book clubs, and have been serialized in newspapers and magazines, both here and abroad, translated into foreign languages, excerpted for anthologies, and optioned for television movies. He lives in New Jersey and Massachusetts.

His book, *The Best Kept Boy in the World,: The Short, Scandalous Life of Denny Fouts*, a biography of the 20th century's most famous male prostitute, continues to be a best-seller for Magnus Books.

Other Riverdale Avenue Books Titles
You Might Enjoy

A Starr is Born
By Ryan Field

Sleepless in San Francisco
By Ryan Field

Pretty Man
By Ryan Field

A Christmas Carl
By Ryan Field

Valley of the Dudes
By Ryan Field

Dancing Dirty
By Ryan Field

You Must Remember This
A Gay Retelling of Casablanca
by John Michael Curlovich

Made in United States
North Haven, CT
21 February 2024

48972246R00143